FEATHERS AND FAE

By

Crystal L. Kirkham

KYANITE
Publishing

Copyright © 2019 by Kyanite Publishing LLC

All rights reserved. No part of this publication may be reproduced, distributed, or transmitted in any form or by any means, including photocopying, recording, or other electronic or mechanical methods, without the prior written permission of the publisher, except in the case of brief quotations embodied in critical reviews and certain other noncommercial uses permitted by copyright law.

This is a work of fiction. Any characters, names, places, or likenesses are purely fictional. Resemblances to any of the items listed above are merely coincidental.

For permission requests, please contact the publisher, Kyanite Publishing LLC, via e-mail, with subject "Attention: Permissions Coordinator," at the e-mail address below:

info@kyanitepublishing.com

ISBN
Hardcover: 978-1-949645-87-3
Paperback: 978-1-949645-85-9
eBook: 978-1-949645-86-6

Cover design by Sophia LeRoux
Interior design by B.K. Bass
Editing by Sam Hendricks
Cover image © depositphotos.com
Interior images © shutterstock.com

www.kyanitepublishing.com

This book is dedicated to that madcap league of scribblers in which I found a virtual home and very real friends. Without them, this book would never have been written. *Literally*.

Chapter One

Emmett glared up at Kami, waiting for an answer. He had found her sprawled across the top bench of the old wooden bleachers half watching the local baseball team practice in the hazy summer heat. Mostly, she had been doodling in one of her notebooks. There wasn't much else to do in Blakely Grove on a late August afternoon. With an exasperated sigh, she closed her notebook and turned to look down at him.

"It's not the end of the world, Em." Kami brushed back a strand of hair that had fallen in front of her eyes. This month it was a vibrant blue that faded to navy at the tips. "I can't believe you rushed over here because of something silly like that. You could have just called or texted or something."

"I wanted to talk about it face to face. Besides, your mom didn't think it was silly," Emmett frowned.

"She thought you had decided to go to Lakeland Community with me, too, not run away to the city."

Kami jumped down from the bleachers to stand at eye level with him. She elbowed him lightly in the ribs and grinned, trying to make light of the situation. "So, what? We're just going to different colleges. It's not like we promised each other that we were going to go to the same one."

"You're right, we didn't promise that, but we've always talked about it. We got accepted into all the same places. We chose which one we wanted to go to together and you went and changed your mind without telling anyone," Emmett knew he could transfer after the first semester or try a late enrollment, but that wasn't the point. He couldn't shake the feeling of dread that had been bothering him for days. He didn't want her to be hours away where he might not be able to get to her in time if something happened.

"Sorry, but it was a spur of the moment decision," Kami shrugged. "They have a better art program and I thought 'why not?' so I did."

"How am I supposed to keep you safe if you're at another college? You're always managing to get yourself into trouble." Emmett crossed his arms.

"Aw, I just changed my mind last minute. Don't be angry, Em. Besides, I don't need you to always keep an eye on me," Kami said, rolling her eyes.

"I do need to keep an eye on you though," he insisted. "This is exactly what I'm talking about. You never think things through. Seriously, I'm going to worry about you the entire time. Did you even think about that?"

"I just need to get away from this place. Find a little excitement maybe." Kami turned to watch the guys playing baseball down below. "Aren't you tired of this place?"

"Of Blakely Grove?" Emmett asked. "Naw, it's quiet here. I like it."

Kami plopped down on the ground with a sigh. Emmett joined her and watched as she plucked at the grass. He leaned back and stared up at the clouds to give her some time to gather her thoughts. He frowned as he watched a flock of strange birds fly through the sky. They reminded him of a distant memory he would have preferred to forget.

Another sigh took his attention from the birds to Kami. Her brow was furrowed as she plucked at the grass.

"Come on, give. What's really bothering you?" he asked.

"It feels like I should be doing something more than this."

"More than lying in the grass and staring at the sky?" Emmett knew that wasn't what she meant but he didn't want to think about that. Neither of them was ready for that conversation.

"You're staring at the sky. I'm staring at the grass." She flung a handful at his face. "And you know that isn't what I meant. It's just that this all seems so…so…"

"So what?" Emmett glanced over at her. She wasn't looking at him, she was staring at a distant point in space. He poked at her thigh. "Life is what it is, Kami. There isn't more to it than this."

"I don't know," Kami reached out to tousle Emmett's dark hair. "You need a haircut."

Emmett batted her hand away. "I hate when you do that."

Kami stuck her tongue out as Emmett sat up and brushed the grass from his face. He glared at her before continuing what he was going to say. "All of that is beside the point. You should have told me that you wanted to go somewhere else. I could have chosen to go there, too. Someone needs to keep an eye on you."

"Don't you think you're being a little overdramatic? I just feel like I'm missing out on something," Kami grinned at Emmett. "I want some excitement in my life."

"Excitement is overrated."

"Says the boring maths major," Kami snorted. "Some days I don't think you'd know what fun was if it slapped you in the face."

"Fun and excitement, you mean like the time you swore you could jump the creek in the forest and broke your leg?" Emmett asked.

"Oh, come on." Kami punched him in the shoulder. "That was fun until it hurt, and you were able to get me back home."

"Yeah, and I got in trouble because of it. You just weren't there to hear that part." Emmett wagged a finger at her.

"Seriously, Em, I'll be fine. You worry too much."

Emmett bit his tongue on the first response that came to mind and changed the subject instead. "We can finish talking about it later. It's getting late. We should get home for dinner."

Kami jumped to her feet, grinning. "Race you?"

"You're on." Emmett was a second behind her as she took off running.

"Hey! Watch where you're going!" an elderly man yelled at Kami as she nearly ran full tilt into him.

"Sorry, Mr. Velman!" she called back over her shoulder without breaking stride. Neither of them paid any attention to his response.

"Ha, I won you slowpoke!" Kami cheered as she reached the far end of the park and stopped to catch her breath.

Emmett wasn't far behind her. "You cheated. You didn't wait for me to get up first."

"Guess you better be more prepared next time."

"Right," Emmett frowned as he glanced up at the bright summer sun as the sky seemed to darken slightly. "We should probably get going."

"What's wrong?" Kami looked up as well, but there was nothing to see.

"Nothing," Emmett grinned. "Just wanted to see if I could make you look."

"Right, whatever." Kami made a face at him before turning to head through the old industrial area. "Let's go this way, it's faster."

"It may be faster, but I don't like it." Emmett pulled back against Kami, but she refused to be dissuaded. "It's not safe."

"Come on, don't be a scaredy-cat," Kami goaded. Emmett sighed and allowed himself to be dragged along. It seemed like it had always been this way for as long as they had known each other. She was hard to resist sometimes and if he didn't follow her, she'd go off on her own anyway. If he was with her then she had someone to watch over her.

"You know I'm not scared. You're just being irresponsible again. I swear—"

"You swear that one day I'm going to get myself or someone else killed. Blah blah blah. Insert tired old lecture here," Kami finished for him. "Hasn't happened yet."

"'Yet' being the operative word," Emmett pointed out.

"And without me, you'd never have any fun," Kami laughed as she picked up her speed. Emmett glanced up at the darkening sky and frowned. It was far too early for it to be this dark and there wasn't a cloud in sight. He would have glanced at his watch to be sure, but he knew it couldn't possibly be that late.

He tried to brush it off as an overactive imagination, like the odd birds earlier, but instincts told him that this wasn't right at all. He wished he could ignore his instincts.

He hesitated when she tried to drag him down a dark alley. He'd been down this alley several times before during both day and night, but something seemed different this time. He could feel goosebumps rising on his arms the closer they got. He tried to stop, but Kami kept pulling at him in a hurry to get home.

"Kami, let's go another way," Emmett insisted. No lights illuminated the shadowy confines between the buildings. Something was in there—he knew it, he could feel it. Nothing moved in the shadows; it looked normal to his eyes, but his instincts told him that the alley wasn't as empty as it seemed. He could sense an ominous presence waiting in those shadows, one that was familiar to him. His rational mind tried to insist that it was impossible.

"Nuh uh. We're late," Kami tugged harder on his arm. He knew her well enough to know that he wouldn't be able to dissuade her. At this point, all he could do was follow her into the dark alley. He did his best to look in every direction at once as they crossed the threshold between the buildings. He needed to be ready for anything.

Halfway through, Kami's pace faltered. Just a few steps, but that was all it took for Emmett to be even more on edge. He tried to see what it was that had caught her attention but saw nothing. Her pace quickened. He was happy to be moving faster towards the end of the block because he still couldn't escape the feeling that there was something unnatural here. He was eager to reach the comfort of the streetlights.

"Kieeeeeevahhhh." It was barely more than a whisper on the breeze, but it caused Emmett to nearly trip over his own feet. He had not heard that name in longer than he cared to think of. He hoped that it was just his mind running wild, but he couldn't take that chance. Every hair on the back of his neck stood on end and he pushed Kami to move faster. He was grateful when she didn't resist.

"Kieeeevaaahhh." It was more distinct this time. Kami glanced back, her eyes wide. This time he knew that it wasn't his imagination. Emmett uttered a single word, "Run."

She didn't have to be told twice. Kami ran towards the light that didn't seem to be coming closer. Emmett thought he heard a rustling in the breeze behind them. He glanced back. All he saw were shadows that appeared darker than was natural.

A comforting orange light washed over them as they stumbled out of the alley. A few faltering steps brought them to a halt. They both turned to look back at the shadows. Nothing moved and no sound echoed in the street beyond their own laboured breathing. Kami giggled nervously. "Aren't we ridiculous?"

Emmett didn't answer. He needed to be sure that his suspicions were right, even as he hoped he was wrong. A shadow moved within the darkness of the alley. He tried to ignore it, but he couldn't. He couldn't stand here and pretend that nothing was wrong. It wasn't natural for the sky to be this dark. Not in August. He gave Kami a nudge to keep moving. "Come on, let's go."

"Yes, sir," Kami barked at him with a wink before doing as she was told. Emmett glanced over his shoulder. This time no shadows dared to move. Not wanting to let her get too far ahead of him, he hurried to follow her down the street. Every few steps he looked back behind them and up at the too dark sky. It didn't take long for Kami to notice his distraction.

"What are you looking at, Em?" Kami demanded. "Scared of the shadows?"

"Everyone should fear the shadows," Emmett said. "There are things that hide in the darkness."

"You are such a dork," Kami laughed and gently punched him on the arm. "And so am I for letting my imagination run away with me like that."

"Right…" Emmett agreed, while his eyes scanned the shadows for something that was more than darkness.

"Let's get home," Kami said and slowed her pace to a more casual walk. "I think it's going to rain or something. It's way too dark for this time of day."

"Okay," Emmett mumbled not willing to argue with her and thankful that she wanted to keep moving away from the alley.

"Kieeeeeevahhhh." Emmett spun around at sound. It was louder this time, stronger. All he could see was the strengthening breeze blowing a few leaves around.

"What was that?" Kami instinctively moved closer to Emmett. He shushed her as he searched desperately for the source of the sound. He needed to be sure. Nothing moved. All he could hear was his own pulse beating in his ears.

Bzzzzzzt-click. Emmett watched the light closest to the alley flicker and go dark. *Bzzzzzzt-click.* Another bright orange light flickered and went out. Darkness was approaching and there was no doubting the movement in it now.

"Em, maybe we should..." Kami's voice trailed off as another light went dark. She pulled frantically at Emmett to get him to move. She was right to panic, but he couldn't go until he was sure of what was in the darkness. Kami struggled desperately as another light died. Emmett narrowed his gaze. An ethereal figure stood in the shadows—a figure he recognized. One he had thought he would never see again.

"Emmett, please," Kami begged. He'd seen enough. There was little he could do now without risking Kami's safety, so he turned and ran, dragging her with him. He needed to find somewhere with lots of light and people. If he was right, it would be enough to keep the nightmare at bay. For now, anyway. He would worry about tomorrow once they were back home. He knew he should be more concerned about how they had been found, but right now all he could concentrate on was escaping.

He could feel Kami beginning to lag. He needed to find something quickly before they both grew too tired to run anymore. A glowing sign gave him hope. A 24-hour gym was just a bit further down the block. Normally, a pass was required to get through the front doors, but he could handle that.

"Just a bit further," he urged Kami onwards. A few more steps and they would be safe. He took a deep breath and tried to summon a power that he had been repressing for a long time. He slammed his hand against the sensor and let the energy flow from him, willing the door to open. He yanked on it and it swung far more easily than he expected. He shoved Kami through the entrance ahead of him but hesitated for a second to look back. His eyes met the gaze of someone he had thought long gone.

"Asèth." A name Emmett had not uttered in many years slipped from his lips. There were no words in the angry screech and something solid within brushed against his hand. Fiery pain burned its way up his arm. It was enough to put him in motion as he threw himself through the doorway.

His foot caught as he stumbled his way into the too-bright building. He struggled to remain on his feet, reaching out for something to grab but found nothing. He lost his balance, his head hitting hard as he fell. As everything went dark, he swore he could hear birds singing.

Chapter Two

Emmett's head pulsed with a blinding pain. He hadn't used his powers in such a long time that it had taken a toll on him, and the bright sunshine was no help. Sunshine...something seemed wrong about that. Sunshine didn't belong inside a gym. His eyes flew open. He shoved himself into a sitting position, wincing at the pain in his hand as he did so. He looked down to see a black streak marring the back of it. He wiggled his fingers; they moved freely. He was concerned about the wound, but there were more important things to worry about right now.

He stared at the unfamiliar trees, their leaves gilded with silver that flashed and sparkled in the bright sun. It was beautiful, but this was not where he had expected to be. He wasn't sure where they were, but he was sure of where they weren't—this wasn't Blakely Grove or any place on Earth that he knew. He looked for Kami to see that she lay prone only a few feet away. He scrambled over to her and breathed a sigh of relief to find that she was alive.

He searched his pockets and pulled out his phone. He wasn't surprised to see that he had no service here at all. He had an idea of where they were, but he still needed confirmation. He shook Kami's shoulder with no response.

"You had to go ahead and be difficult again, didn't you?" Emmett grumbled as he pushed to his feet. "I told you we shouldn't have gone down that alley."

He knew that the fault wasn't solely hers. He had decided to call on power that he had not used in several lifetimes. In his panic to keep her safe, he must have used more than was needed to circumvent the lock. He wasn't aware that he was still capable of such feats. How it happened wasn't important, Emmett reminded himself, his focus needed to be on getting Kami back to Blakely Grove.

He shook Kami again—harder this time—but she stayed stubbornly unconscious. He was going to have to carry her out of here. With some difficulty he hoisted her on to his shoulder. He staggered a little under the extra weight, but he didn't see any other option. He wasn't willing to be more than he appeared, and he didn't want to stay sitting here.

"Some things never change," Emmett mumbled to the unconscious Kami as he headed down the only path that there was hoping it would take them someplace safe. "You would think that just once you would actually try listening to me, but no. Stubborn, bull-headed woman that you are—that you've always been. Running down dark alleys and endangering your life at every turn. He almost had you. I can't let that happen. There's too much at stake."

Emmett stumbled under her weight as he tried to avoid tripping over rocks and roots. Kami groaned in response. "That's probably the closest thing to an apology that I'll ever get. Not that I expected one. You have no idea what I've given up."

Kami groaned again. Emmett leaned against a tree to catch his breath. "Cussing you out won't get us anywhere, will it?"

He pushed onward trying not to think about how lost they might be. "I should probably be worrying about how to get you back home… and about where in the realms we might be. I have my guesses, but that doesn't do us any good."

He knew that any trail he chose would take them somewhere eventually, but he would rather not spend days wandering through these woods. He idly thought about being above the trees so that he could see the lay of the land. It did him no good to think of such things, he had reality to deal with and flying should be the last thing on his mind. He pushed himself onwards down the trail.

"You're getting heavy," Emmett mumbled at Kami. If she didn't wake up on her own soon, he would have to try to find a healer or doctor. "Please, wake up already."

"Umph. Stop jostling me so much."

Emmett lowered Kami to the ground as gently as he could. She looked a little worse for wear, but other than that she seemed okay. "How are you? Are you okay?"

"Where are we?" Kami ignored his questions as she grappled her phone out of a pocket and started waving it around in the air looking for a signal. "This is definitely not home. I have no service at all here."

"You noticed that, too?" Emmett grinned as he plopped down onto the ground beside her, thankful for the rest. "I have no idea where we are, because the last thing I remember was running into a gym."

Kami frowned and tilted her head as she stared at him.

"Don't you remember? There was something chasing us and I pushed you into that 24-hour gym…" Emmett let the sentence trail off. It was obvious that something else was bothering her as the perplexed look remained on her face.

"Yeah, what was that about? I mean…" Kami's voice trailed off and she frowned. "I mean, I thought there was something in the dark chasing us, but that couldn't be real; it wasn't real."

"Unless we're sharing a dream, then I would say that it was very real." Emmett flexed his injured hand and pain shot up his arm. He frowned at his hand. It looked like the mark was spreading. That was not a good sign. "Unbelievably real."

Kami yanked his hand towards her. "What the hell happened to you?"

Emmett bit his lip to keep from crying out in pain. He stood up, gently removing his hand from her grip as he did so. "I'm fine. We should get moving. Can you walk?"

"I didn't ask if you were okay. I asked what happened." She stared up at him stubbornly, not moving.

Emmett tried to ignore the look on Kami's face and held out his other hand to help her to her feet. He wasn't in the mood to answer questions about things he'd didn't want to talk about. She stared at his hand, not budging an inch.

"It's not that important. We can talk about it later," Emmett insisted. He grabbed her arm and tugged. Kami tried to resist, but Emmett was stronger. He yanked her onto her feet. "Right now, we need to find a way out of these woods before dark."

She cocked her head to the side, looking perplexed. "Okay."

He had been prepared for an argument, not agreement. "Can you walk?"

Kami nodded, still looking confused about something. She followed a few steps behind him on the narrow trail. Emmett resisted the urge to glance back to see if that look was still on her face. He had more important things to worry about—like how Asèth had escaped and found them. It shouldn't have been possible.

"What's that?" Kami's voice piped up from behind him. He turned to see her pointing up at the sky. "Is that smoke?"

Emmett followed her gaze to see wispy curls of smoke in the sky ahead of them. He inhaled deeply and could smell the faint hint of wood smoke. He had been too preoccupied with his own thoughts and worries to notice it earlier. "It must be coming from a house somewhere up ahead."

"How do you know that?"

"Just a guess." Emmett picked up his pace. He had no idea what they would find but he hoped that it would give him a clue as to where they were. Once he knew that, then he could try to figure out a way to get them back to Blakely Grove.

He stopped at the edge of the forest. Ahead stood a quaint cottage alone in the clearing. Smoke wafted casually out of the chimney which meant that someone was probably home. He studied the clearing and the little hut. He had no idea who or what lived there and that worried him. It was likely that whoever it was would be harmless, but he wasn't ready to take that chance.

"What are you waiting for?" Kami barged past him and ran towards the cottage without waiting for an answer.

She was banging on the door and calling out hello by the time Emmett caught up to her. He wasn't sure if he should be thankful or not that no one answered.

Kami tried calling out louder when there was no response from inside.

"Maybe no one's home?"

"Someone has to be here," Kami reached for the door handle, but Emmett stopped her before she could touch it.

"Let's not go barging in where we're not invited. Obviously, no one is here," Emmett let go of her hand.

"There is smoke coming from the chimney, which means there is a fire, which means someone is here," Kami reached for the door again. Emmett grabbed her arm and held it in place.

"Yeah, but are they friendly?" Emmett asked, trying to drive his point home. "We don't even know if they speak English."

"Then we'll draw pictures." Kami ripped her arm away and reached for the door handle again.

"And just what do you think you're doing?"

Kami and Emmett whipped around towards the unexpected sound of a woman's voice and saw nothing.

"Well, I'm waiting. Explain yourselves," demanded the apparently invisible woman.

"Uh..." Kami's voice tremored with uncertainty.

"That is not an explanation of why you were about to enter my home without permission."

"I apologize for the actions of my friend." Emmett looked pointedly at Kami who had decided to keep her mouth shut. "We're lost and looking for some help and guidance. Would you be so kind as to lend us your assistance?"

"My assistance? After you tried to break into my house?" a voice purred from near his feet. Emmett looked down into the fluffy face of a silver tabby cat.

"Once again, I'm truly sorry. My name is Emmett." Out of the corner of his eye he saw a puzzled look flash across Kami's face, but he chose to ignore it for now. "And this is my friend, Kami."

"Mrow."

It was not the response he had expected from the cat. Someone chuckled from behind them. "Don't mind her. Come on in. I was just putting some tea on."

Emmett turned to see that the door to the house had been opened. There was still no one in sight besides the cat who brushed past them and leapt onto the table. Emmett shrugged and followed the cat; it would have been rude to do otherwise. He remained on high alert for anything suspicious as he crossed the threshold. Kami hesitated a bit longer before following. They jumped as the door swung closed behind them.

"May I ask, who are you?" Emmett inquired. He kept his voice neutral and pleasant. He didn't want to anger their mysterious host.

"I'm Tithoriea and these are my lands. I share this abode with my friend, Malawli," her gentle voice echoed around them. Emmett knew of only a handful of creatures that could speak without being seen in such a way and he hoped it was one of the nicer of those creatures. He did the only thing he could do.

"Well, we do appreciate your kindness. Would it be possible to see with whom I'm speaking?"

"I prefer this form around those I do not know. It is common for my kind to be reserved in such things."

"Your kind?" Emmett asked

"Dryads," she said.

"That means this is Mythos." Emmett smiled as it dawned on him where they were.

"How do you not know where you are?" Malawli stopped grooming herself long enough to ask.

"It spoke." Kami's eyes widened as she pointed at the cat.

"Of course I spoke." Malawli responded, her nose twitching as she did so. "I'm a witch. If I couldn't speak, I would be a very poor witch indeed."

"What about you two travellers? Neither of you are from around here, that much is obvious, but how did you get here without knowing where you are?" Tithoriea asked.

"That's a bit of a story, and we're rather eager to get on our way," Emmett said. He had no wish to explain himself to strangers. Especially ones that he wasn't sure he trusted yet.

"It must be quite the tale indeed," Malawli said as she studied their guests, her nose still twitching as she sniffed at the air. "A nasty wound like that one can only be caused by the darkest of magic."

"We had an encounter with a creature not near as friendly as either of you." Emmett looked down at the mark on his hand that still appeared to be spreading. "I was hoping it would heal on its own."

"Silly creature, wounds like that do not heal on their own. Sit." Malawli ordered.

Emmett didn't want to hang around here too long, but they needed help. So far, these two had been nothing but hospitable. He obeyed Malawli's command, sat down, and placed his hand on the table. She sniffed at it intently, her whiskers twitching rhythmically as she did so.

"Yes, yes," she mumbled to herself. "This is terrible magic indeed. I haven't seen anything like this since..." Malawli looked up at Emmett, her eyes narrowing. "How did you get this wound?"

"As I said, we encountered something that was less than friendly," Emmett said. He saw no reason he had to expand on that. He could easily plead ignorance. "One minute, we were in our little town of Blakely Grove in Mundialis, trying to get home for dinner, when something in the shadows started chasing us and the next thing we knew, we were here."

"Hmmm," Malawi's nose twitched in the direction of Kami. "Still, I have not seen a wound like this since the dark days of the war. Since the Erlkrönig tried to rule these lands."

Emmett kept his face resolutely neutral. "I have no idea what attacked us, only that it did."

"Blakely Grove. That sounds beautiful." Tithoriea said to break the awkward silence that had descended on them.

"Yes," agreed Emmett. He watched as Malawli jumped off and on the table, retrieving various items from around the kitchen. He tried not to wonder how clean the cat's mouth was as she dropped the bandages on the table in front of him. "There are many small forests within the town and every street is lined with maples and poplars. It was gorgeous."

"Was?" Asked Malawli after she dropped what she had been carrying. "Is it not still?"

"Hard to know what something is when you are not there to see it yourself." Emmett retorted.

"Of course, that is very reasonable of you. Tea?" Tithoriea asked.

"That would be—Ow!" exclaimed Emmett. Malawli was in the middle of putting a salve on his wound.

"Hold still," Malawli growled at him. She picked up a tied sprig of herbs and brushed them over the wound a few times. She spat them out before sniffing at the wound again. "That should take care of the pain and stop it from spreading, but I cannot heal a would like this. Perhaps a fae could, if you could find one."

"Thank you." Emmett relaxed into the chair. He was glad that their hosts had turned out to be not just friendly, but helpful as well. Emmett watched a teacup float across the room followed by a pot of tea that poured itself into the cup. Emmett nodded toward the spot he thought Tithoriea might be standing. "Ta, Tithor... Tithah... Tithy."

"Did you just call me Tithy?" she asked with a dry chuckle. "That is a first."

"I mean no disrespect, but your name is quite the mouthful," Emmett said as another teacup placed itself on the other side of the table and more tea was poured. Emmett looked at Kami who was still standing near the door in silence. "Kami, are you going to just stand there and be rude, or are you going to sit down and have a cup of tea?"

Kami stared at him as if he'd sprouted a pair of wings. With a shake of her head she turned, threw the door open and bolted outside.

"Um, will you both please excuse me for a moment?" Emmett stood up and bowed his head towards his hosts before he dashed out after Kami. He was relieved to see she hadn't gone far. She was standing in the middle of the clearing, her back to the hut. He was sure she was just feeling overwhelmed and a bit scared. He couldn't blame her feeling that way after the sheer number of strange things they had encountered today. He decided that it would easier to play dumb right now.

"What in the world is going on, Kami?" Emmett asked, trying to manufacture as much annoyance as he could—he had a lot of years to pull from. Mostly, he was worried that she would take off on her own and that was something that he could not allow to happen.

"You tell me." She turned to look at him. "Why are you lying about everything?"

"What are you talking about?" Emmett scratched his head, confused and worried at the same time. "I haven't lied about anything!"

"That," she growled, "is a lie."

"What the heck are you talking about?" Emmett tried to keep the worry out of his voice, but the accusation had shaken him. He had not expected something like that from her. His mind spun with a million possibilities and explanations, but few of them made sense and the one that did was not a possibility he wanted to consider.

"I don't know!" Kami shouted and began pacing, her hands making a mess of her hair. "All I know is that you've been lying about everything. I don't even know how I know that, but it's true."

"What are you talking about, Kami? Come on, you know me. We've been friends forever." Emmett grabbed her shoulders and looked her steadily in the eye. "I'm Emmett, your friend. Your best friend. Why would I lie to you?"

"I don't know." Kami closed her eyes and took a deep breath before opening them again. "I don't even know who you are because every time you say your name, I know it's a lie. Who are you really?"

Emmett let his hands drop and considered his answer carefully. "I'm Emmett, I'm your friend, and maybe you hit your head harder than I thought."

"That. Is. A. Lie." She punctuated each word with poke of her finger on his chest. "Tell me the truth. Who are you and why did you bring me here?"

"Oh, my word, Kami. I didn't bring you here. This is not my fault." Emmett turned his back on her, took a deep breath, and tried to gather his thoughts.

"Well, that was almost the truth," Kami spat at him as she grabbed his shoulder and turned him to face her. "Except I still don't know who you really are or why you think this is your fault."

"I don't know what you want me to say. I'm your friend and maybe, just maybe, I'm more than that. I can't tell you anything else. It wouldn't be safe for either of us." Emmett waited for her to say something to that, but all she did was stare at him. He could see the pain and fear in her eyes, and he had no idea what he could say to fix it. "Kami, please, trust me."

"Tell me the truth," she insisted. "Don't you think I deserve the truth?"

"Of course you deserve the truth!" Emmett said and regretted his words the moment he saw her eyes go wide.

"You don't even believe that!" Kami shouted at him.

"Kami, I—"

"No, you don't get to even try to apologize for that," Kami said, her voice wavering as she fought back tears. "If you were really my friend you would have told me the truth already."

"It's not that simple."

"It is that simple." Kami wiped the tears from her cheeks. "You can tell me the truth, or you can leave me the hell alone."

"Kami!" Emmett tried again, but she turned her back on him. He could still hear her sniffling and he had no idea what he could do or say that would calm her down. His only recourse was to do something that screamed against every protective instinct he had. "Have it your way. Don't believe anything I say, but I'm going back inside. I'm going to talk to those two nice beings, and I'm going to find a way out of here. You are welcome to join me."

With still no response forthcoming, he turned and headed back to the cottage alone. He resisted the urge to slam the door behind him as he did so. He wasn't angry at her and he knew it. He was scared and worried. Worried that he wouldn't find a way back and worried about what might be waiting for them if he did succeed.

And he was worried that he had just made his biggest mistake ever by walking away, but he needed Kami to choose to stay with him. Things would not go smoothly if he tried to force the issue. She had to choose. "I'm sorry about that. Thank you both so much for your hospitality."

"That one is a little touched, isn't she?" Malawli asked, looking up from her own cup of milky tea. "Not quite herself or anyone else."

"You could say that again," Emmett mumbled and collapsed into the chair he was sitting in earlier.

"Why would I say it again?" Malawli blinked and tilted her head to the side. Emmett decided it was best to ignore her comments for now. Cats tended to be finicky no matter what world one found themselves in.

Knock, knock.

Emmett glanced at the door as it opened to reveal Kami standing there, looking only a little ashamed of her earlier outburst. She fixed her gaze on Malawli, deliberately ignoring Emmett. "Sorry for that, this is all a bit overwhelming. I'm not entirely sure where I am or why I'm here or even where here is."

"Strange things always happen in this realm. It's the nature of Mythos," Tithoriea commented. "Which is where you are right now. Travel between the realms isn't easy and the weak spots between them grow fewer as the centuries progress."

"Mrew. Ever expanding, ever changing. It's a wonderful thing," Malawli added cryptically.

"Yes, and we would like to return to Mundialis." Emmett tried to ignore the way Kami's jaw tensed as he spoke. "Do you know how we can get back?"

"No," Malawli said bluntly. She looked awkwardly at the area where Tithoriea's voice was coming from. "However?"

"However," Tithoriea continued, "we can tell you the name of a seer who may be willing to help you. It is a difficult journey to cross the realms."

"I'm always up for a challenge," Kami stated grimly, giving Emmett a sideways glance. He ignored the look and the comment that he knew was mostly addressed to him. Their earlier conversation was nowhere near finished. He was sure that she wasn't going to keep letting him get away with lying to her.

"Her name is Jewel," Malawi told them. "You'll find her in the village of Abernath just a few hours walk to the west of here."

"She is easy to find as she is well known," Tithoriea added. "Now, let us give you a bit of nourishment to take for the journey. Consider it a gift for such an important undertaking. We're glad to be a part of your story."

Kami raised an eyebrow at Emmett which he pretended not to notice. He wasn't about to explain that comment to her either. She could stew on it for now and he would think up a suitable explanation later.

Chapter Three

Emmett hoisted the small pack up a bit higher and peered at Kami from the corner of his eye. She hadn't said a word to him since they had left the cottage. It was going to be a long, difficult road ahead, and it would not be made any easier with the rift that had come between them. There was little Emmett could do to ease her mind, but he had to try. "Kami?"

"No." She quickened her pace and he lengthened his stride to keep up with her.

"Come on Kami, we've been best friends since we were little. You know me," he pleaded with her. He was willing to say anything to get her to talk to him. Her anger he could deal with, but not her silence.

"Do I? Because I don't even know your name except that it's not Emmett." Kami stopped so that she could look at him. He could tell that she was barely holding herself together and clinging to her anger to do so. "I have no idea what's going on here. I know if you're lying or telling the truth which shouldn't even be possible. And it's not just you. I could sense the same things from those…whatever those two things were back there. I don't understand any of it, but I know it's real."

Emmett bit his lip, trying to find an answer to give her that wouldn't be a lie. He had a good idea about why she had this ability, but he wasn't willing to broach that subject, not yet. "Kami, I don't know what to tell you."

"No, of course not." Kami rolled her eyes. "Since the moment I woke up in this place almost every word out of your mouth has been a lie. Give me one good reason why I should bother listening to you at all?"

"Because I care about you, Kami." Emmett chose his words carefully—he needed her to trust him, but there was so much that he couldn't tell her. He was afraid that if he was honest with her it would be too much for her to handle. "I don't want you to get hurt—least of all by me."

Kami thawed a little at his confession, but he could still see the anger and confusion in her eyes. And the fear that she was trying so hard to hide. "Finally, something true."

"Of course it's true. Why do you think I've spent so many years trying to keep you safe?" Emmett struggled to keep his tone calm. "You are important to me. I care about you."

"I believe you and I'm sure you have your reasons for lying," Kami said, "What I don't understand is why?"

"I don't have a choice, Kami. It's better this way. You have to trust me on this." Emmett wanted to reach out and sense her emotions, but he couldn't risk doing that any more than he could tell her the truth about everything.

"You do have a choice. Even you know that because I can tell you're lying about it!" Kami shouted.

Emmett was torn between his desire to shout back at her for being so difficult and wanting to hug her and make her fear and confusion go away. Neither solution would do any good. Getting angry would just push her further away and she was too worked up to allow him to hug her. Instead, he took the middle route and tried to reason with her. "Kami, I—"

"No," she interrupted. "Please, Em or whoever you are, don't lie to me. I can't handle it right now. Not on top of everything else. I'm stuck in a strange place with someone I once thought was my best friend. Turns out he's been lying to me my entire life and I don't even know why. Do you know what that's like? Do you even understand what I'm feeling? I need something real and true to hold on to right now."

Emmett closed his eyes and tried to find the words that could fix it all. It hurt him to see the pain in her eyes. He wished desperately that he could tell her the truth, but this was not the time or place for that. He needed time to think about their situation, to consider all the possibilities before telling her even a fraction of the truth. There was far too much at stake.

Emmett opened his eyes. "I do understand what you're feeling, and this is what I can tell you: I have dedicated my life to watching over you and keeping you safe from harm. I'd like to consider you a friend, but you are more than that. Who I am, where I come from, and why I'm watching over you are things I cannot tell you. Not yet. But trust me when I say that I have your best interests at heart."

He allowed her a moment to absorb his words before asking an important question. "Is that going to be enough for you right now? Enough to trust me for just a little bit longer?"

"For now, maybe, but I deserve some real answers. I mean, what am I even supposed to call you?" Kami asked.

"Em, like you always have." He gave her a lopsided grin that he knew she wouldn't understand.

"Okay." She drew the word out as she thought about it.

"And you do deserve answers," he added, "I don't know when, but I will tell you what I can when I can. I promise."

"I'll hold you to that," Kami said. "So, I guess we should get going?"

"Yes, onwards." Emmett wondered what was going through her head. Nothing he had said was a lie, but his mind couldn't stop circling the fact that the longer they remained here, the harder it would be for him to keep the truth from her. He couldn't stand the thought of losing her friendship, which meant that he would need to find ways to talk around the truth that she couldn't detect.

It wasn't long until they reached the town that Tithoriea and Malawli had told them about—Abernath. Bare dirt streets wound their way between ramshackle wooden huts that sat next to meticulous stone buildings. It wasn't an impressive village, but where Mythos was concerned looks were often deceiving. This was a world where magic still existed, and little was as it seemed.

Kami said nothing as she followed him through the maze of streets until they found their way into the village square. Here, the buildings all looked well cared for and identical in shape and size. Only the choice of building material stood to differentiate each one.

"We should find a place to stay for the night," Emmett said as he studied the buildings that faced towards the water fountain at the centre of the square. "We can find that Jewel person tomorrow."

"All the buildings look the same to me and not one of these places has a sign to tell us what is where." Kami frowned at the buildings.

"We could ask someone?" Emmett suggested. He wasn't hopeful. It was getting dark and the amount of people wandering the streets was quickly dwindling. "Or we could go there."

Kami looked towards where he was pointing. It was a slightly larger building a little bit down from where they stood. She nodded and followed him towards it. Emmett could only hope that his instincts were right. He kept his worries about how they would pay for their accommodations to himself.

"Hello weary travelers and welcome to The Inn of Abernath," a pudgy proprietor called out from behind the counter as they stepped through the doorway. His grin was welcoming even if his appearance was rather intimidating. Emmett could hear the sound of merrymaking coming from an adjoining room to the foyer. More than likely that would be the public house. Emmett stepped forward to deal with getting checked in.

"Good evening, sir." Emmett sauntered closer to get a better look at the proprietor, trying to guess at his species and utterly failing. He looked like a cross between a human and a troll that had been painted orange. It wasn't possible since trolls were barely more than animals and would rather eat a human than breed with one. "We're looking for accommodations for a single night, possibly more depending on how our business here goes."

"We do have several rooms that are available. What have you got in the way of currency? We take most valuables as trade."

Emmett knew that they had little to use for barter, but he wasn't about to spend the night outside.

Although he doubted that it would be worth much, he took out his wallet and rifled through it for what little cash he had. "I have some paper and metal currency from Mundialis, will you accept that?"

He handed the money over so that proprietor could inspect it, which he did closely. It wasn't much, but he had no idea what anything from Mundialis would be worth in this place.

"Interesting. We don't get many people from Mundialis crossing the border anymore. I can barely remember the last time I saw an ordinary human." He glanced back at Kami and then to Emmett again. "And the last time, if I recollect correctly, they tried to kill a friend of mine. You two aren't planning on doing any killing around these parts, are you?"

"What? No!" Emmett jumped at the sound of Kami's voice coming from behind him. She had sidled up closer to the counter while he had been occupied with watching the proprietor.

"Good, but I'm afraid to say that this is not enough to secure a room for the night. I mean, paper currency? Don't you have anything more interesting? Like, that thing she's wearing on her neck?" Emmett turned to see that the proprietor was pointing at the small golden necklace that Kami was wearing. Her hand immediately went up to cover it.

"No," Emmett said before Kami could respond. "That is not for sale or barter."

"This was a gift from my Grammie," Kami said, her voice quiet, "but if it's all we have..."

"No," Emmett insisted again.

"Pity. Got anything else of worth or interest?" the proprietor asked, not sounding too hopeful.

Reluctantly, Emmett reached into the far corner of the billfold and pulled out a small wooden coin that he kept hidden there. For him the value was only sentimental, but to anyone on this world it was worth a fortune. He held it tightly in his fist for a moment before placing it on the counter. "What about this?"

"Well I'll be damned, pardon my language," the proprietor said with obvious shock as he stared at the rainbow hues that shimmered within the pale wood. "Now, that's something you don't see these days. Those few who have trinkets from Castus don't like to let go of them. Where did you get this?"

"It was a gift." Emmett stated, knowing that a lie of how he came to have such a rare treasure would bring less questions than the truth.

"That's some gift. You're willing to give it up?" The proprietor narrowed his eyes in suspicion at Emmett. "Said you were from Mundialis, right?"

"Yes," Emmett said firmly, knowing that Kami was reading every lie in this conversation. He would figure out the answers to her questions later. Right now, they needed a way to pay for room, food, and supplies. "For the right price."

"Best room in the house and food."

"We're going to need supplies." Emmett wasn't going to let him get away with that good of a deal. He knew the worth of the coin he was offering.

"Deal." With a grin, the proprietor pocketed the wooden coin and held out his hand. "Name is Dyff, and welcome to the Inn."

"Thanks." Emmett smiled as his heart sank. He hated having to use the coin as currency, but it was all he had that was worth anything here.

"Lemme show you to your room." With a hop and whistle, Dyff took them to a room on the second floor. Two beds with thankfully clean linens, stood starkly on one side of the decently sized room, a simple nightstand beside each of them. A table and a couple of chairs that looked ancient occupied the other far corner. A door led off to what he assumed was the luxury of a private bathroom. Although the room was sparsely decorated, Emmett had no doubt that this was the best available in this establishment.

He waited for the door to close and then flopped onto the bed with a sigh. He was exhausted, but he knew that Kami probably had questions for him. He waited for the barrage, but she remained silent. He sat back up and saw that she hadn't taken more than a step from the door and was staring at him intently. "What?"

"What was that thing you used to pay for our room?"

Emmett weighed the consequences of telling her the truth and decided that he was better off not lying about it. "It was made in a place called Castus. It was given to me as a reminder of who I am and where I'm from. It's rare, which makes it valuable here."

"And I already know you won't tell me who you are, so I guess the where you're from is going to be off the table. I know you lied to him about that too," Kami said, turning away from him to study the room. He gave her time to think things through, but he wasn't used to silence from her.

"I'm sorry, Kami," Emmett said, needing to break the silence, but grateful that she wasn't about to make an issue of the secrets he needed to keep.

"Hm." Kami dropped her pack where she stood and walked over to the window to look out over the town. She lapsed into another long silence as she watched the sun set in the distance.

He nearly jumped when she finally spoke again. "So, we crash here for the night, we get some good food in us, and we find that so-called seer in the morning. Is that the plan?"

"So far, yes." Emmett stared at Kami's back, wanting to be thankful she hadn't given him the third degree, but instead he was worried. She had always been the type to ask a million questions.

"Are you okay?"

"Don't be stupid." Kami turned back to face him. She leaned against the wall, her arms crossed. "What do you think?"

"You're right. Sorry."

"So, are you ever going to tell me who you really are or is that something you can't say?" Emmett tried to not wince at the vitriol in her tone of voice. He couldn't blame her for how she was feeling. He tried to put himself in her shoes, in this strange place, unsure of everything and everyone—even the person she thought she had known best. He was sure he'd be feeling a bit angry himself.

"I…" Emmett had no idea what to say to her. He wasn't sure that there was anything he could tell her that would help in this situation. "I wish I could."

"But you aren't going to." Kami turned away from him to stare out the window again. "Do you know what was chasing us?"

"Yes." He saw no point in lying about that fact, but he didn't have to be any more specific. Still, he couldn't help but to add one more detail. "He's dangerous."

"How dangerous?"

"Very." Emmett didn't want to scare her, but at the same time he needed her to understand the gravity of the situation.

"He?" Kami asked.

"The thing that was chasing us back in Blakely Grove," Emmett responded, "is a he."

"And do you know why he was chasing us?"

He could have told her any number of half-truths, but he didn't want to do that. She deserved better than a half-truth from him. Emmett chose his words carefully. "Yes, he thinks I took something that belonged to him. I didn't, but he thinks that."

"What did you take?"

Emmett sighed. This was one of the topics he had wanted to avoid talking about. "It's complicated. I want to tell you, but—"

"But you can't tell me," Kami finished for him. "I get it."

"No, I don't think you do." Emmett insisted, needing her to fully comprehend how serious this was, even if he couldn't tell her the reasons why. "This is a very delicate situation and there is only so much that I can say without risking our lives. Do you understand that?"

Kami took a moment to consider his words before nodding. "Are we safe here? Are our families safe where they are? Our parents must be so worried about us."

"They're fine," Emmett assured her.

"And us?"

"He won't stop searching for us and his power will be stronger here than in Mundialis," Emmett said. "However, he might not know we're here, which means that if we move quickly he might not find us."

"Okay then." Kami turned around to face him again. "I get that from every which way this seriously sucks for both of us. I get it, Em. I have no idea exactly what is going on, but I can deal with that. It hurts that you don't think you can tell me the truth or that I can't handle it or that—"

"It's not that," Emmett interrupted her. "Well, not just that. There are certain things that, if known, could put us in even greater danger. I don't want to put you in harms way more than I already have. I can't take that risk, Kami. I can't."

"How about this? You tell me what you think I need to know when you think I need to know it," Kami offered. "And don't look so shocked. I've been known to be reasonable on occasion."

"On occasion," Emmett smirked. "And okay."

"Just don't hold me to being reasonable all the time. You know me."

He laughed and nodded in response. "I do."

"One more thing." Kami walked over and sat on the bed beside him. "Do you think we will find our way home?"

Emmett considered her question carefully before answering as honestly as he could. "I don't know."

"Okay." Kami fiddled with her locket. Emmett knew that habit and wrapped his arm around her shoulders.

"It's going to be okay. Don't worry."

Kami sniffled. "You don't believe that but thank you for trying to make me feel better."

"I'm so sorry, Kami." Emmett squeezed her a little tighter. "I'm going to do my best to make sure you get home safe. I promise. Whatever it takes, I'll do it."

"I believe you," Kami said, trying to stifle a yawn, "and I appreciate it. It's been one hell of a long day. We both could use some sleep. Good night, Em."

"Good night," Emmett whispered as she wandered off to the other bed. He laid down and stared at the ceiling. A part of him hoped that they would make it back to Mundialis, but another part of him wondered if it was a good idea to go back. He knew that if Asèth had found them there once then he would find them even easier next time. But Mythos was hardly safer. This realm was once the place he had called home and his spies were still here.

Emmett closed his eyes and tried to calm his thoughts. He needed to get his rest.

"Where are you?" Emmett heard the sinister voice clearly, as if Asèth were whispering in his ear. He sat up and looked around the room. No one else was here, but the voice had seemed so real. He laid back down. Tossing and turning, Emmett eventually fell asleep and dreamed of times long gone to him.

Chapter Four

The sun was shining high in the sky before they wandered out of their rooms to the public house below. Last night, they had seen a few creatures that had caused Kami's eyes to widen, but they had all been at a distance. Walking into the public house, they were faced with a lot of oddities eating a late morning meal. Emmett noticed Kami's hesitation when she saw the collection of creatures in the room. He grabbed her by the elbow and guided her to a seat in the corner, doing his best to block her view of the other patrons.

"Relax. Think of them as your strange cousins." Emmett pushed her into a chair at an empty table as far from the other customers as possible.

"It's covered in hair and nine feet tall." Her eyes flipped from one exotic creature to another. "And that thing over there looks like a reject from one of my worst nightmares and—"

"Relax, *she* is a yeti and *he* is leyak," Emmett explained, trying to speak to her in the most soothing voice he could manage without drawing any attention to himself.

"Its lungs are dragging on the floor."

"It used to be a cannibal of the human variety. It's probably been a long time since it had the chance to feed on real human flesh so if I were you, I would keep my voice down," Emmett growled. Kami opened her mouth to say something, but decided it was better to say nothing and closed her mouth again. "Good. Most of the creatures that you'll find in towns and civilized areas are just that—civilized. So, don't worry."

Emmett sat down in the other seat and glanced at the leyak from the corner of his eye. They weren't usually found in Mythos since they were technically the undead. It should have been in Immortui—the realm that belonged to such creatures. Although, it wasn't entirely unheard of for the undead to find their way into Mythos. Emmett couldn't help but wonder that if the leyak was in this realm, could its queen, Rangda, be here as well? That was not a thought he relished, but he didn't think a creature like that would ever be able to crossover.

"What can I get you folks?" Their server looked like a female version of Dyff. He could only assume that this woman was his wife or a relative of sorts. Either way, it was apparent that they were of the same species. She waited patiently for one of them to speak.

"Eggs scrambled and topped with cheese, bacon soft, shredded hash browns with onions and mushrooms and topped with more cheese. A large mug of blue mountain coffee, medium roast. Oh, and toast. Dark rye toast with extra butter." Emmett thought a little more about his order. "Could you throw in a stack of pumpkin pie pancakes with maple syrup and a bowl of fruit as well? Kami?"

Kami looked at him like he had lost his mind. Emmett suppressed his laughter at her confusion, but he couldn't stop his grin from spreading. "This is Mythos—the realm of all things magical. I'm pretty sure they could make anything your stomach desires."

"Anything? Anything at all?" Kami asked.

"Pretty darned near anyway." Their server grinned. "We've got an incredible kitchen witch working for us. You should see the things she comes up with on her own. I swear some of those ethnic fusions are to die for, although if you're not careful that could happen. Not every species can eat the same thing."

"Well then," Kami smirked. Emmett knew she was about to take full advantage of the situation. "I'll have an order of Belgian waffles made with a touch of cinnamon and served with a side of maple berry compote and a large bowl of whipped cream. Bacon, lots of it, extra crispy. A pitcher of fresh squeezed navel orange juice. And throw in a side of chicken fried steak with that. Cream gravy, of course. And ummm...."

"And that will probably be more than enough," Emmett laughed. "Thanks."

"Sure enough. I should have it all in about fifteen minutes. Holler if you need anything else." She waddled over to the kitchen to give their order to the kitchen witch. True to her word, their table was heaped with food in a short time. They dug in with gusto; both aware that they had no idea what their future would bring. For all either of them knew, this could easily be their last meal together.

They leaned back in their chairs with bellies bulging and let out contented sighs of relief. Emmett sipped at his coffee as Kami nibbled on another piece of bacon. They polished off most of what they had ordered. Emmett closed his eyes and enjoyed the moment for what it was before anything could ruin it.

"So, is there anything you think I need to know? Maybe something along the lines of how you know so much about this place. What was it called? Mythos? Or should I just follow your lead in ignorance and trust you?" Kami asked. There it was, his moment of peace now ruined. Though she kept her tone light, he could hear the edge of frustration that she was trying to hide.

"I would prefer it if you would trust me, but I'll understand if you don't. Things have gone a little sideways since we got here." Emmett took another sip of his coffee to delay the inevitable. He knew he needed to tell her something, something true, but how much he should tell her was still a matter of much self-debate. "I can tell you I've been to this realm before. More than that, I'm not sure I can say."

"When was that?" Kami pushed around the food on her plate.

"A long time ago."

"Okay." Kami nodded holding up a finger for him to remain silent while she processed what he had said. "You keep saying that it's dangerous for you to tell me things and every time I know that you are telling the truth. Or it is to you, the truth. What would happen if you did tell me?"

Emmett considered his answer. "I don't know exactly what would happen. There are things that I can't say simply because I have been sworn to secrecy in such matters. A lot of it would take too long to explain and time is precious to us. I'd like to get you home as quickly and safely as I can."

"But how is it dangerous?" Kami crossed her arms and leaned back in her chair.

Emmett frowned. "It can be dangerous to be in possession of certain types of knowledge. Some of the things I can't tell you are best not known. We're in enough danger as it is, I don't want to increase it."

Kami nodded. "I guess that means it's time to see the seer and grab some supplies."

Emmett swallowed the last sip of his coffee and headed outside with Kami on his heels. At midday the town was far busier than it had been the night before. This time Kami seemed to be able to mostly ignore all the fantastical beings that surrounded them. On occasion, she would crowd a little closer to him for comfort, but it wasn't too often.

It took more than a few questions and a couple of wrong turns before they found themselves in front a humble hut at the end of an alley; this they had been assured, was the home of the seer that they sought.

"Think we're expected?" Kami nudged Emmett in the ribs. "She is supposed to be some big seer and all."

"If she didn't expect us than maybe we've found the wrong seer and we should see someone else?" Emmett grinned. "It doesn't look promising that no one has come to greet us yet."

"I see," Kami drew the two words out as she struggled for something clever to say. "I think we should see the seer and if the seer sees things that we don't want to see we can saw her in half."

Emmett groaned. "That was horrible."

"I agree," a new voice chimed in. Both Emmett and Kami jumped. They turned to find a woman standing behind them, a smirk on her face. She stood less than five feet tall, but her intense golden gaze held their attention. "My name is Jewel and I'm sorry for running late, but there are a few things that even I can't foresee. Come in."

Jewel brushed passed them, carrying several bags in her arms. The door swung open at her approach and she went inside. Emmett and Kami followed her in. Neither were surprised by the door closing on its own behind them. A day in this place and Kami was already becoming accustomed to many strange things.

"So, the two little old biddies in the woods sent you my way and you want to know how you can get home. Perhaps a look at what dangers may await you on the way. Does that sound about right?" Jewel dropped her bags haphazardly on the nearest table. She had yet to even look in their direction.

Emmett and Kami exchanged a look before Emmett spoke up. "I suppose that sums things up fairly well."

"Glad to hear it. On occasion I can get things a little muddled. The problem with being a seer is keeping all the visions and thoughts that you get separate. There is so much that needs to be sifted and sorted and it's not always clear which future is the right one." Jewel turned to face them. "However, the past can often be easier to see than the future. There are so many little things that can affect a timeline, too many things that haven't been decided, so many gray areas. It's a difficult place to navigate, the future, but you came to the right place."

"You seem extremely sure of yourself," Kami said. Emmett held his breath and tried not to groan. It took more than strange surroundings and certain danger to keep Kami's impulsive nature from interfering with things. Emmett had been wondering how long it would take for her to start acting more like her careless, bull-headed self again.

"Of course I'm sure of myself." Jewel giggled. "If I wasn't than I wouldn't be a good seer, would I?"

Kami laughed. "No, you'd be a pretty bad one I guess."

"So then, shall we get this done and see about how to get you two back to Mundialis?" Jewel pushed aside a curtain that lead to another room. "Not many go there anymore. I've always found it rather sad how all the realms are drifting away from each other. Each one expanding within its own plane, but those planes keep moving further apart. You know, eventually each realm will expand to a point where it has hit its limits and will either spill over into other realms or collapse completely. It's difficult to see that far in the future. Takes a lot of energy…and I'm rambling. Sorry, I tend to do that when I meet new people."

She ushered Kami and Emmett to some cushioned stools before sitting down herself. "Sometimes I do get a little ahead of myself. I'm sure neither of you want to know the reasons why it's been getting harder to cross between the realms. Let's focus on what you're here for—how to get you back to Mundialis."

"Yes," Emmett agreed, "and the sooner the better."

"Are you sure of that?" Jewel asked, her face revealing nothing. "I mean, he who was chasing you might still be there on your return—waiting and watching for his chance. Or perhaps he has returned to his place of banishment in the outer reaches of the nothing. Is this something you would like to know?"

Emmett hesitated to ask her what he longed to know the most. As she had said, there were a lot of grey areas in the future and little was ever certain. Emmett chose a question that she would be able to tell them about with confidence. "What would you recommend that I ask you about?"

He hoped that she could see enough to know that there were things that would be better off not mentioned. Instead of answering him, she held out her hands to them. Emmett took it reluctantly. Kami showed no hesitation as she grasped the proffered hand. Jewel closed her eyes to focus.

"Well, some things are decided. You should attempt to return; that much is easy to see. This is a journey that was destined to happen. A necessity in both your lives. You will have to travel to places you have never been before. There will be many who will want to stop you. Passage between the realms is hard to find and what few routes are known are guarded by those who serve him, but there is a place, a realm that is not a realm that connects everything. A temporary harbour in the storm, but...."

Jewel opened her eyes and looked first at Emmett, then Kami, and then back to Emmett. "This is not going to an easy journey for anyone involved and there are many things in your futures that are blocked from me. It makes it hard to descry the best path for you to take. However, I'm sure that the realm that is not a realm would be the best route for you."

"A realm that is not a realm?" Emmett mumbled, mostly to himself as he tried to wrap his head around Jewel's cryptic words.

"Most don't know it exists, but it is the safest and most constant connection between almost all the realms. A constant." Jewel explained. "It's not actually a realm in the way most people think of these things. More like a place between and the only way that cannot be monitored by those who search for you."

"You're talking about the Ether, aren't you?" Emmett asked. "But no one is allowed there except the reapers and the dead. It's forbidden."

"Forbidden is such a strong word." Jewel winked at him. "There are ways, but few know of them. Would you prefer I gave you another option to seek?"

"I'd rather a choice other than that," Emmett said stiffly, "because what you are suggesting cannot be done."

"All other routes will lead to death and destruction," Jewel explained. "It would bring about the mayhem that you wish to avoid. Although, the longer you tarry the harder such a fate will be to avoid. There is much darkness in many of the roads I've searched. Many that even I cannot see beyond."

"Your way is going to trap us in the Ether until the end of time. It's insanity," Emmett argued. "I will not spend the rest of my days waiting for them to figure out the paperwork. I've heard the stories."

"Paperwork?" Kami asked, but they both ignored her.

"There are ways for it to be avoided. It is your best option. Perhaps the only option left to you," Jewel insisted.

"The Ether." Emmett slumped in his seat. "That was not the advice I wanted to hear."

"Your other option is death." Jewel stood up and stretched.

"Wait!" Kami shouted. Emmett knew that stubborn look on her face too well. He braced himself for the questions that were about to come.

"Yes, I know," Jewel sat back down. "You have questions. So many questions, but there are things that cannot be answered at this point. And there is no time for the long explanations you would need to help you understand. However, I will answer the ones that I can."

"Fine," Kami agreed reluctantly.

"Many of the questions that you have will be answered by the end of this journey. You should trust in your friend here, for he will never steer you wrong," Jewel attempted to assure her. "Does that help you at all?"

"Yeah, some," Kami mumbled. Emmett could see she was considering Jewel's words very carefully.

"Now, let's get the supplies organized and we can leave in the morning. I've already bought most of what I need personally, and my affairs are in order." Jewel hopped to her feet again.

"Wait, what?" Kami and Emmett asked at the same time.

"Well, yes. You see, I can't tell you where to find the passage because even if you found it you would be unable to use it. Reapers are notoriously hard to ask a favour of and, frankly, you two would be hopelessly lost without me. You need me on this journey." Jewel grinned.

"What are you talking about?" Emmett asked, trying to wrap his head around everything she had said.

"Right, of course, I didn't mention it, did I? Any good seer would have to be from the other side." Jewel giggled. "Have you ever seen what happens to other species when they get gifted with the sight? Some of the more magically inclined species, like the elves, are equipped to handle it, but for many it is not a good thing."

"You're a reaper?" Emmett asked.

"Retired," Jewel said with a little shrug. "Anyway, we should get you both the necessary supplies."

"Um, no offense, but we don't even know you. And you said it was dangerous. You don't look like you can handle yourself, I mean...." Kami stuttered as she stared down at the tiny dark-haired woman. "You're sort of a little slip of a thing."

Without even twitching so much as finger, Emmett watched Kami shoot upwards towards the ceiling. Her look of surprise was mirrored on his own face as she floated in the air. Jewel grinned. "Physical size is hardly a way to judge. There are many things that are littler than I, but even I would fear them."

"Point taken." Kami crossed her arms and glared at Jewel. Emmett wanted to laugh, but he knew better. She was not the kind of person who liked to be laughed at. When her feet were once again planted firmly on the floor, she relaxed a little. "I guess it'll be useful to have a witch or whatever with us on this journey."

"Not a witch, a retired reaper and a seer who decided that Mythos would be a good place to set up shop. I have very limited magic use, and this is one of the best places for me to expand my talents." Jewel shrugged. "It took a lot of time and energy to learn what I have, but it can come in handy."

"Magic is learnable?" Kami asked with a gleam in her eye. "As in anyone can learn it?"

"Oh, not everyone. You need a little bit of certain Mythos-type blood in you," Jewel said. "I had a great, great grandfather who was elvish. Back when the realms mixed more easily."

"And our journey would have been far easier," Emmett sighed wistfully. "Almost anyone could find a portal back then."

"You certainly wouldn't have needed me." Jewel pushed them both towards the door. "Now, as I said, I already have what I need and I dropped a list off with Dyff so you guys are taken care of, but we need to go get a map now."

"You mean you didn't have that ready as well?" Kami asked, rolling her eyes.

"Of course not. Only some things are certain and there are always a few things that cannot be foreseen and certain people whose decisions are hard to discern." Jewel glanced briefly at Emmett as she said it. "Usually more to do with who I'm dealing with than anything else. And I always do prefer to lean on the side of caution when I cannot be one hundred percent on things. "

"Safe policy," Emmett agreed, hoping that Kami had missed that pointed glance. "It's nice to know that you're not a guesser if you don't have the info. That will certainly allow me to put my confidence in your decisions and advice."

"Besides, I need your input on the conversation and without knowing your exact words I will not be able to form the right opinion." Jewel led them back towards the main the square. "This is not something that I could have decided beforehand."

Kami and Emmett nodded as they followed.

"I know this great little outfitter who does magical maps. Far easier to use, but they have their limits. While you would always know where you are on a map and where your route is, it shows you far less outside your route than a traditional map." Jewel continued talking about their map options, but Emmett had already tuned her out. Kami seemed far more intent on listening to what Jewel had to say.

He lagged back a step to watch the two of them as they chatted away about maps and the journey ahead. He was happy to have Jewel coming with them. Her help and advice could prove to be invaluable on this journey, but he knew that he would have to watch her closely. He had a feeling that she was suspicious of his origins and possibly Kami's as well. There were some secrets that he needed to keep—even from a seer.

Choosing a map and a route proved far more difficult than Jewel had let on during their walk to the outfitter's shop. The helpful guide tried his best to give them good advice, but they only had a vague idea of where they were going and that was not something that made choosing a route any easier. There were many things that they had to avoid and many routes that they could take—it was a matter of weighing a lot of options.

It was near dark by the time they left the outfitters—much to the relief of the poor young dwelf that was helping them. Emmett wanted to do nothing more than have a giant meal and a long night's rest. He was far more exhausted than he had thought possible for having done so little.

He glanced over at Kami who seemed to be dragging a little herself as well. He nudged her in the ribs and winked. "Ready for another magical meal of all we can eat?"

"I could eat a horse!" Kami exclaimed and then winced. "I think this may be one of the few places where I would get that if I did order it."

"I'm thinking a roast chicken with potatoes, carrots, and pearl onions. Some nice gravy to top it off with I think, and...." Emmett paused to think a bit more, then grinned. "How about a flagon of mead?"

"A what?" Kami shouted, her step faltering. "You're too young to drink. Hell, you won't even try a sip of the punch at parties."

Emmett chuckled. "You're right, I'm not a drinker. However, when in Mythos..."

Kami shook her head and grinned. "How do you know so much about this stuff?"

"What stuff?" Emmett asked, feeling like he had just been thrown out on thin ice. He mentally cursed himself for getting too comfortable.

"Realms and stuff." Kami kicked at the random rock. "I mean, I can draw conclusions. I get that you can't tell me all about a lot of things. Fine, I can deal with that, but you know a lot more than just about this place. It bothers me, all these gaps in information."

Emmett decided to stick with the truth. "Well, I learned a long time ago that there are five known realms that help keep the balance between the light and the darkness—or if you will, good and evil. There is a realm of pure light and a realm of pure darkness and three others that are in between those two in terms of the balance of good and evil. That's sort of the basics of it all."

"I see." Kami kicked at the rock again as they walked.

"It's not what you wanted to hear is it?"

"Not really," Kami sighed.

"You want to know *how* I know what I do," Emmett said as Kami kicked at the rock again. He watched it hit the ground awkwardly and bounce out of their path. She nodded but didn't say anything. "That is a long story that I don't really want to get into tonight."

"I know. I'll get the answers eventually."

"Eventually," Emmett agreed.

She grinned at him. "Well, I suppose that'll do for now. I promised to accept the limits of what you could tell me, and I will do just that."

"Thanks." Emmett threw an arm around her shoulder. Kami tried to half-heartedly shrug it off before accepting its presence. For the moment, it was like old times again, and Emmett longed for the time before they had landed in Mythos. It had been so much easier just a few days ago. "Now let's eat."

"Food. Yes, food is good."

Chapter Five

Bang, bang, bang.

Emmett sat up straight as a demanding knock startled him out of a dead sleep. He collapsed back as soon as it occurred to him that it was probably Jewel. Just a hint of pink and orange graced the horizon, and strange stars still clung to the sky.

Bang, bang, bang.

Emmett dragged himself out of bed. He glanced through the peephole to see Jewel raising her hand to knock again, so he opened the door before she could. She bounced in like a little ray of sunshine and he pushed down the unkind thoughts that leapt into his mind. "Morning."

"A great morning!" Jewel trilled as she skipped over to where Kami was hiding under her covers, doing the best she could to ignore everything that was going on. Jewel yanked at the blanket. "Wakey, wakey sleepy head."

"Go away," Kami growled and pulled the blanket back over her head. Jewel grinned and Kami, with the blanket still covering her, floated up towards the ceiling. Emmett couldn't help but smile as she grabbed the edges of the blanket and turned herself into a burrito. "I'll sleep in the air if I have to, but I'm not getting up yet. So, go away."

"Maybe we should grab some breakfast while sleeping beauty here attempts to wake up," Emmett suggested.

"I think you could be right." Jewel frowned at the floating burrito and lowered Kami back to the bed. "I do hope you join us soon because we've got a long way to travel today and you might as well start it off with a big meal. We won't be able to eat this good on the trail."

"Shut up," Kami mumbled from inside her blanket burrito.

"Get us a table and I will be right down," Emmett suggested. "I promise I won't be long."

Jewel nodded and slipped out the door. Emmett walked over and sat down on the edge of Kami's bed. "You're going to have get up and join us. I'm getting dressed and going down for a good meal. Jewel was right—who knows how well we will eat on the road."

Kami didn't even twitch in response. Emmett patted the lump he guessed to be her shoulder before doing exactly what he said he would do. Once he was dressed and moving, he felt far better. Jewel waited for him at a private corner table, sipping casually at some strange, smoking grey liquid. He chose a seat across the table from her and barely had a chance to pull his chair in when the same pudgy server toddled over.

"More of that coffee stuff that you had yesterday? And would you like to take some more time to decide on the food?"

"That sounds great thanks…uh…" Emmett realized that he hadn't ever asked for her name.

"Yniff," she grinned. "Thanks for asking. One coffee coming up for you."

Emmett smirked. "Thank you, Yniff."

"Sooooo…" Jewel stared at him from over her glass. "What are you, how did you come to his attention and, most importantly, why?"

Emmett frowned at the unexpected barrage of questions. She wasn't as likely to be able to tell if he was lying as Kami could, but that didn't mean he could lie with ease. She was still a seer and had some limited magic use. It was enough to keep him on edge. "Beg your pardon?"

"Okay, play it that way if you like, but there is this fuzzy blankness when I try to look at you directly. There are only a few races on this plane or any other that I cannot read. And your stubbornly sleeping companion is similarly obscured." Jewel leaned over the table towards him. "So, I'm asking you to be honest with me. Who or what are you and Kami? Because I know what you're not—you're not human."

Emmett placed his hands gently on the surface of table and took a deep breath. "My name is Emmett. My friend is Kami and we're from Mundialis. I don't know why you have trouble seeing either of us, but we're only what we appear to be."

Jewel leaned back in her chair and took another sip of her drink, taking her time to study him. "Okay, don't tell me. I can respect that. There are great events that surround both of you. Despite the obscurification, I can still sense things from the past and see some of the events in the future and it worries me. What worries me most is that…"

Jewel's voice dropped away as Yniff returned with Emmett's coffee and a smile. "Where's your other friend?"

"Still asleep," Emmett replied. "But I'm sure that when she gets here, she'll want the orange juice she had yesterday as well."

"Right-o, will you be waiting for her to join you before ordering food then?" Yniff asked. With a nod from Emmett she toddled off again.

"What worries me most is the," Jewel paused to be sure no one was listening before leaning forward and lowering her voice, "the Erlkrönig."

She glanced around the room again to make sure no one had heard her say that name. Satisfied, she relaxed back in her chair. "Most thought him dead, but many of us knew that he had been banished—by an angel, if one believes the rumours. Those uppity creatures rarely get involved in mortal affairs anymore."

Emmett raised an eyebrow and suppressed his annoyance at the use of a title that Asèth didn't deserve. "I wouldn't know of such things."

"And yet, for some reason, with what little ability he has within these realms, he is not only after you, but you've been marked by him." Jewel narrowed her eyes as she studied the young man who sat across from her. Emmett looked at the dark mark on the back of his hand. "I know what you're doing is important, but the fates be damned if I know why. I do know that you need me on this journey, or your deaths will be certain."

"Is that the reason you're joining us?" Emmett asked, trying to steer the conversation away from himself. "You grew so attached in a few moments that you couldn't bear the thought of us dead?"

Jewel smiled. "Digging, are you? Why not just come straight out and ask me what I saw? No, that would be far too straight forward. Or, perhaps you know that I cannot tell you everything in the futures I saw. Truth of it is, there are few things that strike a seer when they are not looking, and your visit came to me clearly. That is important."

Emmett frowned. He wasn't entirely sure what she meant by that, but the one thing he knew was that any good seer was cryptic at best. "What is important?"

"You, your journey. So, I will be your travelling companion and, hopefully, your friend."

"Thank you." Emmett nodded and then glanced at his hand again. "You seem to have more knowledge than I do about this wound, except you called it a mark. What can you tell me about it?"

"Not much. Only that I can sense his presence tied to that mark. Whatever happened, he attached a piece of himself to you."

"That does not sound promising." Emmett rubbed his hand over the mark. There was no more pain thanks to Malawli, but it seemed a part of his skin now. "Do you think he can track us with it?"

"Maybe. Which means we should make haste." Jewel smiled gently at him. "Nothing in our future is perfectly clear. Will we succeed? I do believe so, but it will not be an easy journey. I will guide you as best I can down the path with the least amount of pain and most amount of success."

"You know, you have got to be one of the few seers I've met who admits that their knowledge isn't concrete; that there are many paths to get us to the same outcome," Emmett stated pointedly.

"Met many seers then?" Jewel asked. Emmett grinned. It had been a while since he'd been able to enjoy this type of banter and it took his mind off less savoury thoughts.

"Fine. I'm here." Kami plopped into one of the two remaining chairs and eyed Emmett's coffee. He passed it over to her and covered his mouth so she wouldn't see his smirk at the look of utter disgust on her face. "How you drink it like that I will never know. That is disgusting."

"It's the favoured choice of psychopaths everywhere," Emmett quipped and took his coffee back from her. He sipped at the dark and bitter liquid. "Ahhhhh."

Yniff wandered over and placed the orange juice in front of Kami. "There ya go dear. I'll give you all a few minutes to decide on food and then I'll be right back for that order."

"You know there will not be much time for sleeping in on this journey?" Jewel told Kami. "As much as there are fancy technological things in your world and magic in this one, this is a place that has clung hard and firm to the old ways. There are no short cuts. We will be travelling hard, we will be sleeping rough, and there will be little time for self-indulgent behavior."

"Yeah, yeah," Kami sighed. "I know. I've never been much of a morning person, but it's far harder leaving a comfy bed than it will be to leave the hard ground."

"Who said anything about sleeping on the hard ground?" Jewel rolled her eyes. "Ah, Yniff, I have decided what I would like to eat. I would like an order of eldergreul, dry krintbred and more enchenvatar please."

"And I'll have banana pancakes with peanut butter, maple breakfast sausage, soft bacon, and more coffee as well. Thanks," Emmett ordered, deciding to take it easy on the food after yesterday's indulgence.

"French fries, bacon-wrapped filet mignon cooked to medium-rare, steamed assorted vegetables, and I'd like to follow that with a cherry cordial chocolate soufflé." Kami grinned at Emmett. "Hey, possible last meal and all."

"Well heck, I wish I'd thought of that one," Emmett laughed. He almost considered changing his order but decided against it for one important reason. "But this is not our last meal."

"No, it is not," Jewel said. "We'll have many more meals ahead. Not as decadent as this since even with magic there are limits on what we can bring on the trail."

"Yeah, those packs were a little on the small side," Kami pointed out. "I looked through the packages that Dyff left in our room. Not sure what all of it is though."

"You'll see soon enough." Jewel assured her as Yniff returned with a tray loaded down with far more plates than she should have been able to carry.

"Good," Emmett mumbled around a mouthful of food. He planned to enjoy every bite of this meal. And he wasn't going to be distracted or rushed. Not if this was his last good meal for the foreseeable future—which meant a lot more when a seer was involved.

Emmett took a deep breath of the fresh sun-warmed air. He hadn't expected to enjoy the beginning of their trek as much as he was. Being this close to a town made it feel more like a casual trail ride instead of a journey that could kill them. It was a well-marked road and occasionally other people sped by them riding strange beasts—and very occasionally an actual horse. There were even a couple of people who were travelling by broomstick, but for the most part, not many people seemed to be heading north.

Emmett patted the neck of his noble looking tragelaph as it plodded along ignoring everything that passed by them. Jewel had assured them that they were the best choice for their journey. Emmett was glad he had agreed to use them—however reluctantly. Like always, he was worried about the danger they might pose, but his fears had quickly been allayed after a few minutes of riding the gentle goat-like beasts.

"How far do you think we'll get tonight?" Kami asked, a placid smile on her face.

"I think we were hoping to get about fifteen or twenty miles in," Emmett said, "so long as problems and distractions are kept to a minimum."

"I foresee no issues today and we won't be branching off the main road until later. The less used road will slow us down slightly. After that, we shall find a good campsite and enjoy a nice dinner," Jewel told them and then nodded at whatever unseen vision was playing in her head. "I think it may be best for you to do the cooking on this journey, Emmett."

"Really?" he asked, raising an eyebrow. Cooking was not one of the things he considered to be a talent, but he was able to boil water without burning it—most of the time.

"Yes, my food will be too bland and you both will hate it. Kami will get distracted most of the time, forget she's cooking, and burn our meals to the point of inedibility. It's up to you." Jewel grinned. "Not that I can see your meals being all that great, but better than what either myself or Kami will be capable of doing."

"Fine." Emmett shrugged and turned his attention back to their surroundings. He'd rather not have to think about mundane things when he could bask in the beauty of nature instead. It filled him with joy. Being here among the trees and in the sunshine reminded him of happier times. Times that were long in his past, but always fresh in his memory.

True to her word, the day passed with little to mark it as special. They found a nice place to set up camp, a field on the edge of the forest, close to a stream. It was a beautiful place to sit and watch the sun set.

"Okay, so magical equipment," Jewel said when they had chosen their spot for the night, "is not that different from non-magical items. Your shelter may appear small, but it is bigger than it looks, and it will keep you warm or cool depending on outside conditions. To set up your shelter, simply unroll it and straighten out the supports that came with it."

Jewel paused while Emmett and Kami followed her instructions. When the supports had been straightened, she continued. "Okay, throw those on top of your shelter in a cross-like formation. That's it. Now, step back."

Emmett watched as the two crossed supports vibrated and the shelter raised itself.

"Could have used that on those damned family camp trips," Kami quipped. Emmett laughed. Those few ill-fated camping trips their families had decided to take together seemed impossibly long ago.

"Remember that time that your dad tried to start a fire?" Emmett prompted.

"And set the tent on fire instead," Kami snorted. "Or when your mom nearly took her eyebrows off trying to light that camp stove?"

"Absolute gold," Emmett chuckled as he remembered. "I don't miss those days. Our parents are more city folk than outdoorsmen."

Kami smiled as she thought about those fond memories. "How'd we end up so comfortable with the outdoors?"

"Perhaps you are just more naturally attuned to it," Jewel said without looking up at either of them as she sifted through her pack for something.

Kami's grin melted from her face. When she looked at Emmett again, he could see the edge of mistrust in her eyes. It hurt him to see that in her, but it was the way it had to be.

"So, let's check these shelters out and then I'll get to work on dinner?" Emmett suggested, trying to distract Kami's train of thought.

"Sure." There was little enthusiasm in her voice. Emmett hoped that her smile would return before they called it a night. He ducked into his own shelter and stopped short. While he wouldn't describe the inside as luxurious, it was far from barren. A comfy bed, raised off the ground, was on one side and a floating ball of light illuminated the interior. More importantly he could stand up straight with room to spare.

Emmett ducked back out to the welcoming sunshine to see Jewel grinning at him. She patted her own small-appearing shelter. "They are handy to have for long trips."

"This is going to be a far more enjoyable journey than I thought. Just wish we could have used something magical to help with the travelling part. I'm not keen on this slow pace." Emmett leaned against a tree. "Are you sure there is no quicker way to get to where we need to be?"

"Not if we want to find the rift quickly," Jewel answered. "There is no magic strong enough to penetrate the Ether—it is a place that does not want to be found. If we tried to pursue the rift with magic, it would move away from us faster."

Kami popped her head out of her shelter grinning. "Guys, this is awesome. Can we take these things with us when we go back?"

"Magic items must stay in the realm of Mythos," Jewel said. "I'm not actually sure if they would even work in a land so far removed from magic."

"It might work in Anabasa or Castus," Emmett suggested. "They have their own type of magic—if you can call it that."

"Yes, in theory, but it's a different type of magic in those realms. Maybe in Castus it could work, but I don't think they'd consider it pure enough to be allowed into that realm," Jewel replied with a sideways glance at Emmett. "And in Anabasa things get twisted and corrupted. It could be a terrible thing. Of course, this is all academic. Those realms are barred to outsiders."

"You're right," Emmett agreed, realizing that he may have given away more about himself than he had intended. "It'll only ever be theory."

"I'm not sure I understand exactly what you two are going on about, so I'm just going to point out that it's late and I'm hungry," Kami said.

"I'm on it." Emmett rolled his eyes, but he was happy for the distraction. Or perhaps it was the lack of questions being thrown at him that made it seem like such a pleasant night. He was almost starting to enjoy himself instead of spending all his time worrying about everything.

Chapter Six

"Wow." Kami stared at the hidden little valley Jewel had led them to. Shimmering sapphire pools cascaded into more shimmering sapphire pools that were fed from some unseen source. It was early in the afternoon when Jewel had suggested the short detour. After several days on the road, no one objected to calling it an early day at the promise of a hot bath and, at the sight of the glorious valley, none of them regretted it.

"This place is incredible, Jewel." Emmett turned a small circle, taking it all in. "It's so well hidden and out of the way, how did you even know it was here?"

"An old friend of mine, a water nymph, calls this her home." Jewel sauntered towards the nearest pond and looked right into the cerulean depths. "Strophia?"

Emmett watched as the water burbled and swirled and rose from the pond. It twisted upon itself until it formed a tower that stepped gracefully from pond to land—solidifying from water to human form, her skin pale, her hair waving in a breeze that didn't exist as if the figure before them was still submerged in the water.

"Jewel." Her voice was higher pitched than he had expected, but Emmett had never met a water nymph before. They were notoriously hard to find. He never thought that he would have the pleasure of meeting one. "It's been so long since I last saw you."

"Yes," Jewel bowed ever so slightly. "It has been far too long. I'm sure you are doing well and that there have been no more issues with your sisters?"

"They have left me alone." Strophia knelt and reached towards the pond. "And my darling panlongs as well."

A small serpent leapt out of the pond to brush against Strophia's hand. Emmett watched in awe as its scales flashed with rainbow brilliance before it disappeared into the water again. Emmett wanted to get closer so that he could see the small water dragon more closely. As far as he knew, there were very few dragons of any kind left.

"I'm glad to hear that. Your efforts at preservation are important." Jewel smiled politely and then swung her arm towards her companions. "I hope you do not mind that I have brought friends with me. We're travelling through to Álfheimr and are in need of rest."

"Why would you go there?" Strophia wrinkled her nose and frowned. "Surely there are better places to go?"

"Few with what we need." Jewel shrugged. "So?"

"Oh, yes." Strophia grinned happily. "Your friends and you are more than welcome to stay a spell and rest in my sanctuary."

"Thank you Strophia," Jewel said. "May I introduce you to Emmett and Kami?"

They both stepped awkwardly forward at the introduction. Emmett was glad for the chance to study the water nymph now that he was closer to her. Most nymphs preferred to stay invisible to the eyes of outsiders—being seen only when they wished to be seen.

"Welcome strangers," Strophia burbled. "You must be on a very important journey for Jewel to agree to accompany you. She only leaves her home if the need is most grave."

"We're just trying to get home is all," Emmett insisted.

"Yes, of course," Strophia drawled as she studied them. He bristled at her tone, but decided it was best to say nothing in return. This was not a conversation that he had any desire to encourage and it was obvious she was already suspicious of them. After a pregnant pause she continued. "Please do stay the night, my springs are warm, and you are welcome to make use of them. I can see that you have been travelling hard."

Kami snorted and Emmett nudged her in the ribs. He knew what she was thinking, and he couldn't disagree, but they still needed to be polite and proper. He smiled at Strophia. "Thank you. We're certainly in great need of a wash and some rest. Your hospitality is appreciated."

"Shall I show them around or would you like that pleasure?" Jewel asked Strophia now that the introductions had been finished.

"Oh, I shall leave that to you. Please avoid the dark waters. Those are the panlong breeding ponds and they do not take kindly to strangers." Strophia walked back towards the pond from which she had emerged. She disappeared quickly and when Emmett glanced into the pond, he saw very little to differentiate it from any other pond he had seen before.

"Dragon preservation, huh," Emmett mumbled to himself.

"Yes," Jewel said. Emmett looked at her, surprised that she had been able to hear him. "Not a very popular hobby, but an important one. There are so few of them left in this world."

"Why aren't dragons popular?" Kami asked.

"They are not the friendliest of animals, but there are few who can tame and handle them. If left to their own devices dragons would overrun and destroy everything in sight." Jewel motioned for them to follow her as she explained. "Most don't understand the beasts, but I believe that just because we do not understand something doesn't mean it should be destroyed and lost forever into the mists of time."

"I would be inclined to agree," Kami said.

Jewel smiled. "You would be one of the few. There are a handful of people who have dedicated their lives to saving the dragon population. However, there are still many kinds that could not be saved. Soon even memory of them may fade."

"Did dragons ever come to Earth like they did in the old stories?" Kami asked.

"Ah," Jewel thought for a moment before continuing. "I do believe a few have crossed over when the trip was a simpler one."

"How come no one has ever discovered their remains then?"

Jewel laughed and stopped in front of a pond from which steam lazily drifted. "Dragons do not leave remains as other creatures do. They are elemental creatures; upon their death they return to their element."

"Oh." Kami looked disappointed and Emmett didn't blame her. He only wished that he could ask the questions that were in his mind, but he knew that they would reveal far too much knowledge of this world. There was no need to make Kami wonder even more about his past.

Jewel smiled. "Now for more important matters. This pond will suffice for our needs. Who's first?"

They all looked at each other and no one spoke up.

"Rock, paper, scissors it?" Emmett suggested. "Or perhaps ladies first?"

"I think I like the second idea best." Kami winked and stuck out her tongue at Emmett. He grinned back at her.

"You are so lucky I'm resisting the urge to push you in there—clothes and all." He turned his attention back to Jewel. "Where should I go wait while you two make yourselves decent again?"

Jewel pointed back the way they had come. "How about you get camp set up in the clearing over there?"

"Sounds good to me," Emmett called back over his shoulder as he walked back the way they had come. "But don't forget that tour. I would love to see more of this valley and its wonders."

He set about putting up the shelters and creating the nicest camp that he possibly could. He took his time, wanting to give the them as much time as possible to enjoy their bath. They had been roughing it for a while, and he was sure that they were enjoying themselves as much as he was going to when it was his turn to slip into the gloriously warm water.

Emmett paced impatiently with nothing else left to do by the time Jewel and Kami returned to camp looking refreshed and relaxed. He was only a little envious, but it was his turn now. He ran towards the pond that the girls had just left and cannonballed in fully clothed. It was a deceptively deep pond; he never managed to touch the bottom before he had to swim back to the surface.

He removed his clothing and scrubbed it as best he could before he laid it over a nearby branch to dry in the warmth of the setting sun. He had no worries about it drying in time—it was one of the benefits of magical items. They dried fast, were tear resistant, and had a few other properties that came in handy for travellers.

"This is just what I needed," Emmett mumbled to himself as he floated in the water, staring up at the sky.

It wasn't until he heard Kami screech that he stumbled his way out of the pool in a rush. Half-dressed and mostly out of breath, he was greeted with the sight of Kami and Jewel flying in the air on sticks—looking much like the witches out of old folk tales.

"Weeeeee!" Kami screeched again as she performed a death-defying flip that made Emmett's heart stop for a few seconds.

"Kami!" Emmett screamed, hoping she would hear him. "Kami get down here now! You're going to get yourself killed! KAMI!"

He could almost hear her roll her eyes as she came zooming in too close. Emmett stepped back, trying to catch his balance. Kami giggled from above him—just out of reach. "Come on, Em, don't be a spoil sport. This is just the kind of fun that I've been missing the last few days. I need this."

"It's way too dangerous. Come on, please?" Emmett pleaded with her, but he knew that she wouldn't listen to him. She never had before when it came to having fun.

"Watch this," Kami grinned as she shot straight skyward again, daring to fly even higher. If it wasn't for his keen vision, he would have had a hard time knowing that the black blob in the sky was a girl on a stick. He could also clearly see the concern on Jewel's face as well.

"Kami, be careful!" Jewel called out. Emmett felt the hair rise on the back of his neck. A worried seer was never a good sign.

"Kami, listen to her! Get down—"

"No!" Jewel's shout cut him off as she shot straight upwards towards Kami, who had begun a series of loop-de-loops and barrel rolls. Emmett watched in horror as another blob—this one he could not identify—collided with Kami before Jewel could get high enough to get her attention. Whatever it was, it had enough force to knock her from the stick she was riding as it too went tumbling.

His heart stopped the moment he realized that she was falling. He had maybe twenty seconds to decide before it would be too late. He watched as Jewel reached out towards Kami, trying to halt her fall with the little magic she was capable of. It wasn't enough; her own stick began to wobble. She didn't have enough power or focus to be able to sustain her own flight while stopping Kami's rapid descent.

Twelve seconds. That's all he had now. There were no more options, nothing he could fall back on now. He had to act. He turned his focus inward to the power and energy he had kept so well hidden for such a long time. He needed just enough, only a little bit of that energy.

It flowed outward from him. A roar escaped from his lips as he stretched his golden wings to their full extent. It hurt, but he had to ignore the pain. He had to save her. He pushed upwards, launching himself upwards toward Kami. He grabbed her and allowed her momentum to pull him downwards. It would do no good to stop her fall in such a way as to hurt them both. He stretched out his wings to catch the wind and slow their descent instead.

They hit the ground harder than he had intended. He'd waited too long to act. Emmett tried his best to set Kami down gently even as his own legs buckled underneath him. He was exhausted, but he forced himself to pull his energy back and hide it away again. Emmett stayed on his hands and knees, trying to catch his breath while waiting for the inevitable.

"You…" Kami said but didn't finish the sentence. She sat there staring at him, mouth open as she searched for the right thing to say.

"Why do you have to be so darn reckless?" he growled. It seemed that was all he needed to do to loosen the words that she hadn't been able to say just a few seconds before.

"What in the hell are you?" Kami shouted at him and he could hear the panic on the edges of it as she scrambled away from him and onto her feet.

"It's not important." Emmett pressed a hand against his forehead knowing that this was going to be one of those conversations that would give him a headache if his head didn't already hurt.

"Really? That's the lie you're going with? No. Just no." She held her hand up and Emmett waited for her to gather her thoughts. He didn't have answers for her anyway. "All this time you could fly, and you never even told me?"

"Because it's dangerous for you to know. It's even more dangerous to me if anyone finds out." Emmett pushed himself up on to his feet, wobbling slightly as he tried to catch his balance. He looked at Kami, trying not to be furious at her. He knew that half his anger stemmed from his fear that someone out there would have sensed even that tiny bit of energy he had unleashed. To those that knew, it was something that would be easily detectable.

"You're a—" Jewel started to say, but a look from Emmett cut her off before she could finish the sentence.

"No," Emmett pleaded with her. "Please, don't."

Jewel stared at him wide-eyed, mouth hanging open. She snapped it shut and gathered her thoughts before speaking. "I never would have guessed. Of course, I'll tell no one."

"Tell no one what?" Kami asked. Emmett winced and turned to face her. He had to tell her something, but the truth was just too dangerous for all of them. He needed to tread carefully here; he didn't want to drive her away with another lie.

"There are things within the realms that shouldn't be mentioned." Jewel stepped in front of Emmett. "You do not understand the ways of all the realms so you may not have a full comprehension of the history and nuances that exist. Just believe that some things are so rare as to warrant their capture, death, or worse."

"Or worse?" Kami asked. "And not a single word was a lie, or even half a lie. So, I guess this is one of those times that I should leave well enough alone?"

"More than you know," a soft voice said from the direction of the nearest pond. Emmett winced again. He had forgotten about Strophia. Another witness to something that was not allowed to be seen. Something he was supposed to avoid doing unless he had no other option. He was still trying to convince himself that there had been no other option this time. "Worry not, this valley is protected by myself and none will know by my word."

Emmett nodded his head in thanks. He knew he had to deal with Kami, but he was more concerned over who may have noticed what he had done. "How protected is this valley?"

"Only enough to diminish the ripples you created, but not enough to stop them." Strophia looked up to the sky. "You are safe here for now."

Jewel wrapped an arm around Kami's shoulders and started walking her away from Emmett. "There are winged creatures of many varieties, but none that can hide them so well. None with wings quite like that. There is so much that you do not know about the worlds. Where you are from is very disconnected from the rest. Sometimes, it is best to stray on the side of caution. Your friend—"

"Not my friend, because this isn't something friends would keep from each other." Kami glared back at where Emmett was. He did his best to ignore it as he considered Strophia's words and wondered how safe they really were here. He was confident that Jewel would find the right words to calm Kami down.

"Your friend," Jewel emphasized, "has risked a lot to save your life. For whatever reason he is your friend, consider yourself lucky. Perhaps even blessed."

"It certainly doesn't feel that way some days," Kami said. Jewel turned her around so that she could look back to where Emmett now stood—the same place where he had placed her back on the ground. He watched from there but made no move to come towards them.

"That boy is a rare kind of friend to have," Jewel said, putting her emphasis on the word friend again. "He will protect you with his last breath and that is not easy to find in any world. Do not turn your nose up at that so easily. He may not be able to tell you everything, but he will never lead you astray. I've told you that before. Trust him."

Kami sighed and stared at the ground "I want to believe that. I do, but too much has happened since we ended up in this place. I just don't know anymore."

"What does your heart say?"

"I want to trust him, but the lies and unanswered questions make it hard. It's all too much. All of this." Kami looked back up at Emmett who waited patiently for them to return.

"You'll know it all soon enough." Jewel squeezed Kami's shoulder.

"Is that a prophecy?"

Jewel nodded slightly. "I'm sure of it."

"I'll keep your words in mind," Kami murmured. They walked back to where Emmett waited, and he looked up at them hopefully.

"Jewel," Emmett pointedly looked over at Strophia who was still watching them, "find out what she meant by 'for now', please."

"I'll talk to her," Jewel said.

Emmett turned his attention back to the more immediate problem of Kami, who was still glaring at him. He wondered what questions she was going to bombard him with this time. He hoped that Jewel's little intervention would keep the conversation more civil.

"So..." Emmett left the unasked question hanging in the air, giving Kami her opening to ask whatever she wanted.

Kami just studied him. "So?"

"I'm sure you have questions and I might as well give you a chance to ask some of them."

"Now you give me a chance to ask questions?" Kami shook her head. "I thought this was one of those tell me if it's necessary things."

"Kami..." he started.

"Don't worry, Em." Kami shrugged. "It's fine. It's whatever."

Emmett wanted to know what was going through her head, but it was better this way. He let her disappear into her shelter without pushing any further. The questions would come eventually. This was just one more thing in her arsenal when the time came.

"She wants us to leave first thing in the morning," Jewel informed them. Emmett jumped a little. He hadn't heard her come up behind him.

"Of course." Emmett tried not to jump again when she stretched her arm around him.

"I may not be able to see everything in your future because of what you are, but I can tell you one thing." Jewel gave him a little squeeze. "There are ties between you two that cannot be undone by even the greatest of powers."

Emmett smiled at the statement, but he could only hope that she meant what he wanted. His smile faded and he shook her arm off. "Tell me the truth, how bad was the surge? Were we noticed?"

"This place is protected, but it still would have been noticed."

Emmett nodded. "Then we need to hurry."

"Yes," Jewel agreed. "We can reach Álfheimr in a few days if we leave early and push through hard. Nothing can enter Álfheimr unseen. We will be safe from those who seek power such as yours."

Jewel looked at Kami's tent and then back to Emmett. "She'll come around."

"Right. Good night then." Without looking back at Jewel, he headed for his shelter.

Chapter Seven

It was dark still when they broke camp down. They hit the road as soon as they could, eating a cold breakfast along the way. Emmett didn't bother to explain to Kami why they were hurrying. He let her draw her own conclusions, grateful that she wasn't in the mood for asking questions. He had a hard time concentrating on their surroundings, his mind consumed with worry. He could see no signs that they were being followed, but that meant little. Every day he felt Asèth's presence grow stronger, and every night he still heard the same words calling out to him, "Where are you?"

They passed through the rolling foothills that lay between Strophia's hidden home on the southern edge leading up to the Verilindore Mountain range, and on to the edges of the great woods that marked the boundary of Álfheimr. Few dared to pass this way and the road showed its disuse having become overgrown to the point of invisibility at times. Elves were not known for their love of outsiders.

Eventually, they stood on the edge of the great forest that was Álfheimr and stared in awe of the trees that stretched far in either direction. Dark and foreboding, the trail ahead of them quickly vanished into the underbrush. A cool breeze rattled the silver gilded leaves as it carried the scent of moss and mulch from the depths of the dense woods. Bird song echoed beatifically from the branches high above. It was both inviting and ominous at the same time, and it gave Emmett a sense of foreboding that he could not shake.

He hadn't been looking forward to this part. Since Jewel first mentioned that the nearest portal was within elfish territory, he'd had his doubts. He couldn't argue with her when she had insisted it was their best bet. Even after she had admitted that everything past this point was unknown to her because of the enchantments placed on this land.

"There's no way to go around?" Kami asked. They both had heard the warnings from the guide at the outfitters. *Do not enter the elven woods.* They did not like visitors—especially the uninvited kind.

"This is the way we need to go." Jewel closed her eyes to concentrate on the visions in her mind. She nodded grimly before turning to look at Emmett and Kami. "Yes, this is the only way to the nearest portal. I can sense its presence deep within these woods. We leave the tragelaphs behind."

"What?" Kami gripped the reins of her mount a little tighter.

"They won't go in these woods. Few domesticized animals will." Jewel slapped her mount on the rear. "One of the reasons I chose these mounts. They'll find their way home. They're very loyal animals."

"Then I guess we're going for a walk." Emmett hefted his pack higher on his shoulder as he marched into the woods, back straight and eyes fixed on the trail ahead. He could hear Jewel and Kami follow him past the first tree that marked the boundary of Álfheimr. They all knew that their presence would be known, and the confrontation would be inevitable.

They walked in solemn silence, doing their best to follow a path that was little more than a game trail. It was getting late when they came upon a small clearing in the forest. A stream burbled nearby, and a clear sky hung above of them instead of a ceiling of branches. It was a small opening, but it was good to be able to see the sky again. It would do for making camp.

"I guess we'll camp here for the night." Jewel announced. "I thought they'd have greeted us by now."

"Maybe they're shy?" Kami dropped her pack on the ground.

"No." Jewel didn't bother to expand on that answer. She busied herself with making camp instead. Emmett and Kami joined her. It didn't take long to get it all set up. Their shelters were huddled together on one side of the clearing as they ate a simple meal in silence. Emmett found himself watching the woods around them. He kept waiting for something to happen. It was a large area that the elves claimed as their own. It would take a week of steady trekking to get through it. Except, they weren't going through it. Jewel claimed that the rift they needed was in the heart of elfish territory.

"I think this worrying and waiting has exhausted me." Jewel stood up and stretched the moment her meal was finished. "I'm not used to being so blind. Not knowing what is coming next is an odd feeling. I'm not sure how you two manage to live like this all the time."

"We manage just fine, thanks," Kami snapped back at her. She looked down at the drawing she had made in the dirt with a stick and frowned. "Sorry, I'm tired too. It has been hard knowing what will happen, but not when."

"Thirded," Emmett agreed with a stretch. "I'm crawling into bed. I will see you both in the morning."

It seemed like hardly a moment had passed before someone was whispering his name and shaking his shoulder. Emmett tried to cling to the last vestiges of sleep, but they slipped away from him. "Go away, Kami."

"It's not Kami," Jewel hissed. "Wake up."

Emmett rolled over to see her worried face only inches from his. She glanced back over her shoulder towards the entrance to his shelter. Her demeanour was enough to bring him fully to his senses. "They're here?"

Jewel nodded and glanced at the entrance again. "Lots of them. More than I would have thought. I don't think they saw me, but they are elves. Hard to fool with a little bit of magic. They probably know I'm in here."

"We expected this," Emmett said as he rolled out of bed, "Maybe not this many, but it'll be okay."

"I don't like not knowing, not seeing. Elves cannot be read by those not their own. What little elfish blood still runs in my veins isn't enough."

"Elves are not violent without cause," Emmett said, reminding her of the exact thing she had told them before. "They just do not like having their world polluted by outsiders."

"You are outsiders to Álfheimr," a musical voice announced from outside. "You are now our prisoners until we decide your fate. It is best not to fight or argue. You cannot win. Please come peaceably and bear no arms against us."

Jewel preceded him out the entrance and he made sure to be close on her heels. It didn't matter to him how many reassurances he got about the normally gentile nature of the elves; there were still other, unsavoury tales of them at the back of his mind. He had never met an elf before, but he knew enough of their basic history to know that they had pulled away from the worlds when the realms began to separate.

Over time, they had become a secluded and paranoid race.

Emmett stood silently beside Jewel, staring at the first elf he had ever met. He was short, only a few inches taller than Jewel. He blended so well with the surroundings, he looked as if he had been carved from the flesh of the forest itself. His soft eyes reflected the lavender of the torches that were held by those that surrounded their encampment. He was stunning to look upon. Emmett knew his own race was often considered beautiful to see, but this was more than that. The only race that he considered nearly as fair was that of the sælig and there were few of them left in any of the realms.

It was an awkward few moments before the figure turned his attention to the remaining tent—Kami's shelter. She had yet to emerge. Emmett tried not worry. She was a deep sleeper and there was chance that she had not heard the elf announce his presence. It wasn't likely, but it was still possible.

"Female occupant, please, come outside," the elf demanded. Emmett thought he could hear a tinge of annoyance in the tone of his voice. "No harm will come to you as of this time."

Kami poked her head out of her shelter and looked around. Even in the dim light of the lavender flames he could see her eyes widen at the sight of the elf in the middle of their encampment before ducking back inside. "I don't know you. Why should I trust you?"

"My word is my bond. My kind does not lie," he assured her.

"And I'm supposed to believe that?"

Emmett suppressed his grin at the angry look that flitted across the elf's face. He knew that look so well. It was the same look that had graced his own face many times. Kami had a way of doing that to people. Annoyance was one of her greatest talents.

"My word is my bond," he insisted once again, as if repeating the same thing would change Kami's mind. "I would rather not have to send anyone in for you. I would prefer you to come peaceably."

"Anyone you send in after me is going to have a fight on their hands. I'm fierce!" Kami shouted. "I have weapons."

"My warriors," he emphasized each word carefully, "are well trained and well-armed. And we're elves."

"And I'm a human, ever heard of us? We're vicious and venomous and dangerous!" Kami shouted. "Be warned."

He chuckled and nodded towards one of the shadows in the trees. "I've known humans. While time has passed, they are not that dangerous to my kind. They are silly things with silly ideas."

Two elves entered the circle and approached Kami's shelter. Emmett knew that she would put up more of a fight than these elves expected, but it wouldn't be enough to stop them. He was confident that she was not in any real danger yet. For now, he would be patient and let things play out. He exchanged a glance with Jewel as sounds of a scuffle came from inside the shelter and tensed slightly, worried about what he would do if he had to intervene. He tried to assure himself that no matter what, elves did not waste life wantonly. Still, Kami had a way of pushing things and he knew it was best for him to be ready to intercede on her behalf.

Most of the words coming from the shelter were muffled, but occasional Kami's voice rang out clearly with such gems as, "Oh hells no you pointy-eared bastards," and "Take that, you twisted Rapunzel."

After a few minutes, they came out with a struggling Kami between them, looking much worse for wear. A chunk of hair was missing from the head of one of her escorts, which was probably where the comment about Rapunzel had come from. Kami's enthusiastic resistance wasn't making it easy on them as they dragged her in front of the elf who had originally addressed them.

"My name is Quynn. Your attempts at resistance are futile, and they do not hold you in good stead with my people. We're not a violent race, but we will not take abuse with a gentle hand. Be warned." He attempted to stare down Kami who stubbornly refused to look away.

Emmett wanted desperately to ask permission to speak, but since it was unlikely to come, he decided to just go ahead and say what was needed. "Kami, relax. We're fine. While waking weary travellers in the middle of the night can be considered poor etiquette, no one has been too badly harmed."

He refrained from adding 'except a couple of elves', but it was tempting. Quynn glared at Emmett who ignored him and continued. "Just chill and it will all be okay. I'm sure these elves treat their temporary guests with great respect and care, but you know how it is. We've got to show them respect in kind."

Kami sighed and rolled her eyes at him. "Yeah, yeah, yeah."

"And?" Emmett raised his eyebrow.

"I'm sorry to have caused an issue. I don't like being woken in the middle of the night. Perhaps you should have introduced yourself first." Kami stuck her chin out stubbornly. It was not a real apology, but Quynn seemed slightly mollified.

"If you would be so considerate as to come along with us, you may rest when we get back to the village." Quynn nodded towards the shadows again. Four more elves entered the clearing—two each for Emmett and Jewel. Kami's escorts had yet to release their grip. "You will need to be blindfolded. Do not worry, we will keep you safe."

Emmett submitted to the blindfold willingly. It wasn't a problem for him since he had an incredible sense of direction. Even without his eyes, he knew he would be able to find his way back easily. He let the two elves take his arms, but he wasn't prepared for them to lift him completely from the ground. It felt as though they were flying through the forest and he enjoyed the sensation of the air whooshing by.

Even with the speed they were moving at, Emmett had expected the journey to take longer than it did. He was surprised when they came to a halt after what seemed like a short time. He guessed that they couldn't be more than a third of the way through the woods. Wherever they were, he could hear very little noise beyond those natural to the forest.

"Welcome to Ouras, the great village of Álfheimr and home of the Elder Council." Quynn announced as their blindfolds were removed. "It is they who will be deciding your fate."

Emmett opened his eyes to see that they stood below a village that extended high into the trees. Fires of all colours lit the area, and gems embedded in the woodwork glittered in their flames. It was as beautiful as the people who lived in it. Prisoner or guest, it didn't matter to him, he was grateful for the chance to see it.

"Wow." Kami whispered. They only had a few moments to take it all in before they were steered towards a ground-level structure. It was simple in its elegance, but still beautiful in a way. Despite the arches and ornate engraving Emmett recognized the building for what it was—a cage.

"You will not be permitted to wander Ouras. This is a sacred place to us, and we cannot allow you to ruin it with your presence," Quynn informed them as they were ushered into the building. "Even now the elders are deciding your fate. If necessary, one of you shall be requested to speak to them. Until then, you remain here. A guard will be posted. If you need anything, you have only to ask."

"But you haven't asked us our destination," Jewel said. Quynn did not answer, and the door shut silently.

"So, what now?" Kami asked.

"We wait." Jewel sat down in a chair and stared at the door.

"For how long?"

"I don't know," Jewel sighed. "I had hoped that it would go better than this, but to be honest, I'm worried."

Chapter Eight

"How much longer are we going to be stuck here for?" Kami asked. She paced the edges of the common room they were in, occasionally kicking at the walls or doors as she passed. It had been three days since they had arrived in the Ouras. They had spoken to Quynn only once since their imprisonment; they were in limbo, and it didn't look promising.

"There are far worse places to be stuck," Emmett answered, shrugging. "And they are treating us fairly. The accommodations are comfortable. I'm sure things will be sorted out shortly and then we'll be on our way."

Kami stormed towards him until her face was an inch away. "How are you remaining so calm? You're the one that keeps saying we must hurry and now you're content to sit here?"

Emmett was saved from answering when the door to their gilded cage swung open. Quynn stood stiffly in the threshold, looking annoyed. "It has been requested that one of you address the council. They wish to speak to the one called Emmett. Which of you is Emmett?"

No one said a word. Both Jewel and Kami looked at Emmett and he sighed. He didn't know why he had been chosen; he had little interest in speaking to the Elder Council. "That would be me."

"Follow me, then." Quynn pivoted and marched out. Emmett trailed him and was immediately flagged by another two elves as he exited the building. It was his first chance to see Ouras during the daytime. They were the only ones standing on the ground and, naturally, his gaze drifted upwards. Elves moved with silent ease along branches that had been grown into bridges. Light filtered down from far above. There were no stairs or ladders anywhere—the elves didn't need them, as they leapt the great distances and heights between the branches with ease.

"Ready?" Quynn asked. The elves that flanked Emmett each grabbed one of his arms. He nodded and prepared himself to experience a different way of being airborne. It was strange being dragged along through the air by quickly leaping elves. He would have preferred flying and he briefly considered doing so before deciding against it. He could just imagine the looks on their faces as he shot up to the sky. While he knew elves would have no want of his feathers, he was conditioned to never take an unnecessary risk. Not to mention, it would likely hurt and drain him. He was out of practice with his powers.

Emmett was not surprised when they came to a rest at the highest building in the trees. Outwardly, it looked no different from any of the other buildings, but on closer inspection the carvings here were far more ornate, and more jewels were embedded into the designs.

Quynn put a delicate hand up to stop him as he walked towards the entrance. "Please show more respect for the elders than you would your own gods. Remember, we were once considered to be gods ourselves. This has never been forgotten," he informed Emmett, as if he were talking to a child. Emmett only nodded in response. As far as he was concerned, gods didn't exist. Unless they lived in a realm that no one knew of, but that was an entirely different conversation on which no one could agree.

"Thank you," Emmett said, attempting to sound respectful. It was hard when all he felt was annoyance. Quynn held aside the light curtain that hung over the entrance and motioned for Emmett to enter. He had only taken a few steps when he realized that Quynn had not moved to follow him. "Are you not coming in?"

"The Elder Council is not a place for spectators."

Emmett ducked through into a dimly lit room. Bright squares of buttery sunshine filtered down through the skylights to highlight dancing motes of dust. Until his eyes adjusted it was all he saw. Slowly, the figures in the shadows became clear to him. It was a simple room. No furnishing or decorations could be seen; just six elves sitting cross-legged on the wooden floor with their eyes closed. They gave no indication that they knew he was here.

He stood awkwardly, unsure of what to do or what was expected of him. He didn't know who should speak first, but if they were like any other pseudo-gods he had met, it was best to let them speak first. He studied the elves as he waited for them to finish with their powerplay and begin. Although elves did not age much in appearance, these six managed to seem ancient even to him.

"Welcome Emmett, as you choose to call yourself in this form." Each one only spoke a few words before the next continued the sentence seamlessly. "We knew of your arrival. Your goal and methods as known to us have been assessed." It dawned on him that this was not just a circle of elder elves. It was more than that. These were their eldest prophets. Their power and range expanded by a linking of the minds. He had heard of it before, but he had never known of anyone who had witnessed it. "We cannot allow you to reach the Ether through our lands. Fates have decreed it to be irreconcilable with the needs of our people."

"What?" Emmett was unable to hide his confusion. He had not expected an outright refusal.

"No argument will change the decision that has been made. It is in the best interest of all parties involved."

"If I cannot change your mind, why was I summoned?" Emmett struggled to contain his frustration at the pronouncement. He knew they would not tolerate a childish outburst from him. As much as he wanted to argue his point, he knew that their decisions were absolute.

"So that we may pass on our decision officially. Such things should not be done through an intermediary."

"I see," Emmett pushed the reluctant words out through gritted teeth, "and what would that be?"

"We believe that if you return to Mundialis, you will fail completely. Therefore, we will not allow for this to happen."

"What do you mean you won't 'allow' it?" Emmett found himself losing the fight to keep his anger from erupting forth.

"Your journey ends here. We have seen many paths of the future. Most end in darkness and destruction. We cannot ignore that which the Fates show us."

"You're going to keep us here against our will?" Emmett asked, the meaning behind their words sinking in.

"That is the best choice we have. You shall be our guests indefinitely. Consider it an honour. Very few have ever had the chance to visit these lands and even less have been allowed to stay."

Emmett was speechless. It was the last thing he expected to hear, and his mind spun with a million questions and thoughts. At one time, he would have understood why they were doing this. He had once been bound by the strict rules and beliefs of his own race, but that was a long time ago. Things looked different after a few centuries of living in the realms.

He took a deep breath and managed to force a single word. "Why?

They paused. It had probably been a long time since anyone had dared to question a decision they had made. "We believe that no matter what path you choose, you will fail. How you fail, though, that is the mystery that remains. That is the question that begs to be answered. That is the reason you cannot be allowed to return, for there is only one conclusion, and we do not like it."

Emmett tried to gather his wits about him. He should have known better then to ask such a vague question. "If we cannot pass, why have you not escorted us off your lands and told us to find another way?"

"This is the best path to preserve what is most important to us."

Emmett clenched his fists tightly as he spoke—it was the only outlet he had for the anger he felt. "Is that what this is all about? Preserving your race?"

"A long time ago, we secluded ourselves from the world. We were a dying race. Our blood lines were dirtied by other creatures. We needed to save ourselves, so we pulled away. We left the impure behind. They no longer belonged with us. Now it is rare that we let others within our forests, and even rarer still that we allow them into the very heart of our home. We do this today because preservation of our race is far more important than allowing the impure into our lands."

Emmet stared at them. He didn't care about their blood purity and he had no idea what it had to do with the question he asked. His uncomprehending silence seemed enough to prompt them to continue.

"It is the safest path. Only a path far too narrow for any to follow could lead to success. You will fail and not only our race will be the ones to suffer from it. This is for the greater good."

"Greater good? This isn't fate, it's fear," Emmett growled at them through gritted teeth. "You may think you're the closest things to gods around here, but you are nothing more than scared little children, hiding in your woods while the real world is passing you by."

"We're not the ones who are afraid."

Unwilling to listen to another word the elders had to say, Emmett stormed out of the room, wincing at the blinding sun outside. Someone grabbed his arm and pulled him back. His eyes adjusted to see that he had nearly walked off the branch. He shook off Quynn's grasp and tried to calm the burning rage that had risen inside of him. His kind was not normally emotional; he wondered if he had spent so much time pretending to be human that he was starting to act like one.

"Ahem." A thoroughly unimpressed Quynn waited with his two lackeys to take Emmett back to the ground. "You'll be allowed to rest the night. We will take you to a permanent habitat in the morning," he said stiffly. Emmett didn't bother with a response. He held out his elbows and allowed them to carry him safely back to the ground level, where he was immediately ushered back into the jail. Jewel and Kami waited with expectant looks on their faces.

"They have no intention of allowing us to use the rift. They have decided in their infinite wisdom to extend our current stay," Emmett informed them.

"What do you mean?" Jewel asked, her voice barely a whisper.

"I mean they want to keep us prisoners here forever." Emmett watched the shock of his announcement spread across their faces. "We can't allow that to happen. We're escaping tonight. We need to try. Even if we fail, we need to try."

"Well, that wasn't what I expected from you—or from them," Jewel said, matching his tone as she leaned in closer. "Have you got a plan?"

"Not a good one," Emmett shrugged, "but it's the best I got unless someone has a suggestion."

"Burn all these stupid twerps to the ground," Kami growled. "Every last one of them."

"That might be, uh, a bit excessive," Jewel stammered. "They may not be the nicest people in the realms, but they are not inherently evil. If they were, then they would not be here and their decision would be something less acceptable than lifetime imprisonment."

"That is a matter of some debate. This is a neutral realm," Emmett interjected, "and there will be people and races that run the gamut of good to bad. None of them will be pure goodness or true evil. However, I'm no fan of elves right now."

"Okay, plan." Jewel spoke up before Kami could start arguing. "What is it?"

"I bust down the door. We run as fast as we can and try to make it to the rift. Where is it from here?" Emmett asked.

"Northeast, a day's journey. But we can't outrun the elves on their own turf."

"Can you hide us somehow? Stop them from seeing us?" Emmett asked. Jewel shook her head.

"That," Kami groaned, "is a terrible plan. Seriously, that was the best you could come up with? We run?"

"I said I was open to suggestions." Emmett glared at her. "So, if you have a better idea, share it."

After a few minutes of silence Jewel grinned. "Okay, I have a plan."

"Is it a good plan?" Kami asked, not sounding hopeful.

"My plan," Jewel stated, "is to follow Emmett's plan. We'll probably fail no matter what we do, but at least we'd be doing something. And frankly, I'm growing fond of your idea, Kami, to hurt an elf or two. I'm sick of their holier-than-thou attitudes."

"As much as I want to bust some heads, I doubt it'll do any good," Kami mumbled. "Not that I can think of anything better. Those things are fast. If we make it out of town, I'll be surprised."

"Me too," Emmett muttered under his breath. He walked over to the door and placed both his hands against it. "Ready?"

Jewel and Kami both nodded. Emmett pressed all his weight and strength against the door. It didn't even wiggle. He frowned and took a few steps back. "It's enchanted."

"So that's it?" Kami asked.

"Nope. It's just going to take more than brawn to open it." He cracked his knuckles and grinned. "Be ready."

Emmett took a moment to gather himself. Much like with the door to the gym, he needed only a small amount of energy to do the job. It would barely be noticeable—he hoped. He charged the door and pushed the energy he had gathered ahead of him just before he made contact. It was more than he needed. The door shattered, sending wooden shrapnel flying in all directions.

Even with the energy spent, he had gathered a good momentum and found himself trampling over one of the unconscious guards. He didn't slow down as he glanced over his shoulder to be sure that Kami and Jewel were close behind him. He got a quick glimpse of Kami on top of the second guard, her fist raised. He was pretty sure she was shouting something obscene before Jewel grabbed her by the shirt and dragged her along.

The elves' response to their actions was quick. They charged towards them and dropped down from above. Emmett wanted nothing more than to go full strength on them, but it wasn't something he dared to do. He was still worried about someone picking up the residual energy of him having to use his wings earlier. To go full tilt was far too dangerous an idea. Instead, he fought as a man.

He was shocked that they had made it so far when he realized they were outside the colourful flames that lined the edges of the village. How they had not been captured or injured seemed a small miracle to him. He had been fighting for all he was worth, and it had been enough against a superior foe. He could only attribute it to the element of surprise. The elves were far too arrogant to believe that their prisoners would resist them.

Kami struggled with an elf that had gotten a good grip on her. Emmett rushed towards her, but she managed to get her teeth clamped on to its forearm before he could get there. He tried not to laugh at how quickly the elf let go. It was a moment's distraction before someone else noticed him. She drew back her bow to fire from the treetops above. It was an easy dodge, but he wished he had something more than the trees to hide behind—elves rarely missed their targets even in the most crowded of battlefields. It made him wonder, as he pulled Kami into the relative safety of the trees, why they weren't firing into the village. He looked around for Jewel when someone tapped him on his back. He turned, ready to strike, and was relieved to see it was her.

"Run." She didn't need to tell them twice. Although she was the shortest of them, she was a fast runner and Emmett found himself struggling to keep up. Elves flanked them on each side and arrows flew around them. Emmett was sure they were missing on purpose, trying to scare them instead of trying to kill them. It gave him a small glimmer of hope, but it ran out quickly.

A group of elves stood directly in their path. Jewel deked to the right to get around them, but they were soon flanked on all sides. There was nowhere left to run, and little they could do as the elves stood with weapons drawn. Emmett watched as they closed in on them. Kami struck out first, launching herself at the nearest one, tackling her to the ground. Emmett ran in after her, swinging at anything unfamiliar that moved. No matter how many elves they took down, two more replaced them. Eventually Emmett found himself in the hold of four elves—unable to escape without drastic measures. He struggled uselessly in their grip as Jewel and Kami were likewise restrained.

Quynn marched before them as soon as they had all been secured. Emmett wished that he had been one of the first ones out of the trees. He wanted a chance to take a swing at that smug face. Killing may be something that he could not do, but that didn't mean he couldn't hurt a being in a non-fatal way. It was frowned upon, but not forbidden.

"Your actions are contemptible. You have been treated fairly among us and this uncalled-for attack cannot be ignored." Quynn stared directly at Emmett before saying the last part. "It is especially offensive coming from one such as yourself." He paced back and forth in front of them. "You have injured ten of my people in this useless attempt of yours. There will be consequences. You have proven to us once again why outsiders should never be permitted within our lands."

Quynn pivoted and marched away. The elves that were holding on to them followed him, never loosening their grip. They were deposited into a different ground level hut. This one was more basic then the previous one. "You will know your fate in the morning."

Although the attempt had failed and a new threat hung over their heads, Emmett grinned as soon as the door had closed behind their escort.

"What have you got to grin about?" Kami asked. She took a half-hearted kick at the door.

"We pissed them off and we got to knock a few heads together." Emmett shrugged. "We knew our chances were slim at best, but, for what it's worth, we showed them that we will not allow ourselves to be pushed around."

"For all the good it did us." Jewel's eyes twinkled in the dim light. "Still, I think I actually enjoyed that. If we must move on to the next rift, we're going to have to become far better fighters. It is not an easy path. I had hoped that the elves would let us use this one."

"Not that it will matter if they decide to behead us or something," Kami mumbled as she collapsed onto the floor, her back against the wall.

"I don't think they will do that," Jewel said softly. "However, if we prove to be enough trouble for them, perhaps they will change their minds on keeping us here and let us continue on our journey."

"Maybe," Emmett said, not wanting to voice his own fears. "And maybe we should all get some sleep."

"That seems like a good idea." Jewel yawned and stretched. "Nothing to do but wait for morning to come anyway."

Kami said nothing. She laid down where she was, as there were no beds in the small room that they had been placed in. Emmett did the same, but he doubted that sleep would come.

"Wake up," Quynn demanded from the doorway. It was barely light out as Emmett wiped the sleep from his eyes. As soon as everyone was passably awake and looking in his direction, Quynn continued his announcement. "It is obvious that any attempt to keep you in our lands will continue to be met with belligerence. As such, the elders have chosen the next best course for you as decided by the Fates. You will be left on the northern edge of our lands, and we will not be so kind as to retrieve your items. We will leave shortly."

Quynn slammed the door closed behind him. Emmett kept his cheer muted so as not to let the elves know that he was happy about the turn in events. He couldn't supress the grin on his face, though. "I think we got lucky."

Kami moped. "Lucky? Without our stuff this is going to suck."

"It won't totally suck." Jewel winked at Kami. "Remember when I put those runes on everything?"

"Vaguely."

"Well, so long as it is intact, I can summon it."

"Okay, then maybe that distraction was worth it after all." Kami smiled and then yawned.

"We might as well get a few minutes more shut eye before they drag us out of here," Emmett said, muffling his own yawn. He had no idea what the coming day would bring, but if he remembered the map correctly, things would be getting more interesting from here on out.

Chapter Nine

Emmett tried not to be impatient with Jewel as she sat crossed legged on the ground, trying to summon their items for the fifth time. She had warned them that it would not be instant or easy and that patience was key. Still, it seemed to him that she was starting to get frustrated with the lack of progress.

She opened her eyes with a sigh. "I can feel the items. If the elves are planning to destroy them, then they haven't done it yet. I'm having a hard time forcing them to move through the woods to our location. It might be that these woods are bound to the elves and, thus, are somewhat resistant to outside magic. I will keep trying."

Emmett plopped down near a small apple tree and Kami joined him. They sat in silence, looking out over the rolling hills that gradually gave way to steeper peaks. Far to the north, white-capped mountains soared tall over everything. After a few minutes, Kami laid her head on his shoulder. "I miss this."

"What? Running for our lives, fighting elves, and spending most of the time worried and confused?" Emmett asked.

"Ha ha." Kami rolled her eyes. "You know what I mean. Back home we were always hanging out in the woods. It was our spot to get away from the world. Seems like a bad joke now, doesn't it?"

"It would be fair to say that we've gotten away from the world," Emmett said, chuckling. "I know it seems like everything has been turned upside down and dropped on its head, but some things don't change."

"Like the fact that you'll always be watching out for me."

"Hmmmm." Emmett leaned back and stared up at the sky.

"Is that all you have to say for yourself?" Kami jabbed him playfully in the ribs with her elbow.

Emmett grinned. "Always is a long time, but I will for as long as I'm able."

"That's a funny sort of thing to say. Why would you say that?"

Emmett didn't know how to answer. It was a complicated topic to explain to her; to anyone really. "Because it's the truth."

They watched Jewel in silence for a few more minutes before Kami interrupted Emmett's wandering thoughts. "You're pretty powerful, aren't you?"

"Yes," he answered without a second thought.

"That's what I thought." Kami sat up straighter, a wide smile on her face. "Finally! Looks like the supplies are arriving."

Emmett got up and helped Kami to her feet. They joined Jewel who was grinning from ear to ear. One by one most of their supplies flew, tumbled, or wobbled their way out of the woods and into the clearing. Emmett made sure to double check everything as it arrived.

"Looks like we got almost all of it!" he cheered. "Good job, Jewel. Glad we have you with us."

It took time to get everything sorted before they were once again loaded down with packs and ready to head to their next destination. It was much further north than they had intended to go. They were running low on supplies and there weren't too many places near here where they could stock up. With the map spread out before them, they considered their best options. Jewel pointed at a town near where the foothills gave way to the peaks that formed Verilindore Mountain range.

"This is Gibborim. We'll need to go here to get supplies before we will be able to go any further towards the next rift, which is deep inside the caves of the dwarves. Hopefully, they will be more welcoming than the elves. We'll get a guide in town because we need to go through here to get there," Jewel tapped the map where several sharp peaks were marked with the word Jötunheimr, the land of the giants.

Jewel bit her lip as she studied the map, her finger tracing over the route several times. "I'm not sure how easy it will be to cross through the mountains this time of year."

"Of more immediate concern is that we don't have enough food to make it from here to Gibborim," Emmett pointed out. They were all aware that they only had enough for another day or two at most. "What is the quickest route?"

"We have two choices. We can go to Lorrac, which is northeast of us and closer than Gibborim. It's still several days further than our supplies will last and the quickest way there takes us through the foothills, which is not easy terrain to pass through. Not to mention, we'd be heading into sælig territory. Our other option is to head straight west to the flood plains where the main trading route is. There is a good chance we'll encounter someone from whom we can buy from or trade supplies with. We'll have to cross through Baksüz Bog, though. It covers too large of an area for us to go around, but the route will be easier once we're through it." Jewel pointed at the map as she spoke.

"Are these seeley things dangerous?" Kami asked, studying the routes that Jewel had pointed out to them.

"Well—"

Emmett cut Jewel off before she could continue. "We're not going through sælig territory. We'll go through the bog."

"And what about the bog wogglies and the chirbatti?" Jewel asked.

"Bog wogglies only eat children and chirbatti don't exist." Emmett slung his pack over his shoulder and stood up. "We're going through the bog."

"Whoa. I didn't think this was a dictatorship." Kami stood up to face him. "What gives you the right to decide for us?"

Emmett bit back the harsh reply that immediately came to mind. He knew she was right. It wasn't his place to decide for them. He sat back down. "Fine. Which way do you guys want to go?"

"Both ways present their own unique challenges," Jewel said, "and I'm too tired to dedicate much effort to seeing all the paths. Either way we will find ourselves in Gibborim. That is the one thing I can guarantee. Much like you, I would prefer to avoid sælig territory. If the Erlkrönig has returned it is the last place any of us would want to be."

"The what?" Kami asked. She didn't miss seeing Emmett wince at the question and turned her attention to him before Jewel could answer. "Seriously? What lie are you going to tell me this time?"

Emmett said nothing. There were no lies he wanted to tell her or truths that would suffice. Jewel frowned at the tension that rose between them and shook her head. "There are many things that he hasn't told you for good reasons in his mind, but there is no point in keeping this information from you. You should know what you are running from."

He glared at Jewel, but it didn't stop her from continuing. "There was once a great time of darkness in this world, when a powerful sælig rose from these lands. His goal was to steal all the magic of the other races for his own. No one really knows why. He was eventually banished."

Kami frowned. "What does that have to do with what chased us here?"

Jewel looked at Emmett in hope that he would continue the narrative, but he looked away from her. He had no wish to think about such dark times, let alone speak of them. With a sigh, Jewel carried on. "He is attempting to return from banishment and for some reason he is searching for you two."

"Why?" Kami asked.

Jewel fixed Emmett with a glare that could have melted a glacier. "That I don't know, but I have a feeling we'll find out if he catches up with us."

Kami and Jewel both stared at Emmett for an answer, but he remained silent. Kami cocked her head to the side. "Em, what did you take?"

"Take?" Jewel asked.

"Yeah, he said to me when we first got here that he had taken something that this dude thought was his." Kami furrowed her brow as she tried to remember the conversation. "He didn't say what it was, only that it didn't belong to this—what did you call him? Earlcroney?"

"Erlkrönig," Jewel corrected her. "Not that it matters. We should get moving before we lose too much daylight."

"I'd rather be climbing hills than trudging through muddy water." Kami wrinkled her nose at the thought.

"It's a peat bog so there are paths through it," Jewel said, smiling. "There are dangers to consider on both routes. It's easy to lose your way in a bog that large. There are many who have met their end simply because they are unable to find their way out."

Kami grabbed her pack from the pile. "If we get lost, I'm blaming Em."

Emmett almost smirked, but he was still upset about what Jewel had told Kami. He was glad that she hadn't tried to force him to answer Kami's question about what he'd taken, though. "I've got big shoulders, I can carry that burden."

"West we go then." Jewel pushed herself to her feet and with the sun to their backs, they began their trek down to Baksüz Bog.

"Wow." Kami stood, stunned, on top of a small rise. Ahead, the land was painted with the fiery reflection of the setting sun on water that dotted the landscape ahead. It spread far and wide, dark green blotches and sparkling water creating an unsolvable jigsaw puzzle.

"Baksüz Bog." Jewel announced, although it was unnecessary for her to do so. It stretched out as far as they could see. "Come on, you won't be as impressed once you're close enough to smell it."

"Smell it?" Kami followed Jewel down the hill.

"It's a bog at the end of summer," Jewel explained. "Have you never been near a bog before?"

"Isn't it like a big marsh?" Kami asked.

"Not quite," Emmett chuckled.

Kami glared at him. "What's so funny?"

"You'll find out." Jewel decided to change the subject. "We need to focus more on finding a place to set up camp for the night. Something semi-sheltered would be ideal."

"There's a few trees over there, small ones, but I don't see much else," Emmett said, pointing towards the south. It really wasn't much. Nothing tall seemed to grow around here; there was just the bog in the distance and a few hillocks that could barely be classified as such.

"It'll have to do." Jewel marched over to the trees. It took little time to get camp set up. As soon as they were done, Jewel pulled an item out of her pack and smiled. "Ohniska mulciber."

"Um, English please?" Kami said, staring at the red stone that Jewel held up as if she had discovered something incredible.

Instead of explaining, Jewel placed the stone in the middle of the campsite. "Inardesco!"

Where the stone had been, a fire now roared. Kami and Emmett approached it cautiously. Heat emanated from it like a real fire. Emmett grinned. "Neat trick."

"I picked it up just in case. Limited usage on them, but great for things like this." Jewel sat back on her stool and stared into the blaze. It didn't take long before her confident smile turned into a grimace as she swatted at something. "However, there are things that may be attracted to it. If you don't have your protection charm on you, I would suggest doing so now."

Emmett touched the small charm bag that was attached to his belt. He hadn't bothered to take his off since they had hit the trail. Jewel and Kami both fished out similar pouches from their backpacks.

"I'm going to get started on dinner," Emmett announced. He used the compact cook stove to make the meal, sitting on the opposite side of the fire from where Jewel and Kami relaxed in its warm glow. He listened to their lighthearted chatter about the path ahead. He was happy to hear Jewel glossing over the more dangerous creatures they might encounter. Eventually, he interrupted them with an important announcement. "Dinner is ready."

"That looks disgusting." Kami wrinkled her nose before taking a bite. "Tastes okay though."

"I don't have a lot left to work with here, but I'm glad it tastes okay." Emmett laughed and dug into his meal. He had to admit that it didn't look like much, but he was trying his best to be conservative about using their supplies.

"I'll set a perimeter warning. After the elves, I'm not ready to have any more middle of the night surprises," Jewel announced the moment she had finished her meal. "Then I'm going to focus on finding a route through the Baksüz Bog. I'll be in my tent if you need me." After a slight pause Jewel added, "Please, don't need me."

Emmett chuckled quietly as Jewel disappeared into her tent. "I don't know about you, but I'm not looking forward to this trek."

"You have only yourself to blame for that. Besides, blaming you is what I plan to do."

Emmett rolled his eyes and chuckled. "Point taken. Still, I hope Jewel finds us a safe way across. Even if I don't believe that chirbatti exist, I've heard the stories."

"What are those anyway?" Kami asked.

"They're kind of like the will-o-wisp myths back home, except far more dangerous." Emmett explained. "Will-o-wisps are mischief makers. They lead travellers astray. Chirbatti though, they lead the traveller not just astray, but to their yōkai. Now the myths about those are extremely vague at best, but the stories never end well."

"Never end well, how?" Kami asked.

"Those who encounter a yōkai are never seen or heard from again," Emmett said. "But I don't believe that the chirbatti or yōkai actually exist."

"I used to think a lot of things weren't real. Like dragons, for example, or girls who are made of water," Kami pointed out. "Why do you think these things don't exist?"

"None of the stories I've heard have been verifiable. Simple as that. In a place where it is so easy to believe in almost anything, a little bit of disbelief is a good thing."

"I'll keep that in mind." Kami yawned and stretched. "Right now, I think I'm going to get some sleep."

"Good plan," Emmett agreed, and did his best to not dwell on the possibilities of what they might encounter in the bog as he tried to fall asleep.

Chapter Ten

Emmett left the warmth of his shelter and stepped into a fine drizzle that permeated everything. There was a chill in the air that reached down into his bones. He wrapped his jacket tighter around himself as he set water to boil. Neither of the girls had emerged from their tents to greet the murky dawn yet.

Emmett tried to remember the words to turn the fire back on, but it escaped him. He'd have to wait for Jewel to get up. Instead, he stayed as close to the camp stove as he could. It was little comfort, but the rich, earthy smell of coffee brewing warmed him in another way. He poured the dark liquid into a mug and walked to the edge of camp to stare out at the bog barely visible through the rainy haze. He did not relish the idea of being in that mess for the day or two it would take to cross it, but it was better than encountering a wandering sælig. There was a chance of being recognized if that happened and, if the Erlkrönig had returned, then that was where Asèth's influence would be the strongest.

For now, though, there were only the beasts of the bog to worry about. Not many intelligent creatures—mythical or otherwise—would choose to make a home here. He could fight anything that dared to challenge them, and if that was all that stood between here and home, it would be an easy journey. He wasn't so sure it would be, though.

"Where are you?"

Emmett stiffened at the sound of the words that haunted him every night as he closed his eyes. This time, his eyes were open, he was wide awake, and he heard Asèth's voice as clearly as if he was standing beside him.

A figure coalesced in the fog. Emmett stood his ground, and for the first time, he answered. "Why can't you stay gone?"

His only response was the wind rattling through the reeds. The figure dissipated as quickly as it had appeared. He tried to find it again, but there was nothing there. Only him, the fog, and the wind. He heard rustling from the tents behind him. Kami or Jewel had awoke. He gave his head a shake to clear it and focussed on preparing a meal of unexciting porridge. It would be filling and just what they could use on a day like this. He hurried about getting it ready before either of the girls left their tents to greet the damp and chilly morning.

They did not tarry by the fire after breakfast. It would be a long walk to follow the meandering ribbons of land that made the only decent paths through the Baksüz Bog. Emmett hoped that the fine mist would dissipate to show a sunny day; the gloom of their environment seemed to weigh heavily on all of them as they took down their camp in silence. Miserable grey mist slowly solidified into an unrelenting rain as they started their journey.

"What is that smell?" Kami wrinkled her nose as they approached the edge of the bog and the scent of rotting vegetation permeated the air.

"That is the bog. It would be worse if it was sunny out." Emmett could hear the smile in Jewel's voice as she spoke, though she kept her focus on the route ahead. "I told you that you would find out."

"I hate you, Em," Kami grumbled.

Emmett grinned. "No you don't."

Rain pounded at them mercilessly. As the day wore on Emmett worried that they might never be able to get out of the bog. Jewel's choices appeared random, although they always managed to stay on land.

"Shit." Jewel stopped and Emmett looked to see what had caused their normally calm companion to swear. Ahead of them the ribbon of land they were following disappeared underwater. There was nowhere else to go—they had reached a dead end.

"Um, Jewel?"

"It's this place. I saw the path we needed to follow clearly last night, but today everything has changed. Nothing looks like what it's supposed to look like. Nothing is where it was supposed to be. Even when I tried doing it on a junction by junction basis, nothing turned out as my visions have show me. I don't understand." Only the slightest tremor in her voice gave evidence of her worry and fear.

"You mean we're lost?" Kami asked.

"Yes," Jewel admitted, "we're lost."

"I hate you, Em."

This time Emmett didn't contradict her words. He had to own part of the responsibility. Wallowing would do no good, so he forced himself to focus on the important things. "How is that possible?"

"It shouldn't be possible." Jewel's shoulders slumped as she spoke. Emmett felt bad for her—first the elves and now this. "It's a bog. It's not intelligent, it's not magical. It's a damned bog!"

"It's not like the elf thing where it's all obscured and protected and stuff, is it?" Kami inquired hopefully. Jewel shrugged and shook her head.

"Maybe it *is* intelligent." Emmett kicked at the sodden, mossy ground in frustration. He knew there had to be a solution, a reason why they were lost. Not that he knew what it was. There was only one thing they could do now. "I guess we backtrack and try another route."

There was little room to move around where they stood, so Emmett ended up leading them back the way they had come. After a few moments of walking he stopped and looked around at the water that surrounded them. He continued for another ten minutes before stopping again. "Something is wrong here."

"And by 'something is wrong here' you mean we should have passed an adjoining trail by now?" Jewel asked.

"Yeah, that."

"I remember having passed some by now as well," Kami added.

"So, where are they?" Emmett asked. "I don't care how hard it's raining; whole paths don't disappear that quickly. Are you sure this place isn't enchanted?"

"To be honest I have never been north of the Álfheimr. I only know this area by story," Jewel admitted. "I'm sorry. I was hoping my sight would be enough, but I have failed us again."

"You didn't fail us, Jewel." Emmett assured her. "It was the elves that failed us. You have done your best to keep us safe and on track. Right now, the question remains, how in all creation are we going to get out of here?"

"We do the only thing we can do; we keep going." Kami surprised Emmett by being the voice of reason for a change. "I still hate you, though."

"I know, I know," Emmett sighed. "It's all my fault."

Day gave quickly into night and the rain continued to beat at them. It felt as though they had little hope of finding their way out of this watery labyrinth. It became hard for them to see far enough ahead even with the fireball Jewel created to help light their way.

Splash. Emmett whipped around, fully prepared to jump into the water after Kami, but she still had one leg on solid ground. The sodden surface had given way when she stepped too close to the edge. Emmett gave her hand to help her back up.

"Sorry," she mumbled. "I'm tired."

"We need to find a place to rest," Jewel said, stating the obvious. They were all exhausted and it seemed that they were only wandering deeper in.

"Tell that to the bog," Emmett mumbled under his breath. Louder he added, "We might not have the choice of finding a decent sized hummock or anything big enough."

His statement was only met with silence as they trudged on. He chose directions at random. Emmett thanked what little luck they had when the rain abated. It wasn't long before stars began to show above them.

"What's that?"

Emmett turned to see what Kami was talking about. She was pointing at something out over the water. A ball of light danced and played in the distance as a second ball of light joined it.

"Wisps, or as they're more properly known, will-o-wisps." Jewel said softly. "They're harmless, mostly. But don't ever allow one to will you into following it. That's how they work, they live on the despair of others. Those who come unprepared will follow the beautiful lights until they are well and surely lost."

"We're already lost," Kami pointed out. No one argued with her as they watched the lights blinking in and out; dancing, twirling.

Emmett turned his attention back to the trail ahead. Watching the wisps wasn't going to get them closer to finding a place to rest for the night. "Let's get moving."

He had taken only a single step forward when one of the lights charged at them. It stopped above the path in front of them and floated out of reach. He took another step and it flared brighter. He stepped back and it dimmed. Emmett moved forward again and the same thing happened. He looked towards Jewel in hopes of an explanation.

"That is not normal wisp behavior." She sounded as confused as he felt.

"Okay. Now what?" His question was met with silent stares. He tried to walk forward again and was greeted this time, not only with a brightening of light, but a change in colour to a bright and angry red. It flitted towards him and back again. Emmett got the picture and stepped back to where he had been standing before. "Can these things actually hurt us? They're just ghost lights, right?"

"Right—if it actually is a wisp."

"What else could it be?"

"A chirbatti," Jewel responded.

"They don't exist," Emmett insisted once again. "Why wouldn't it be a wisp?"

"Maybe because it's trying to physically stop us rather than entice us to follow it?" Jewel suggested. "And how about the fact that wisps never get this close to people? Not to mention that rather than being an ethereal light it looks kind of solid. Choose your favourite."

Jewel glared at him. It was a challenge and she was going to win. He had no way to argue against her on this.

"Of course, if you want final proof, we could follow the damned thing and see if it leads us to a yōkai."

Emmett threw up his arms in frustration. "Fine then! Into certain death we march."

"Fine."

"Um, don't I get a say here?" Kami asked.

"No!" Emmett and Jewel responded in unison.

Emmett ignored Kami's pout as he turned his attention back to the patiently waiting ball of light. "Okay, whatever you are, where are we going?"

It responded immediately to his words, changing from red back to a soft bluish-white. It sped straight at them, narrowly missing Emmett, and charged off in the direction they had come from. Emmett raised an eyebrow at Jewel. She ignored him and pivoted on her heel to follow the ball of light along the twisting, changing paths of the bog. They followed it until it came to a sudden stop and began to pulse.

"Now what?" Kami griped.

"I don't know," Jewel murmured. They waited to see what would happen. Emmett prepared himself for anything. Just because they hadn't encountered danger yet didn't mean that they wouldn't. It pulsed even brighter and took off to the right across the water, then stopped about nine feet away. The fact that no reflection showed beneath it told Emmett that it hovered over something other than water.

"Now what?" Emmett asked. They all stared at the ball of light that appeared to be waiting patiently. He couldn't tell if it was floating over land or something else that was non-reflective—he couldn't see far enough.

"I can't jump that far." Jewel frowned as she squinted at the spot where the light hovered. "I don't know what we'd be landing on. I can't see that far, either."

"I can jump that far," Kami said. She sounded afraid that they would both yell at her again, but her face was set with those stubborn lines that Emmet knew too well.

"No," Emmett spoke softly, "you weren't able to make a jump this far with a run. From a standstill it's near impossible. And we have no idea what you are jumping towards."

"I know I can do it. Besides, what other option is there?"

Jewel interrupted before the conversation could become an argument. "Even if you could Kami, we don't know what is over there. While there are few dangerous monsters that call a bog their home, that doesn't mean there aren't any. If I wasn't so exhausted, I could float someone over there."

"Or one of us could wade across if it's shallow or swim if it's not," Emmett suggested.

"I wouldn't recommend it." Jewel knelt at the edge of the trail and stared into the water. "Bog wogglies normally go after children, but if you disturb them they will attack an adult as well. Hard to see where their nests are, but we would really want to avoid those."

"So, stalemate then?" Kami sat down, the sodden land squelching.

"I didn't want to have to suggest this, but," Emmett took a deep breath before continuing, "if the only way across is to have you float us through the air then I can lend you the energy."

"What?" Jewel furrowed her brow. "How? Some who have studied dark magic can steal the life force of others to increase their power, but no one can give energy."

Emmett reached out to touch her with a single finger. It was easier this time, pulling that miniscule amount. He hoped that it was a small enough gesture to go unnoticed.

"Oh!" Jewel exclaimed, her eyes wide. Emmett smirked at the look on her face. He had never done this before and was glad that she could feel it.

"I'm not from around these parts. Remember?" Emmett shrugged slightly. "There's a lot the other worlds don't know about my kind. They like it that way."

"They?" Jewel asked. "Those in charge in your realm?"

Kami raised an eyebrow. Emmett chose to ignore it and nodded at Jewel. "Will it work?"

"I don't know, but what else can we do? Just take it easy."

"I don't really have a choice." Emmett flattened his hand against her arm. "I'm still worried about being detected."

"Hurry it up guys." Kami looked up from where she sat in between them. "I'm tired. I want to sleep."

"We all are," Emmett said, smiling at her. "Now let me concentrate."

Each time he pulled at the source of his energy it was getting easier. His connection had faded with time and distance, but it wasn't gone yet. It took effort and, if he wasn't careful, he could hurt Jewel as well as himself. "Is it working?"

"It's like being plugged into a lightning rod, but in a good way," Jewel said, pausing to concentrate. "I think I can control how much energy I pull. This is amazing. I think that's enough."

Emmett pulled his hand away. Jewel opened her eyes slowly and looked at him with a smile. Weariness no longer weighed her down. She took a deep breath of the cool night air.

"Okay, I'm going to take myself over first and then bring each of you over. Emmett, I'll bring you first in case I need another boost. Does that sound good?"

Kami and Emmett nodded. Jewel floated upwards and towards the wisp of light. She studied her landing spot carefully before descending. "It's land. There is land here."

"Solid land?" Kami shouted back.

"Yes," Jewel informed them. "Okay Emmett, I'm bringing you over."

Emmett didn't have a chance to respond before his feet lifted from the ground. It was a strange feeling—a different feeling from flying—as he watched the dark water pass by beneath him. It didn't take long until he was standing on solid ground beside Jewel. He looked around at what appeared to be a small hummock, unattached to any trail.

"Okay," Jewel shouted back to Kami, "your turn."

It took only a few seconds before Kami was standing beside them. She asked the question that each of them was wondering the moment she had a chance to look around. "Now what?" They all turned to look at the floating light that had been their guide. It gave no response to their question. Kami yawned and stretched before she sat down on the ground. "I guess we stay here."

"Sun should be up soon," Jewel said, glancing towards the east. Emmett could see no sign of the coming morning, but he trusted her judgement. "There isn't enough space to set up three shelters here."

"Is there room for one?" Emmett studied the small island trying to do the calculations.

"Barely." Jewel frowned. "We'd be best off wrapping ourselves in the fabric to stay warm and dry."

"No shelters?" Kami looked like she was about to cry at the thought. Emmett couldn't blame her—he felt miserable as well. All he wanted was to curl up in a nice warm bed and fall asleep.

"No and—" Jewel ducked as the light that had been floating nearby charged towards her. It narrowly missed her before diving into the murky water. There was no sound, no splash at all, it just disappeared. "We should probably get some rest. I want to be up while it's still light enough to see what is going on."

Chapter Eleven

Bright sunlight assaulted his closed eyes and, reluctantly, Emmett allowed himself to wake up. Kami still slept peacefully nearby, while Jewel sat with her eyes closed in meditation. He tried not to breathe too deeply as he stretched, although it was hard to avoid the stench of rotting vegetation that permeated the humid air. Water glittered in every direction; no new trails had appeared.

He did his best not to think about that and instead focused on the feeling of the warm sun on his face. After yesterday's sodden trek, it was glorious. Emmett closed his eyes and basked in the sun. Until Jewel was ready to talk there was no point in doing anything; he didn't want to disturb her concentration.

"Good afternoon."

Emmett opened his eyes to see Jewel smiling at him. He was surprised that he had nearly fallen back to sleep. "Is it afternoon already? Are you hungry?"

"Yes, yes," Jewel helped Emmett to his feet, "and I think I finally know what is going on here."

"Oh?"

"Let's wait until Kami is awake before discussing it."

"Of course," Emmett agreed. "Food first is my motto anyhow."

"Sure it is." Jewel wandered over to a small bush whose roots ran into the murky water. She picked a berry off and popped it in her mouth. "Mmmmm. How about some warm bread and fresh jam?"

"Sounds good." Emmett went over and helped her pick enough berries to make a quick jam, then threw them in a pot with a bit of sugar. "What else?"

Jewel dug into the various packs, pulling things out as she went. Emmett grinned at her and wondered if she had been honest with him about her cooking being too bland. She always seemed to have good ideas on what to make. She started throwing things at him and he mixed a few ingredients together. Before long he had a basic fry bread cooking in a pan. At one time, he never would have attempted to make something like this; now it seemed almost easy.

"Something smells good," Kami mumbled, as the scent of fresh bread and jam enticed her towards consciousness.

"Nice of you to join us." Emmett smiled even though he knew she couldn't see it. "I'm making some food."

"Ya don't say," Kami drawled. He could hear fabric rustling as she crawled out of her cocoon. "Thanks so much, Captain Obvious."

He glanced up when he felt her hand on his shoulder. "Fry bread and fresh, warm mystery-berry jam. Jewel says they're safe to eat."

"Hmmm." Kami didn't elaborate and Emmett saw no point in asking her to. He removed the jam and bread to allow them to cool slightly before they ate. From Jewel's demeanour, he could tell they were in no hurry to go anywhere at the moment. They all took their time to enjoying the meal before anyone spoke.

"So, I spent my morning searching the winding paths that form the history of this area to find out why this place is the way it is." Jewel brushed the crumbs from her hands. "And now I know why we're having trouble finding our way out of this maze." She paused to look at them. "I'm sorry. I should have seen it before. I should have known. This place, this entire bog, is a magical sinkhole. A place is rarely sentient, and this bog is no exception to that, but it seems to have some sort of rudimentary awareness or instinct. It feeds off lost magic and, to it, we're a feast."

"Wait, that doesn't make sense." Emmett furrowed his brow as he tried to figure out everything else. "If it feeds off magic, then what about the wisps?"

"Oh." Jewel's eyes went wide. "I hadn't thought about that. Chances are they're as lost as we are."

"Then what are we following?" Emmett regretted the words as soon as he said them. He knew exactly what she was going to say about that.

"A chirbatti." Jewel didn't add an 'I told you so' for which Emmett was grateful. "They're not magical themselves. They're trapped souls in the service of a yōkai—or are you going to claim those don't exist either?"

"Okay, so maybe I was wrong," Emmett muttered.

"What was that?" Kami said, with far too much cheer.

Emmett sighed and repeated himself more clearly. "I said that maybe I was wrong, okay?"

"About time you admitted to that." Kami said, grinning. "Now for those of us who don't speak freak—what does it mean?"

"I'm only guessing, but I think we need to forgo all magic usage." Jewel kicked idly at the ground, unhappy with her own conclusion. "Moving forward, I believe it will be best if we follow the least magical of our group, which would be you, Kami."

"No," Emmett blurted without thinking. He scrambled to soften the harshness of the statement. "I mean to say that she isn't unmagical, she has the ability to detect lies. We're better off choosing directions at random."

"Right." Jewel's eyes narrowed in suspicion, but she didn't add to that statement. Instead, she turned to Kami. "What do you think?"

"Uh—me?" Kami stuttered, surprised that someone was asking for her opinion. "I don't know. I could try, but I have no idea where I'm going. I'd rather follow that chirbatti thing."

"And the yōkai that it'll be leading us to if the myths are right?" Emmett pointed out. He still wasn't sure he believed in either thing, but he could not deny the current evidence. What little he knew of the yōkai made him want to cling harder to his disbelief.

"That's a chance we're going to have to take." Jewel stood up and started putting things away, her back towards them. He could tell she was mad, but he wasn't entirely sure why. He decided to leave it alone for now.

"So, we leave at nightfall then?" Kami asked.

Emmett smiled at her. "You got it. Wisps and the like don't come out until after dark."

"Kay." Kami looked pointedly at Jewel and then back at Emmett and raised her eyebrows in a silent question. Emmett shrugged in response. She raised her eyebrows again and nodded her head towards Jewel.

He got the message and walked over to where Jewel was steadfastly ignoring them, struggling with getting things into her pack. "Jewel?"

"What?"

"Is something wrong?"

"What would make you think that?"

Emmett glanced back at Kami who glared at him in return. She motioned for him to continue. "You seemed to have ended that conversation rather abruptly."

Jewel struggled with the bag a bit more before throwing both the pack and her sleeping roll on the ground. "What do you want me to say? That I feel useless? That I should have seen this coming? Seers aren't perfect, but this, this is so big. I should have sensed something. I risked my entire comfortable existence because everything told me that you needed me on your side in this journey. I have a very specific set of talents and they are all useless here. And do you know what the worst part is? Do you?"

"Um, no."

"I don't know why." Jewel turned to face him. "If I weren't a true seer, I would have shuffled you on over to the nearest outfitters and wished you luck after a few charming lies." Jewel closed her eyes and pressed her fingers to her temples. "So many paths, so many possibilities. I'm frustrated and it's getting to me. I'm sorry."

Kami pushed Emmett aside and wrapped her arms around Jewel. "No one is perfect. We knew this wouldn't be easy."

"I didn't know it would be this hard." Jewel stepped back and smiled. "I've spent so much time trying to pull these puzzles apart, I forgot that there are moments even a seer has to sit back and let life happen."

"There are moments when that is all any of us can do," Emmett said. "Anyone who lives long enough learns that lesson."

"And how long have you lived for?" Jewel asked. Emmett saw the realization of his otherness flash across Kami's face at that question. It had never occurred to her that he was older than her, only that he wasn't human.

He saw no reason to lie, but that didn't mean he had to tell the truth. "Long enough to learn that lesson. We should probably get some more rest if we're going to be following a ball of light all night." Neither of them responded to his comment. Emmett glanced up at the sky. "It's still a few hours until night fall."

"Right," Jewel said, looking at her dropped pack and the sleeping roll she had failed to shove into it. "Guess it's a good thing I never quite got that in the bag."

"I'm not tired." Kami crossed her arms and sighed. "I know, get some rest, right?"

"Your choice," Emmett said, shrugging, "but I'm not tired either. A quick nap before nightfall should be good enough. Any suggestions on what to do on this little island?"

"Sure. You want the strange and slightly hazardous? Or do we go straight to the really weird and likely to get us killed ideas?" Jewel winked. "Seriously though, I'm not sure what we can do."

"Well..." Kami smirked. "Em's a really good juggler."

"No." Emmett crossed his arms and glared at her. "I'm not juggling for your entertainment. I haven't even done it in years. I probably can't."

"Come on. Entertain us," Kami pleaded with him.

"Don't know unless you try." Jewel tossed a rock at him. Emmett caught it with ease.

He threw the rock in the air and caught it. "Fine." Emmett picked up a couple more rocks and tested their weight before starting to juggle the three of them. His focus was on the stones when he heard the girls giggling. He stopped juggling, caught the rocks, and glared. "What?"

"Your..." Kami was laughing so hard she couldn't keep going.

"Face..." Jewel continued for her, before breaking out into full laughter.

Emmett chucked one of the rocks towards Kami. She ducked it easily and it splashed in the water behind her.

"Missed me," she teased.

"How about an apology?" Emmett growled, even as he grinned. He tossed a second rock towards Jewel who also ducked it, her laughter starting to fade.

"Sorry, but your face!" Jewel exclaimed. "You were making this face and..."

Kami snorted with more laughter. Emmett casually tossed the last stone into the water behind him. "Fine. Have it your way. We will sit here in silence then."

He sat down with his back to them and crossed his arms. He was planning on making a good show of the fake pout. It would keep them occupied for a few more minutes. Beneath him the ground trembled. He ignored their laughter and half-hearted apologies as he focused on the steady trembling of the ground. "Do you guys feel that?"

He turned around to face them and asked again after receiving no answer the first time. "Do you feel that?"

"Wha—" Jewel stumbled forward as the island gave a violent heave and water rushed into the air. They scrambled to the far side of the small piece of land, stumbling as the shaking continued. They could only go so far before the ground turned into watery bog. With nowhere else to go, they turned to see a creature rise on a tower of water.

Numerous dark eyes of varying sizes stared down at them. It walked towards the island on six hairy legs. Emmett couldn't help but notice how each leg ended in a single, bony spike. The creature stopped at the edge of the little island, still standing on the water.

"Hello there." Its mouth appeared as nothing more than a small dark hole in its bulbous head. "I'm Anukabi."

Emmett exchanged glances with Kami and Jewel. He had no idea how to respond to the creature or what it was. From the look of it, Jewel had no clue either. They stared at Anukabi, who stared back at them.

"Are you able to speak or has the Baksüz taken your minds?"

"Er, um, no?" Emmett hadn't meant for it to sound like a question, but he was at a loss for words. He had no idea what he was speaking to or why it had confronted them.

"Oh, that is good." It flailed its legs. "So many I meet here have lost their minds to the Baksüz. It's been so long since I have spoken to those who were not lost beyond all hope."

"We haven't been here long. We quickly realized the nature of this bog." Jewel took a step forward and bowed slightly. "I'm Jewel, and my friends are Emmett and Kami. We're travelling through to Gibborim."

"You chose a difficult path, but a good path."

"Good?" Emmett let the word roll off his tongue. He had no idea how being lost in this place was a good thing, but he was willing to hear the creature out.

"Well, it's an interesting route and interesting can be good."

Emmett chuckled. "Not always."

"I suppose, but we would not have met had you not come in this direction."

"That is a fair point," Emmett conceded. He didn't add that it would all depend on what happened next.

"May I inquire as to what you are?" Jewel asked quietly. "I have never met one such as you before."

"I'm Anukabi."

Jewel locked eyes with Emmett, her eyebrows raised in an unspoken question. He glanced back at Kami who hadn't said a word yet. Her lips were pursed, deep in thought about something.

"Well, Anukabi, I will say that it is a pleasure to meet you. Would you like to sit and share a meal with us?" Jewel offered. "We welcome your company and it would be an honour to break bread with you."

Emmett wanted to applaud her diplomacy and was quick to add his voice in agreement. "Yes, we would enjoy your company greatly."

"Such a generous offer, but alas, I cannot set foot upon the land or I would be subject to the same fate as those who lose themselves to the Baksüz." Anukabi waved an arm at the maze of paths that ran through the bog. "It is a good thing that I like the water."

"Wait, does that mean we have to slog through the water to get out of here?" Kami piped up.

Anukabi turned to stare at her. "It was never the water that was cursed, but the land itself which is of unnatural origin. It is the Baksüz."

"It is alive." Emmett barely heard Jewel mutter those words under her breath before she continued more audibly. "You have been here for a long time then?"

"I was here when there was only a trickle of water that became a lake that was turned into a bog," Anukabi said. It sounded like the creature was wistful, longing for a time that had long since passed. It was a feeling Emmett understood.

"You know this place well. Can you help us get out of here?" Kami interrupted. It was just like her to skip the niceties and get straight to the point. Emmett hoped the creature would not perceive her direct request as an insult.

"I could."

"Will you?" Kami walked towards the edge of the island, as close to the creature as she could get. "Saying you can is not the same as saying that you will."

Emmett winced at her words. She was right, but diplomacy was not her strong suit.

"Aren't you a bright child?" Anukabi leaned down to meet Kami's gaze. "You are right, of course. I did not say that I would, only that I could. Why should I show you out? It has been a long time since I've had the pleasure of sane company. I would much rather you stay here and talk to me."

"About what?" Kami placed her hands on her hips and stared defiantly into its eyes. "Current politics? The weather? And for how long would we be forced to sit here and wait so that someone can keep you company? Until we die or go crazy?"

Anukabi leaned in even closer until its was only inches from Kami's unwavering gaze. "You have no idea to whom you address such statements."

"I don't care who I'm addressing. You're being rude and inconsiderate."

With a sigh, Emmett joined Kami near Anukabi and placed a hand on her shoulder. "She means no disrespect, Anukabi. It has been a long and troubling journey for us. Please forgive her rudeness."

"Don't tell me what I mean." Kami shrugged his hand off her shoulder. "I meant plenty of disrespect. I will not be held captive by another creature in this world."

"Captive?" Anukabi leaned back. "You would not be captive. You could leave now if you so choose to. I would not stop you."

"And be lost forever." Kami wasn't backing down.

Jewel stepped up, a placating smile on her face. "She is not wrong in that, Anukabi, even if her approach to the situation is less than polite. We would like to reach Gibborim as soon as we can. We're on a journey of some urgency."

"Nothing is ever as urgent as mortals believe it to be. You cannot change the tides of time. Everything will go as it goes. Everything will be as it always has been."

Emmett bit his tongue on the topic of mortality. He still did not know what the creature before them was, but he knew that no matter what it thought, it was not truly immortal. He had never met a being that was. However, Anukabi was right. There were certain things that would always go as they were meant to go, and no efforts of any being from any realm could change that.

"And what events do you foresee as unchangeable by the likes of us?" Emmett asked, his voice softer than that of his friends. All of Anukabi's eyes focused on him and it was like the creature was seeing him for the first time.

"You know my words are truth better than most." Anukabi weaved intricate and abstract patterns in the air with four of its limbs. "Such is the way of the many planes, the many worlds that balance the forever."

"That hardly answers my question," Emmett pointed out. He was beginning to grow exasperated. All he wanted to do was get out of this place and go back to where Kami would be safe.

"And you are more than capable of getting out of here without my help. Why do you choose to let the bog weigh down on you? Why choose to play with the mortals?"

"We're all mortal." Emmett had no interested in having this conversation with Anukabi. "I'm no better than any other who stands here. All who live will eventually die—this is unchangeable."

"You do not believe in immortality?"

"I do not believe in wasting my time playing word games when so much more hangs in the balance."

"More?" Anukabi drawled.

Emmett stole a sideways glance at Kami and bit his lip. "Things are often more than what they appear to be."

"Yes," Anukabi agreed readily, "that is a great truth, but the opposite is often true as well. It is easy for any with immortal wisdom to know that you have had many lifetimes to practice your own kind of deception. It leaves a trace."

"If you think you are so wise, then you should know by now that we must be allowed to pass," Emmett insisted as he stepped forward, nearly within touching distance of the creature. "You should know which truth is mine."

Anukabi leaned forward, its limbs reaching towards Emmett, but not quite touching him. It eyed him closely. Kami and Jewel held their breath, not knowing what Anukabi would do. Its limbs traced patterns around Emmett who stood still, staring it in the eyes, waiting for a response. Satisfied with whatever it was doing, Anukabi leaned back. "I will need a tribute. A shiny bauble. Her necklace for example."

Emmett's eyes followed Anukabi's outstretched leg to see it pointing at Kami. "No. That is a gift she treasures. It is not for barter."

"Em..." Kami put her hand on his shoulder. "I appreciate that you care enough to let me keep it, but if it's what gets us out of here, then it's my decision."

"No." Emmett looked hard at her. "We can trade something else."

Kami took the necklace off and placed it in Emmett's hand. "We have nothing else."

"It does not matter," Anukabi gestured with a single leg towards Emmett. "Even if you had something else, I would only accept that necklace. Nothing else will do."

Emmett gripped the locket tightly and took a deep breath before holding it out for Anukabi to take. He couldn't watch as Anukabi reached for the necklace, its claw looping gently through the chain. But instead of taking the necklace, it leaned in close to Emmett, its mouth only an inch from his ear.

"I can see far and long in many directions. Not only here but through time as well. I know the truth of your words and I know the darkness to follow. This is one bauble that you have no further need of. Do not fight what cannot be changed," Anukabi whispered, before leaning back with the necklace still looped over its claw.

"The way is open to you. Take the water and follow the chirbatti tonight. Do not touch land. You will reach the other side shortly," Anukabi said, loud enough for the others to hear. "I bid you well on your journey." Without waiting for a response, Anukabi slipped quickly below the surface of the water. Not a ripple showed where it had disappeared. It was as if it had never been. They stared at the stagnant, murky water in silence.

"That was…" Jewel started.

"Odd." Emmett finished for her. "Very odd."

"What was it?" Kami asked.

"I don't know. If what we followed was a chirbatti, then it's a yōkai. Maybe." Jewel stepped back from the edge of their island. "If it was a yōkai, then they are nothing like what the stories tell us about them."

Emmett moved to sit in the centre of the island. "It doesn't matter now. There is little left for us to do but follow the chirbatti until we lose our minds or find our way back to dry land."

Kami flopped onto the ground with a groan. Emmett understood exactly how she felt. None of them were looking forward to trudging through the filthy water all night, but that was what their future held. As promised, the chirbatti appeared at dusk.

As the first vestige of dawn coloured the eastern sky, they dragged themselves from turgid water to dry land. Exhausted and chilled to the core, they made it only a few steps before collapsing. Jewel pulled the fire stone from her pack and placed it on the ground between them. "Inardesco."

A bright, warm flame erupted, and Kami let loose an audible sigh. They gathered around it as close as they dared. Though hungry, none of them had the energy to eat. Instead they fell asleep as the sun rose, enjoying the warmth the fire provided.

Chapter Twelve

"Finally," Kami exclaimed, at her first sight of the village in the distance.

"I can't wait to have a hot shower," Jewel mumbled, her pace quickening slightly despite the exhaustion they all felt. Emmett didn't say anything, reserving his energy for the last bit of distance they had to go today. It wasn't until they crossed under the open wooden archway that marked the main entrance to the village that he let his pace slow to take in what Gibborim had to offer.

It was a small, prosperous village. Like most villages, there were many different beings to be found—although there seemed to be a higher percentage of fur covered creatures this close to the mountains. Emmett was sure that they would be able to pick up a few special items they needed to traverse the mountains that they had hoped to avoid at the beginning of their journey.

"We should find an inn to stay at for the night. We can ask the proprietor where the best place for supplies is." Jewel glanced around. There were more than a few options to choose from. She pointed to one on the far side of the village. "That one there."

"Why that one?" Kami asked.

"It looks prosperous enough to be clean, but not so prosperous as to be overpriced," Jewel said. "It'll be our best bet with our rather limited funds."

"Limited or non-existent?" Emmett frowned. They had bartered with what little they had on the trade route for food to make it this far. He could feel a chill in the air coming down off the craggy peaks. Their magical clothing, as good as it was, had not been designed for the conditions they might find on the mountains. They also needed more than food. If the rift within the caves of the dwarves turned out to be inaccessible, he had no idea what they would do.

"I still have a bit on me—and I'm a seer. Anywhere I go I have a way to get what I need." Jewel winked and grinned. "Never mess with someone who can see the future."

Emmett laughed. "Only when you're paying attention."

"Spend a day in the head of a seer and you'll know why I'm not always tuned in. It can get crowded in here if I don't take the time to block it out."

"I bet," mumbled Kami. "It's busy enough in my head with just me in here."

"Exactly," Jewel agreed. "It's not easy and it takes a lot of skill and effort to do it successfully. I'm usually successful."

"Usually?" Emmett teased as he ducked through the door of the inn Jewel had chosen. It looked exactly like the sort of place she had described. Comfortable, but not overpriced. What he hadn't expected was the unusually large yeti that stood behind the counter, staring at a ledger, with comically tiny glasses perched on his stub nose. An old brass bell chimed as they entered.

"Welcome guests," the yeti roared politely, removing his glasses and placing them aside. "I'm Bob, the owner of this fine establishment."

"Bob?" Kami asked, unsure if she had heard correctly. Emmett didn't blame her for the confusion, it wasn't the sort of name he had been expecting to hear either. "Like, legit—bee-oh-bee, Bob?"

"I'm not entirely sure what you mean by 'legit,' child, but, yes, my name is Bob and that is how it is spelled."

"It's an unusual name for these parts," Emmett said, shooting a quick warning glare at Kami. "We were, perhaps, expecting something a little different."

Bob laughed. "It's certainly not your typical yeti name, but my parents had a thing for odd Mundialis names. It took me a bit to forgive them for that, but now that I'm older I've come to enjoy it."

"Well, Bob, we're looking for a comfortable room for a night or two and some advice on the best outfitter to visit for supplies to continue our journey," Jewel told him, before they got too sidetracked.

"I should be able to help you with both those requests." Bob scratched his chin. "A couple of nights? A suite perhaps? We have our pick, not a lot of visitors to Gibborim this time of year."

"A suite would be ideal, but we may have to talk trade on the price."

"I'm willing to barter a little," Bob grinned. "You might have less luck with an outfitter though. I might be able to help you with that as well. I assume you're heading on through to Neerlandia?"

Jewel looked at her companions with a raised eyebrow. Emmett gave a little shrug, as did Kami—neither cared if the innkeeper knew their destination. "No, we're not heading through the Angrums Pass. We're looking to make our way to Dwergenhellar."

"Whoa," Bob boomed. "Those are not words I hear too often. What in the name of Shinje is taking you out that way?"

Emmett exchanged a glance with Jewel, but before either of them could say anything Kami stepped forward. "Why do you want to know?"

"It's not somewhere most reasonable people choose to go. They share their lands with angry jötun, trolls, and many other vicious creatures," Bob explained. "And this time of year the weather is unpredictable at best. There are few who dare to venture up there, even in ideal travelling conditions.

Few ever return. I'm a curious fellow, but I understand that not everyone wants to share their reasons for doing what they do."

"Um..." Kami glanced back at Jewel. "You didn't say it would be that dangerous."

"I said we'd all have to become better fighters," Jewel pointed out. She turned her attention back to Bob. "So, about that room?"

"Yes, you said something about a bit of barter," Bob acknowledged. "What sort of trade were you—"

"No." Kami interrupted, turning to Jewel and Emmett. "I want to talk about this insane journey you've got me on. I want to get home more than anyone, but I don't want to die doing it."

"Let's not do this here," Emmett growled. "We can talk about it later."

"Oh, who cares if he overhears?" Kami insisted.

Jewel sighed. "Do you want to go home?"

"Yes."

"Then this is the way we have to go. We can work out the details later. It'll be fine. Mostly."

Kami frowned. "Mostly?"

"I would prefer to have this conversation in private," Emmett interjected, "but I'm inclined to agree with Kami that the word 'mostly' is concerning."

With a sigh, Jewel closed her eyes in concentration. Bob watched them without interrupting, a lopsided grin barely visible through the thick hair on his face. Emmett got the distinct feeling that their newest acquaintance had seen many odd things in his life and that the three of them didn't even make the top ten.

Jewel relaxed as she opened her eyes and smiled. "Only some things are foreseeable, you both know that, but I think Bob may be of assistance to us. He seems to have knowledge about the area we're heading into."

"Is that so?" Emmett asked.

Jewel grinned. "Maybe."

Emmett rolled his eyes and turned his attention to the patient yeti. "Then perhaps we should tell him what we're arguing about. Long story short, we believe there is a way for us to get back to Mundialis through the dwarven caves."

"Mundialis, hmm?" Bob said. "Not too many try to pass into that realm anymore."

"We're trying to go home," Kami added.

Bob leaned forward and inhaled deeply. "You two smell vaguely of that realm, but not quite right. And you," he glanced over at Jewel as he straightened, "are definitely not from there."

"I'm not," Jewel agreed. "I'm someone who decided to help these travellers on their way."

Kami snorted. Bob smiled and nodded knowingly. "I'm sure there is more to the story than that. There's always more, but I don't expect you to tell all the gritty details to a stranger. Mundialis..." he sighed wistfully before anyone else could say anything, "It's been a long time since I've set foot in that realm. Wouldn't have pegged you as being from there."

"Oh?" Emmett asked.

"Realms have their own unique smells." Bob grinned again. "You travel enough, you learn these things. Of course, it helps if you have a nose for it."

"I never knew that." Emmett shrugged. "We've been travelling hard for some time and haven't showered in a while, maybe that has something to do with it?"

"Yeah, that's probably it," Bob agreed.

Kami sniffed and wrinkled her nose. "We do stink. You'd think the elves would have provided us with some sort of cleansing facilities, but there was nothing. Ridiculous."

"Elves?" Bob exclaimed, his already loud voice shaking the room. "Sounds like you three have had quite the adventure. Not too many people have dealings with those elves anymore. Most don't know this, but they don't need to bathe or shower. They have a natural cleanliness to them. Hard to explain. Strange creatures, elves."

Jewel looked at their host a little more closely than before. "Have you spent much time around elves then?"

"I've met a wide variety of interesting people in my time." Bob smiled and then deftly changed the subject. "So, let's get you a room with a shower in it then?"

"Right..." Jewel said, accepting the subject change reluctantly. "As I said, we have little in the way of valuables to barter with, but I'm a seer. I can offer you my services in trade for the rooms."

"A seer? Interesting. We'll worry about the trade in services later." Bob gave a dismissive wave and turned his attention back to Emmett and Kami. "So, from Mundialis are you? How are they managing since most of the portals to the magical realms have been closed? Have they found a way to compensate for that yet?"

"They've developed some advanced technology that helps them get by," Emmett told him, trying to think of how best to explain things. "I'm not sure how long it's been since you were last there."

"Well, to be honest, the few times I was there before the direct rifts closed, I spent most of my time high in the mountains," Bob said. "It's one of the things that attracted me to this village. It looked so much like the mountains of your planet in Mundialis."

"It is beautiful here," Kami agreed, "but, um, shower first, then chat?"

Bob chuckled. "Where are my manners? You are probably hungry as well. Let me show you to your rooms and get you fed. We're not a fancy establishment, but it is good, hearty food."

"Thank you," Jewel said as Bob stepped out from behind his counter to show them to their room.

Their suite was simple, but clean. Emmett glanced longingly towards the bed, wanting nothing more than to collapse into that luxurious softness, but a nap was going to have to wait. He walked past the bed and into the small, functional bathroom that was attached to it. When he finally returned to the common room after his shower, he found a simple, delicious meal of leg of mutton, coarse bread, mead, and fruit waiting. He tucked into it with gusto.

"Okay, so what's up with our helpful host?" Emmett asked, after their initial feeding frenzy had descended into polite nibbling on what was left of the delicious meal.

Jewel frowned. "He is certainly interesting. I have the distinct feeling that he is a good being to have on your side, but at the same time I'm not entirely sure about his motives. I believe that he knows more than he is telling us, though I can't really blame him for that."

"Yeah," agreed Kami, "and he hasn't lied to us about anything."

"There is also the fact that he's a yeti." Jewel pointed out. "More chaotic good than anything else. Most of the time they're in it for themselves, but they're not intentionally malicious or mean. In fact, they're usually downright friendly and hospitable. Which points more at my instincts on him being correct."

Emmett munched on some grapes and found that he couldn't disagree with either of them. Still, he was worried that there was more to Bob than what he was seeing, and Jewel had pretty much confirmed that suspicion. He tried not to obsess about it, but he couldn't help himself. It was in his nature to be concerned and cautious.

Knock, knock.

Jewel rose to answer the door. Bob was holding another pitcher of mead in his massive hand. "Thought perhaps you would all like more to drink?"

"Thank you. Please come in and join us." Jewel stepped aside to let him pass into the room. Bob ducked through a doorway that was not made to accommodate his height. He chose to sit cross-legged on the floor.

"I'm happy to see that the meal was thoroughly enjoyed," he commented, as he placed the full pitcher beside the nearly empty one on the table.

"It was delightful and refreshing," Jewel agreed, taking her seat again. "Exactly what we needed after being the on the road for so long,"

"I'm glad to hear that." Bob grinned. "So, you're heading to Dwergenhellar?"

Jewel nodded.

"Bad time of year for that," Bob said. "We have our share of thrill seekers heading up for an adventure, and the dwarves come down on occasion to trade wares with the passing caravans, but not often. Like the elves, they prefer to keep to themselves. Exceedingly rare for anyone to be heading up to see the dwarves instead."

"You seem to be well informed on things," Emmett commented.

"It's because I'm good at my job." Bob helped himself to a glass of mead. "I also used to be quite an adventurer in my day, but we all must settle down eventually. Me, I got married."

"Yes, many a great adventurer has met such a fate," Jewel said, grinning, "but it is a good fate."

"It is and it was. She was a wonderful soul and a kindred spirit," Bob said with a sigh. "We travelled the worlds together, learning and exploring. Eventually, we settled here in Gibborim. We thought we could be the first to fully map and explore this mountain range." Bob stared out the window that overlooked the snow-capped peaks. "There are more dangers in those mountains than many realize. It is an unforgiving place, even for those so well equipped to their dangers. After it took her, I still couldn't bear to leave. So, I opened this small establishment for other travellers and adventurers. Been here ever since."

Jewel placed a hand on Bob's hirsute forearm. "I'm so sorry for your loss. You must have loved her very much."

Bob nodded and placed his considerably larger hand over top of hers. "Thank you my dear, but we're not here to talk about my past. This is about your future."

Emmett was glad to see the conversation move along to other things. "Yes."

Bob's brow furrowed in thought as he looked at the three of them in turn. "An outfitter alone isn't going to be able to get you through those lands. Why go such a dangerous way when there are closer portals through the realms?"

"That is a long story," Emmett said. "CliffsNotes version, we're looking for the rift to the Ether so that Kami and I can return back to Mundialis. As far as we know, the nearest available rift is somewhere deep within the dwarven caves. As things currently stand, it's the safest way back to where we belong."

"Safe you say?" Bob sounded incredulous. "If that is safe then I would not want to know what waited for you on any other path the little seer may have seen."

"This way led to the best possible of all outcomes," Jewel insisted, her voice soft.

"Hmmm." Bob scratched at his chin as he stared up at the ceiling, as if it was suddenly far more interesting than the three travellers who sat before him. "How about a deal?"

"A deal?" Emmett asked. Even with Jewel's earlier assessment of the yeti he still wasn't sure if he was willing to trust him yet.

"Tell me your story and, in exchange, you can have the rooms with meals included for a few days." Bob looked at Emmett as he spoke. "If it's a good enough story, you needn't visit any of the cheating outfitters in this town. I may not be the adventurer I once was, but I still have all the equipment necessary for traversing these mountains. I could even find myself more than happy to be a guide."

"A guide?" Kami asked. "As in come with us?"

"As in lead you, child." Bob smiled, "Heck, if you're heading for the Ether then I may be interested in a final great adventure. It's been a long time since I've had any excitement in my life. Perhaps it's time."

"How kind of you," Emmett said, sipping at his mead. "But if you choose to come with us, we can't guarantee anything."

"Most of the time, a trip to the Ether is a one-way sort of thing. I'm aware of that." Bob shrugged as if it was an unimportant point. "I was wondering, though, aren't there still a few weak spots between this realm and yours? Special places where the powers can align and those who know how can travel between them? What terrible fates must the little seer have seen on these less perilous routes?"

Emmett stayed silent as he tried to figure out what Bob was insinuating. Jewel hesitated in answering and an awkward silence filled the room. Kami, as usual, was the one to break it. "Jewel told us that they were being watched."

"Watched?" Bob raised an impressive eyebrow. "Why and by whom?"

Jewel's face flushed and she looked down at her hands. "Well, uh. You see...um."

"Perhaps it's time to clear the air. We're being hunted." Emmett was curious about how Bob would react to the information. He met Jewel's questioning gaze and hoped she understood what he wanted.

"By the Erlkrönig. I could not tell you why," Jewel continued. Emmett watched Bob closely for any reaction. He remained unreadable.

"Well, there is a name that isn't heard much anymore," Bob said, his tone even. "Those were dark days."

"Yes, they were," Jewel agreed. "We will understand if you renege on your offer of guiding us."

"May we never live to see such dark days again." Bob smiled gently. "However, that doesn't mean I'll not guide you. It just means I'll need a good reason as to why I should."

Jewel and Kami both looked at Emmett to explain. He had no idea where to go from here. He still wasn't sure he trusted the yeti. Bob turned to him as well, waiting for him to say something.

"It's complicated."

"This is about the things that you won't tell me, isn't it?" Kami crossed her arms.

Emmett sighed. He was starting to wish that they had never met Bob so that this conversation could have been avoided for a little longer. "You're not ready for this conversation yet."

"Don't you think that she deserves to know?" Jewel asked. "Don't you think that we both deserve some answers?"

Emmett rubbed at his temple trying to stop the headache that was forming there. "Yes, but now is not the time to have a lengthy discussion."

"Then when will be the time?" Kami leaned back in her seat, arms still crossed. "Because I've got all night."

Emmett groaned. "I took something from him. He wants it back, but it's not his to have back. End of story."

"Old news." Kami rolled her eyes. "Tell me something I don't already know, Em."

"I've got nothing else I can tell you."

"That's not true and you know it," she insisted.

"What do you want me to say, Kami?" he shouted at her, forgetting the others in the room. "That I'm carrying the fate of all the realms on my shoulders? That I don't know how to stop him and keep you safe at the same time? Is that what you want to hear?"

"Now you're being melodramatic."

"I would give anything for it to be even a partial exaggeration." Emmett slumped back into his chair. This conversation had gotten them nowhere and he was back to feeling exhausted.

"I would normally tend to agree with you, child," Bob grumbled, "but his demeanour and the involvement of the Erlkrönig tells me that he is serious. When that dark creature is mentioned, it is always serious."

Kami frowned. "Well, I would know this if someone would actually talk to me."

"Then," Bob boomed, "we should let him tell us what he can and that will have to be enough. Although, I'm not one of your group and I would understand if you were to ask me to leave."

"Stay," Emmett said. "If you are going to help us, then it would be better if you knew what was going on. I'm not sure where to begin. It's a difficult situation that I'm in. I have been sworn to secrecy on many things. Give me a moment."

Emmett stared at the ceiling as he gathered his thoughts. "Everything in all the realms exists in a delicate balance. After the defeat of the person you know as the Erlkrönig, I was charged with the care of something so important that, if I were to lose it, all the worlds would come crashing down into darkness and chaos.

"When I realized what was chasing us back in Blakely Grove I may have overreacted. I didn't think I was still capable of such things. No matter how it happened, here we are in Mythos. Now, all I'm trying to do is get my friend back to safety, but we believe that he is watching the weak points for us to go back. So, we're going through the Ether instead."

Emmett hoped that he had told enough of the truth to appease Kami and to explain to Bob the importance of his task.

"From Mundialis, huh?" Bob snorted. "Knew you didn't smell right for that realm. I won't ask where you're from. If it were relevant to this conversation, then I'm sure you'd share."

"I still don't get to know who or what you are?" Kami asked.

"Does it matter that much to you?"

After some thought, Kami sighed. "No." She leaned over to put her arm around her friend. "I know you'll tell me one day. Or I'll beat it out of you when I get tired of being in the dark."

"Like you could." Emmett grinned, happy that she wasn't going to push the subject. It was stressful to him that Jewel knew so many of his secrets.

"Friends are important. They are the family we choose, and it is good that you stand beside each other," Bob said, his voice a low grumble for a change. "And anything to vex as loathsome a creature as the Erlkrönig is a noble cause in my books. You'll have my help to make it there."

"You're not worried about the Erlkrönig?" Jewel asked.

Bob shrugged. "There are more important things in this world. Besides, I think I've had enough of life here in this realm. It's time to go to the next, whichever realm that may be."

Jewel cocked her head in confusion at the statement, but she said nothing in response.

"Your help is appreciated. What can you tell us about the journey ahead?"

"Oh, there is a lot I can tell you. We have a difficult journey ahead of us. Travel into the mountains is treacherous at the best of times, but the places you need to go can be deadly. While the jötun are few, their anger towards all that are not their kind is great. We have little chance of surviving an encounter with one," Bob informed them. "But you probably knew that already. Dwarves, although they are secluded, can be quite friendly. Very hospitable under the right circumstances. Unless, of course, they think you are after their treasures. It's generally a good idea to bring them a gift of sorts.

"Now, that's the most likely beings we'd encounter. Those forests are full of many things, including trolls and golems. Our next concern is the weather and terrain. No walk in a park, that's for sure. It is an arduous journey in the best conditions and this time of year, that is not what you will get. Winter is on the way, and the weather can turn from beautiful to deadly in the blink of an eye. There is no easy pass into the lands of the dwarves. We will have to go up high past the tree line, on to the glacier itself. There, we will encounter dangers that are unique to the ice; crevasses that are invisible to the eye but will swallow a jötun whole."

"Well that certainly sounds pleasant," Kami said. "And how long will it take?"

"Nearly two weeks—maybe longer," Bob replied. "It depends on how Mother Nature treats us."

"Does she actually exist?" Kami asked, her eyes wide.

Bob laughed. "No. It's an old saying. Maybe she did exist once. Maybe she's one of the old gods that have disappeared into the mists of time and story. In all the realms, I have yet to meet a single true god."

"There's no god?" Kami snorted. "Guess there are going to be a lot of disappointed people when they die."

Jewel giggled this time. "Weren't you listening when I told you about the Ether? That's where people go when they die. We process them, sort them, and send them on."

"On to where?" Kami asked.

"Wherever they belong. Some go back to their realms, some move on to others. Some get to choose what they do with their afterlife, which is always interesting. Life and death can be complicated things, but out of the two I think dying requires the most paperwork."

"Alright," Emmett interrupted, loudly enough to get everyone's attention. "Let's focus on our more immediate concerns. Like, when should we be leaving? And does our wonderful new guide need to wrap up any affairs prior to closing up shop?"

Bob chuckled. "Not much to wrap up. Business has been slow. There are fancier and newer places the adventurers prefer nowadays. You are my only guests; a few notes sent and I'm done. As for when, the sooner the better I think."

"Are we to leave early in the morning then?" Jewel asked.

"Perhaps the morning after?" Bob treated them to a fearsome grin. "I will leave you three to rest up."

"Good night, Bob," they managed to say in unison. Their new friend nodded and left them to their own devices for the night.

"Can we trust him?" Emmett asked.

Jewel responded with a shrug. "I have a good feeling about him, if that eases your mind."

"Slightly," Emmett admitted.

Kami yawned and stretched. "My bed is calling my name."

"Good night." Emmett watched her leave but remained where he was. As much as he wanted to trust Bob, he still had his reservations. He understood why Jewel had decided to join them on this dangerous journey, but Bob's motivation was a mystery. He doubted their noble cause was enough for most beings to be willing to put their lives on the line.

Chapter Thirteen

Bob woke them with a heavy knock on the door and a tray loaded with food as the first blush of dawn coloured an otherwise dark horizon. Today they were leaving for the mountains. Jewel was the first one up and in the common room. By the time Kami stumbled in to join them, a good amount of the food had disappeared—allowing room on the table for Bob to spread out a map for them to look at.

Kami helped herself to a chunk of meat and plopped down next to Emmett. He smiled at her briefly to acknowledge her arrival before turning his attention back to the map. "Are you sure about that route? I know we talked about it yesterday, but with what you said about glaciers I'm not sure I want to take my chances. Jötuns we can fight, giant cracks in the ice, not so much."

"Trust me friend," Bob insisted, "jötuns are near impossible to fight for our kind. Not without more magic than we have available to us. And that is their burial ground. A jötun burial ground is no place for mortals of any kind. Crossing the glacier is the best bet to reach the dwarves."

"Agreed," Jewel said. "I've been searching all the options, and this is the safest way to go. Bob knows these mountains better than most. He will do his best to keep us aware of and safe from most of the dangers we'll face."

Kami swallowed the food she had been chewing, "I don't even know why you guys are discussing this again. I thought it had all been decided yesterday. Can someone just tell me when we're leaving?"

"Yes, we did talk about this yesterday, but it's important that we're sure of our chosen route." Bob didn't even look up from the map. "We decided on a main route and a couple of alternate paths dependant on certain conditions and events. I'm feeling confident we'll get there in a decent amount of time and with a minimum of hassle. As for when…"

"As for when," Jewel continued for him, "we will be leaving within the hour. Our packs are prepared and ready to go."

"Cool," Kami mumbled, her mouth full of food. She swallowed before continuing. "Glad to know I'm not awake at this godawful hour for nothing."

Emmett stared at her for a second. "Are you feeling okay?"

"A little tired, but otherwise fine. Why?" Kami asked as she reached for a glass of juice.

"You seem a little off today. That's all." Emmett shrugged. He didn't want to make a big deal of things, but he wondered where her relaxed attitude had come from. "Wanted to be sure you're up for the challenge of climbing a mountain."

"Yup. Ought to be a blast." Kami grinned and reached for more food. Emmett bit his lip to keep from saying more. He would enjoy her cheerfulness while it lasted.

Bob folded up the map and shoved it into one of the pouches that were slung across his body. "I took the time to pick up some cold weather stuff for you guys. I don't need it, but since you all are more exposed to the elements, I figured you could use the extra warmth. Most of it is enchanted, so it should fit okay."

"Perfect." Jewel stood up and stretched. "If everything is settled, we should waste no time."

"Agreed." Bob stood as well. "Packs are in the lobby, so we can grab them on our way out."

It took little time to get themselves loaded up and ready to go. Bob paused for a moment as he locked the door to his small inn. He placed one hand against the wooden frame and sighed. "It's been a long time since I've left Gibborim. I may actually miss this place a little."

"You do not have to come with us. We can go alone on this journey," Jewel said softly.

"Naw," Bob turned his back on the place and strode down the street towards the main road that would lead them north. "I've been here too long. It's time for me to go."

Emmett chose to say nothing in response. He understood how Bob felt. Sometimes you just needed to get out of a place and go somewhere new—even if that meant putting your own life at risk. He had never regretted that decision, but sometimes he still missed his home.

Although they left early, they found the north road was already busy. Trading caravans and travellers clogged the well-worn route through Angrums Pass to Neerlandia. Soon enough, they turned off the main road and onto a lesser-used trail. They made their way through the quickly steepening foothills to reach the trail that Bob had told them about—by this point, the path they were following had branched off many times until there was barely a trail to follow.

They made camp beside a teal lake, fed by the glaciers high above them. Trees towered around them. Fewer in number were the bright flashing deciduous trees of the valleys and plains. They had given way to the harsher, sharp-needled trees in hues of green, blue and red. Emmett tried not to look at the mountains that loomed over them. They were far more imposing from here than they had appeared from the town.

Bob took over the cooking. After all his talk of gourmet campfire meals, no one would have it any other way. It left Emmett with a few minutes to himself. He took a seat on a fallen log near the lake and stared out over the placid waters. He let his mind wander where it wished and found himself considering the possibility of failure. He pushed the thought away and cleared his head. It was nice for five seconds not to think; not to worry. Five seconds of pretending that everything was good in the world.

Jewel sat down beside him and interrupted his concentration. "You don't have to be a seer to know that there is something troubling you."

"I'm fine," Emmett said, turning to face her. He could see Kami was pestering Bob about something on the other side of the camp. "Just a little homesick."

"For what home?"

Emmett didn't know the answer to that question. He had only said he was homesick because it was a convenient excuse. He hadn't realized how true it was until the words had crossed his lips. "I don't know."

"I thought that beings from your realm rarely left, hardly ever bothered in the affairs of the mortal realms," Jewel shrugged. "But then there are few true things known of your people."

"Our job is to keep the balance." Emmett said the words he knew by rote. "If things are in balance, there is no reason for us to interfere. My people learned long ago that it is not worth the risks involved."

"Risks?" Jewel asked. Emmett immediately regretted saying anything. The words had just slipped out, and now they couldn't be taken back or brushed off.

"There is the risk of never being able to return again." Emmett decided that he was better off sticking to the truth this time. While he had always put the importance of the realms over his own well-being, sometimes it was nice to be a little selfish. "Anabasa and Castus are pure realms—opposites of each other. To leave a pure realm is to risk corruption by the natural duality that exists in the other realms. Once corrupted, a being can never return to a pure realm."

Emmett let Jewel draw her own conclusions from that explanation. He had spent many years pushing away these thoughts. It had been easier in Mundialis, pretending to be nothing more than human. But here, in lands that were once familiar, old memories came back to haunt him.

"And you?" Jewel asked, after a few moments of silence. "Will you be able to return?"

"I don't know." Emmett frowned. Jewel put an arm around his shoulders in comfort, but he kept his gaze fixed on the fire and figures beyond it. "No one knows how it happens. Some can be gone for hardly any time at all and are never able to return, others have been gone for centuries and re-enter with no issues. I have a feeling, though, that by the time my task is finished I may not be able to."

Jewel squeezed him a little tighter. There were no words that could adequately relay how she felt. She could only let him know that she was here for him.

Emmett shrugged. "Don't worry about me. I'll be fine."

They stared into the fire together. He could hear Kami's laughter at something Bob had said. If not for his worries, he would have enjoyed the peaceful evening.

"Can I ask you something?" Jewel asked.

"I can't guarantee you an answer."

"What happens to your kind when they can't return to their own realm?" Jewel's voice faltered slightly, as if she was worried about what his answer might be.

"We die," Emmett said. He would have left it at that, but the look on Jewel's face made him elaborate. "When the power is gone, so is the immortality that goes with it. And that's only if we're lucky."

"And for the unlucky?" Jewel's voice had dropped so low that he could barely even hear her.

"I think someone familiar with my kind should know the answer to that," Emmett whispered. "Can I ask you something?"

"Hmmm?"

"Have any of my kind ever crossed into the Ether before?" Emmett had never expressed the worry growing in the back of his mind ever since they had decided on passing through the Ether. It was something he had been planning on dealing with when they got there, but now, in the peace of the evening, he couldn't push it away any longer.

"No. Not to my knowledge," she admitted.

"That's what I thought." He could feel Jewel's eyes on him as he stared resolutely into the fire. Her words were a confirmation of what he was thinking. He wasn't sure his kind had the ability to enter the Ether, even while alive, but he was about to find out. Of course, that was still a best-case scenario.

"Dinner is ready!" Bob roared at them. With a heavy sigh, and a heavier heart, Emmett joined Kami and Bob. By the time he was close to them, he had managed to plaster a pleasant smile on his face. There was no need to worry anyone else with his suspicions. After all, there was always the possibility that he could be wrong.

Chapter Fourteen

Each day, they found themselves slogging up increasingly steep terrain. Shimmering deciduous trees disappeared entirely, giving way to the rich colours of the tall conifers holding tenuously to the thin, rocky soil. Despite the warmth of the sun, a chill could be felt in the breezes that flowed down from the icy crags above. Emmett was not looking forward to when they left the protective shelter of the treeline behind.

Dense foliage shaded the rising sun from their view as they scrambled and crawled their way up the steep, narrow path. Like most mornings, they had started at first light. A rocky ridge high above them was their goal before they could take a brief rest. Emmett brushed dust from his eyes as several stones tumbled down.

Panting and exhausted, they were thankful to have a rest on the slim ledge. Emmett took a moment to enjoy the view and luxuriated in the warmth of the sun on his face. From here, they could see out across the valley. It was hard to believe that they had traversed those hills and basins to find themselves high above the plains that they had crossed so long ago. They sat in silence as they allowed the beauty of the panorama before them to sink in.

Bob broke the silence as he pointed towards a small clearing. "Look." Kami gasped in amazement and Emmett smiled at the sight of the two brilliant white unicorns grazing peacefully in the field. It was not something he had ever expected to see. It was incredible. Bob allowed them a few more minutes before he beckoned them onward and upward.

The grueling climb took its toll on each of them as the day wore on. Afternoon gave way to evening, the trees began to thin, and the ground became more rock than soil. Bob called a halt to their ascent as their path entered a clearing. Above them a few hardy trees clung desperately to the rocky terrain. Emmett wrapped his jacket a little tighter around himself in the chill.

"We'll rest here for the night. I don't think we'll find a more sheltered position after this point," Bob informed them. "Past this, it's barren lands and if we're unlucky, wandering jötun. I'd tell you to keep an eye out for them, but they're hard to miss if they are moving and nearly impossible to see when they are not."

Jewel visibly shuddered. "Let's do our best to not run into any."

"Always advisable, little one." Bob grinned. "Let's get camp set up and have an enjoyable and restful evening before we start the trek to the glacier."

Bob sniffed at the air a few times and then stared at the sky. Emmett found himself looking up as well. There didn't seem to be much to see. A few wispy clouds decorated a pale blue sky. Whatever had caught Bob's attention wasn't evident to him.

"Yeah, these trees will give us good shelter tonight," Bob said, a little more quietly then normal. "I think we should set up fairly close together."

"Don't we usually?" Kami asked, a look of confusion on her face.

"Yes, but perhaps closer than usual," Bob said. "It'll make sense later."

"How about making sense now?" Kami grumbled. She dragged her own shelter out of her pack. Emmett turned so she wouldn't see him roll his eyes as he went about getting his own shelter set up.

"I smell snow. It's distant, but I can still smell it. No way of telling if it'll be a few flakes or a full out blizzard, but the scent is distinctly there."

"Snow?" Jewel echoed. She gave the sky a passing glance before dropping her pack and rolling her freed shoulders. "Give me a second and I might be able to see how the weather patterns are likely to flow."

By the time Kami had finished setting up her own shelter, Bob and Emmett had finished theirs and Jewel's. It took little time, but it was enough for Jewel to have reached a conclusion. "From what I can tell, the most likely outcome is a small snowstorm. Although, there were a few strange factors that made the prediction harder than it should have been."

Jewel glanced at where they had set up the shelters according to Bob's suggestions and nodded. "Yeah, that looks good."

"We should collect some extra wood in case the storm turns out to be worse than expected." Bob gave the sky a disapproving look. "Go in pairs in case you run into anything. Don't stray far."

"I'm with Emmett!" Kami shouted. "Come on bud. Just like the forest back home. Promise I won't almost break anything this time."

Emmett grinned. "You better not. There aren't any hospitals nearby." She stuck out her tongue and scampered ahead of him into the woods. "Kami! Wait up! Don't wander in there alone!"

She ducked her head from around a tree and rolled her eyes. "I know better than that. I just wanted to see how long it would be before I could make you say my name in that whiney tone of voice you get when you're annoyed with me."

Jewel giggled and Bob roared with laughter. Emmett just sighed and jogged to catch up. "No more testing my limits, okay?"

"Sure, sure. Whatever you say." Kami skipped along beside him, but it didn't take long before her lighthearted skip slowed into a normal pace. She seemed lost in thought as she collected fallen branches for the fire. Emmett wasn't sure if he should be happy about her silence or worried about what her silence could mean.

As they were toddling their way back to camp, arms loaded down with as much wood as they could carry, Kami paused. "Can I ask you something?"

"Sure."

"What am I?"

Emmett stopped dead in his tracks. "What?"

"That thing you're protecting, that you took from that early-whatever thing—that's me isn't it? It's why you've spent your entire life being my personal wet blanket?"

"That's a little unfair," Emmett argued, happy to divert the subject away from her initial question. He began walking again, at a quicker pace this time so they'd reach camp that much sooner. "I think maybe I would best be described as a voice of reason."

Kami snorted. "You'd like that, wouldn't you? Being called a voice of reason means I'm unreasonable."

"Maybe a little impulsive," Emmett said. He slowed his pace as Kami started to lag.

"Maybe, but calling you a voice of reason is way too nice for all of the nagging I've had to put up with over the years. Besides, sometimes you can be a bit bullheaded." Kami laughed.

"I'm still not a wet blanket." Emmett faked a pout. Initial apprehension gave way to enjoyment at the light-hearted banter. It felt so much like how things used to be that he was almost nostalgic.

"What else would I call you? My guardian angel?" Her voice dripped with sarcasm. Even though the tone was enough to tell Emmett that she wasn't serious, his step faltered, and he dropped a few of his branches. Unfortunately, his stumble seemed to be the clue that Kami needed. Her tone of voice changed almost instantly. "No freaking way."

"Don't be silly," Emmett said, more forcefully than he had intended to, desperate to cover up her all too accurate assumption.

"Right," Kami snapped back at him. "I'm the one being..."

Her voice trailed off into nothingness as they stepped into the small cove of trees to find their camp ransacked. They both dropped their branches.

"What the hell happened?" Kami whispered.

"I don't know," Emmett murmured. He was suddenly thankful that Jewel had insisted he wear a sword when they left Gibborim. He placed his hand on the hilt, just in case it might be needed. "Whatever it was, I hope it's gone."

"Where are Bob and Jewel?"

"I don't know." Emmett took a few steps forward, searching for any sign of their companions.

Ker-thunk!

Kami jumped a little closer to Emmett. He held an arm up in front of her, urging her back towards the trees. He couldn't see where the sound had come from, but something had destroyed their campsite. It didn't take a giant leap of imagination to conclude that the sound was being made by that same creature.

"Stay back," he whispered.

"I can take care of myself." Kami pushed past him, reaching for the sword that Jewel had given her against Emmett's wishes. He knew that she had no idea how to use it, but he let the seer have her way. It wasn't worth the fight. "I don't need you to protect me."

"I don't have time to argue with you right now," Emmett growled, rushing to catch up with her. They crept towards the stones that blocked their view of the rest of the clearing. Emmett was a few steps behind when he heard Kami gasp. Rushing forward, he pushed himself in front of her, ready for almost anything.

A troll, large and ugly, shuffled its way towards them. He had never seen one in person before, but the descriptions he had heard were more than accurate. It was sniffling and snuffling with each lurching, awkward step. Emmett pulled out his sword. He hoped that it would move away on its own, but if it didn't, he would be prepared.

"Rrrrrraaawwwwwrrrrrrr!" A large white blur charged towards the troll. Bob looked small beside the massive creature. He dodged a clumsy blow before charging in again. Emmett searched for Jewel only to see her standing by the far treeline staring up at the overcast sky.

"That thing is going to kill Bob!" Kami shouted. She tried to rush out into the clearing, but Emmett grabbed her arm. She pulled frantically against his grip, but he wasn't about to let her run headfirst into danger.

"Jewel is trying to clear the sky," Emmett said, pointing past the fighting figures. "Bob is just trying to distract him. He'll be okay. They've got this handled."

Kami struggled harder, not caring or understanding what he was saying. "No he won't! That thing is monstrous. It's going to kill him."

"He's a yeti, he'll be fine," Emmett said, with as much confidence as he could muster. He had to admit that Bob didn't seem to be doing well in this fight, but he only had to manage long enough for Jewel to clear the sky. Once that happened, it would be fine.

"He is our friend! I will be damned if you force me to stand here on the sidelines and watch him get hurt or killed!" Kami shouted, just as Bob went flying through the air and landed hard on the ground. The troll turned and started marching towards the prone yeti who was still struggling to get up.

"He's going to be okay," Emmett assured her. Bob barely managed to avoid the fist the troll slammed into the ground where he had been laying.

"You can't lie to me. You don't even believe that. Let me go." Kami pulled harder to get away. Emmett could feel his grip starting to slip. He dropped his sword so that he could keep hold of her. As he went to grab her other arm, she turned and raised the point of her sword towards him. "I said let go. I mean it. I'm not going to let him die for me." She looked him dead in the eyes. He hesitated and she pressed the sword more firmly against his skin. Reluctantly, he let her go. She stared at him for what seemed like an endless second before turning and running towards Bob and the troll. She waved her sword high in the air as she screamed obscenities at it.

Emmett watched in horror as the troll turned to face her. He wanted to protect her, he had sworn his life to that, but it was obvious that she didn't want his help. He knew one day he would no longer be needed; that all would be returned to balance once again. This was not that time.

His feet were frozen with indecision as he watched Bob get thrown across the clearing. Now Kami stood alone against a beast more than ten times her size. There was little he could do about it that would not put them in more danger than they already were. She launched herself forward with no finesse to her attack, just anger and determination. She swung the sword wildly, in unpredictable arcs and jabs, and barely managed to avoid the troll's swinging club and pounding fists.

Bob pushed himself to his feet and launched into the fight again. The troll staggered backwards as the yeti bowled into him. Kami swung her sword again, slicing at the back of the troll's heel. She ducked away before the troll could even begin to swing in her direction. Distracted by Bob's ferocious attack, she found her chance to deke back and swing at its other heel. Bob continued to slam himself into the large creature, pushing it around the clearing. Emmett realized the yeti wasn't just passing time; each attack was herding the troll back towards a cliff.

Emmett grabbed his sword, sheathing it as he ran along the edge of the clearing—staying clear of the fray. It didn't take him long to reach Jewel. Beads of sweat showed on her forehead. He wasted no time with words and placed his hand on her shoulder. He could feel her startle at his touch as he closed his eyes to focus. He felt her concentration falter. She was tired, pushing her talents to their limits. Emmett sent what energy he could to help her, leaving himself open to what she needed. His energy refreshed and renewed her focus. She pulled from him quickly, almost faster than he could handle. Warm sunshine hit his face and he opened his eyes in time to see the troll, now nothing more than stone, tumbling backwards over the edge of the cliff.

Emmett broke the connection with Jewel and collapsed beside her. Clouds quickly gathered, once more blocking out the sun. Snowflakes drifted down, speckling the air around them. Bob limped back towards camp, leaning on Kami for help. Emmett forced himself to stand and helped Jewel up as well. Exhausted, they leaned on each other as they made their way to meet Bob and Kami in the centre of the clearing. Almost as one, they turned to survey what remained of their camp.

"This is not good." Bob lurched forward a few steps to pick up a rag that was once a shelter. He ran his fingers over the shredded material as if doing so would make it whole again.

"No, it's not," Emmett muttered in agreement. Bob took a few more awkward steps. "How badly are you injured?"

"I'll live. I think I twisted my ankle. Nothing a little rest won't fix, but I'm not sure we have that luxury." Bob frowned as he gave the falling snow a disparaging look.

"We may not have a choice." Jewel stared at her feet as she spoke, and Emmett gave her a little squeeze. He could almost feel her guilt as she leaned against him. "My interference caused the weather to worsen. We may be stuck here for longer than we would like. With your injury and this storm, trying to push on could be suicide."

"I'm a yeti." Bob grinned. "I'm made for this weather. Injured or not, I can make my way through it, but your kind is not as suited to it. We must make a decision. Do we continue onwards through this storm, wait it out, or return to Gibborim to restock?"

"I guess that depends on what's left of our supplies." Kami kicked at a crushed cooking pot.

Emmett held out little hope as they moved to examine what was left. Things were strewn about, shelters were torn and beaten; there was little that had not been damaged. Everything they could salvage was placed into piles, depressingly small piles, while Bob took a moment to rest.

"I think this tells us what our decision is going to be," Emmett said, pointing to the smallest pile. It was their food supply. "We don't have enough to wait out a storm, even if we ration it."

"I'm not sure we have enough even if we left now." Jewel picked at the pile, trying to determine how much of it was still edible. "How far was it to the dwarves?"

"In good weather conditions with no delays?" Bob asked, scratching at his chin. "Hmm, a week and a bit I suppose."

"And in these conditions?"

"Longer than that unless we cut through the jötun graveyard," Bob said. "That route would only take about five or six days in these conditions. However, we still have the choice to return."

Emmett ran through the options as he watched the snow cover the piles they had made. It was coming down hard and fast. "If we choose to return, is there any possibility we could still make it to Dwergenhellar before travel through these mountains becomes too dangerous?"

Bob took the time to consider his question carefully before shaking his head. "We're at the end of the shoulder season. Even the path through to Jötunndys could become impassible at any time."

"Then we should go through Jötunndys." Kami glowered at Emmett as he spoke and he was reminded of their argument before heading through the Baksüz

Bog; this was too important a decision to not allow the others a say in their fates, but he didn't want to take the chance that they would be stuck in Gibborim until the spring thaw. "What do you guys think?"

"It'll be more dangerous without good visibility." Bob frowned at the thought. "Jötun are more active when the sun is out of sight, but even they won't wander around in a bad storm."

"I say we should try," Jewel said. She looked at Kami who seemed lost in her own world. "What do you think Kami?"

"You're the seer." She shrugged and turned her attention back to what remained of their supplies. Jewel raised an eyebrow at Emmett. He didn't respond as he watched Kami sort out all the pieces of rope from one of the piles.

"For tonight," Jewel continued, "I suggest we make camp as best we can with what is left and leave as early as we dare."

"Sure," Emmett agreed, his mind not on the conversation. Kami worked a piece of rope between her fingers, looking for weaknesses in it before setting it aside and checking the next. Her mind was elsewhere, too. "What do you think, Kami?"

"Sounds good," she muttered, without looking up from what she was doing. He could hear the dismissiveness in her voice. He wanted to probe further, but not with the others near enough to overhear. They had not finished their conversation from earlier, and he had no idea what he was going to say to her. He could see Jewel watching them from the corner of his eye and he avoided her questioning gaze by sorting through the piles.

"It won't be magical, but I think we can make a shelter out of what is left. It won't be fancy, but it will keep us warm enough if we wrap ourselves in it. There's a larger shard that we can hang like a tarp above us," Jewel said from behind him.

"And we have enough wood to make a large fire," Bob added. "Perhaps, if you can, a little magical help to make it last longer."

"We'll see how much energy I managed to recover, but something like that is simple enough," Jewel said.

Bob struggled to get up and Kami showed the first real sign of life since they had defeated the troll. She was immediately at Bob's side. "You should keep resting. We can take care of everything."

"She's right. If you are going to guide us tomorrow, you need to get that ankle up." Jewel grinned. "And I don't think icing it will be a problem tonight."

Bob chuckled. "No, I don't think it will be at all. The cool temperature ought to keep the swelling down for now."

There was no doubt in Emmett's mind that it would be a hard few days with what little they had left. It almost made him reconsider turning back. He pushed the temptation from his mind and did his best to remain in good humour as the snow silenced the land around them. It wasn't until they curled up in the remnants of their shelters for extra warmth, with Bob snoring and Jewel seemingly asleep, that Emmett tried to get Kami to speak to him.

"Kami?" He kept his voice soft and low. If she was awake, he would hear her—unless she was ignoring him. He tried again. "Kami, please talk to me."

"Talk to you about what?" she whispered back. "How you almost left Bob out there to die?"

Emmett gritted his teeth. He understood why she was angry at him, but that didn't make it any easier. "If you had any idea…"

"I would if you would be honest with me." Kami rolled over to look him in the eye. "I understand that there are things you can't tell me, but I deserve to know more than this. Bob deserves to know why you almost let him die."

"I didn't almost let him die. I helped Jewel clear the clouds to save him."

"Sure, after watching him nearly get killed. If I hadn't gone to help him, he might have died before those clouds cleared," Kami spat.

"But he didn't die. He barely even got hurt. You don't know how to fight. You could have gotten yourself killed rushing in there like that. I'm supposed to protect you and I can't do that if you keep willfully putting yourself in danger. You were right. You are the valuable thing that needs to be protected."

"You can't protect me forever," Kami said, her voice a little softer now. Still, he could hear anger behind the words.

"I can try."

"At least tell me why," Kami demanded. "What makes me so special?"

Emmett had no idea where to begin. She had accepted so much already, but would she be able to accept the whole truth?

"I'm not sure how to explain it," Emmett said. "It's complicated."

"Try."

"You are human, but you are more than that." His brow furrowed as he struggled to find the words to explain what he wanted her to know without scaring her. "There is something hidden deep within you. An energy of sorts. It's this that the Erlkrönig wants to take."

"Hmmmm." She lapsed into silence. "What about earlier?"

"What do you mean?"

"I know why you didn't want me to fight, but why didn't you fight?"

"I did what I thought was best; I went to Jewel and gave her my power, my energy, so that she could clear the clouds. It is not easy to change the natural order of things and she needed help."

"I'm glad you were able to help her." Her voice was soft, her words broken by a yawn. "I wish you could tell me more. I just want to understand."

"I wish I could too," he whispered, so quietly that he wasn't sure she had heard him. He added, louder, "Get some sleep. We have a hard few days ahead of us."

"Em?"

"Yeah?"

"I'm sorry about the sword thing. I don't know what I was thinking." She reached out her hand to him and he grabbed it, squeezing tightly. "I know I don't make things easy for you."

"You wouldn't be you without that stubborn, impulsive streak." He smiled even though she could barely see it in the dim firelight. He knew, better than she did, the reasons behind her actions, but it was best to keep those things to himself. One day, she'd understand.

"Thank you," she whispered, pulling her arm back into the warmth of her sleeping wrap. He laid awake, staring out past the fire at the falling snow and letting his thoughts wander. A single worry pushed for his attention. He tried his best to ignore the little voice that was telling him that the time he had lived in fear of for so long was coming.

"Where are you?"

Within the fire, he saw the outline of a face he could not forget. He listened to the soft sounds of his companions, wanting to be sure they were firmly asleep before he responded. "Give up Asèth. I will never allow you to get your claws in her again."

His statement was greeted with cruel laughter. The image wavered and disappeared as if it had never been. Somewhere in the distance, a scream broke the silence. Emmett shuddered. He wrapped the ruined remains of his shelter around himself and prayed for sleep.

Chapter Fifteen

Blinding, swirling whiteness was all Emmett could see in any direction. Sometimes the wind would shift and he could see the outline of something more solid—his friends, rocks, the occasional lone pine. If it wasn't for the rope guiding him forward, he would have had no idea where anyone else was most of the time. He lowered his head against the biting wind and clung tighter to his only lifeline as he stumbled along, one foot in front of the other, slow and steady.

With each passing hour it was getting harder, but he persisted. He had to. They all had to. This was his only thought as the cold sapped his strength and the endless, encompassing white attempted to play tricks on his mind. *Keep moving.* He had no idea how Bob could manage to lead them through this. He could only trust that the yeti knew what he was doing. It had been this way for nearly two days.

"Halt!" He barely heard Bob's voice over the howling winds. He staggered to a stop, wondering what it was that had brought their slow crawl to a complete stop. Although Emmett could not see it, they had arrived at the beginning of the long entrance to Jötunndys. Before them was an unmapped, rocky labyrinth that was said to be nearly impossible to navigate. It was a place few dared to enter, and those who chose to rarely survived.

A gentle tug on the rope forced Emmett to trudge forward once again. It wasn't long before a solid rock wall appeared on his left, giving them a reprieve from the relentless blizzard. He followed the rope, and the others, into a small cave. He heard Kami breathe a sigh of relief as they left the gale force winds behind them. A light began to flicker and glow. It quickly filled the cave to the point that he could see his friends for the first time since he had awoken to the wintery landscape. He could not imagine a more tired looking group. With the light came the incredible feeling of warmth—a feeling he had almost forgotten.

"Tonight, we rest here." Bob collapsed on the rocky floor. "I don't think I can bring myself to get too close to that place without good visibility."

"It could provide us with cover," Jewel replied, as she too slid to the ground. "Keep any wandering jötun from seeing us."

"Or we could wander right into one," Emmett pointed out. "Be stepped on or worse."

"Stepped on would be the best possible outcome with a jötun," Bob said, managing to force the words out between massive yawns. "They enjoy the taste of mortal flesh. Besides, we would find ourselves beyond lost among those stones."

Kami glared at them all as she plopped down on the ground. "I'm tired and hungry and half-frozen to death. I say we rest."

"Is there any food left?" Emmett asked.

Jewel checked her bag. "I have some dried meat and fruits. Not much though."

"Soup maybe?" Bob suggested as he dug into his meager pack. "I have a few seasonings and dried vegetables in here. It's not much, but a soup will stretch the furthest and fill us best."

Emmett began to unpack his own bag and pulled out the few bits of food that he still had left. They pooled everything they had on a small napkin; it did not fill the cloth.

"How many more days of travel?" Jewel asked.

"Three or four." Bob stared at the pitiful remains of their food. Jewel nodded and took a large pot to the entrance of the cave to fill it with snow. She returned and carefully took a single dried stick of meat, a few dried vegetables, and a pinch of seasoning to place in the pot.

There was no wood to start a fire with, so Jewel did her best to turn the small orb of light into a more significant heat source. Emmett reached out to her. "I have little energy to spare, but what's mine is yours." Jewel nodded and drew from his power. They were all exhausted. There was no denying the toll this journey was taking.

Silently, they sat waiting for their meager meal to be ready, wrapped in the fabric of their former shelters to stay warm. Kami pushed to her feet and dragged her pack towards the entrance. Emmett watched her and smiled at the look of focused determination on her face as she pulled out rope and a length of fabric. She did her best to cover the opening and further block out the wind.

"Cold?" he asked.

"Smart-ass." She pulled the rope taut and tied it off to a small outcropping of rock. "There, that ought to make this a nice and cozy place to spend the night."

"Just like home." Jewel rolled her eyes and giggled, and Bob joined in on the laughter.

"Yes, I think this could be my new favourite vacation spot," he said, barely catching his breath. It felt good to laugh. It was what they all needed. Jewel wiped away tears from her eyes as she announced that dinner was ready. They each took a single mugful of the thin soup. Even though they were cold, tired, and facing their potential death, they were happy to be alive and among friends.

Emmett awoke to Bob's snoring and the relentless grumbling of his stomach. He heard nothing of the wind that had been their constant companion the last two days. Curious about what would greet him beyond their makeshift door, he got up. He kept his sleeping wrap pulled tight around his shoulders to fight the biting chill in the air.

Pushing aside the makeshift tarp, he was blinded by the shimmering brilliance that greeted him. He closed his eyes against the pain and took care as he slowly opened them again to see a landscape made of diamonds—even the air sparkled in the early morning light. The sun had become a brilliant pillar of light, and a smaller version burst out on the edge of the horizon from the shimmering rainbow circle that surrounded it. As the frigid air outside tried to steal the warmth of his breath, he found himself unable to turn away from the silent beauty before him. He might never see something like this again in his life, and he found himself wanting to etch it into his memory.

"Sundogs." Emmett jumped at the unexpected sound. He hadn't heard the yeti approach. "They guard the heat of the Deisolis from being taken by Hiemsenis."

"Yeti folktales?" Emmett asked, letting the fabric fall back into place. Compared to outside, it felt balmy inside the cave.

"Every race has their myths and beliefs. Most of the humans don't even realize how many of theirs are just based on old interactions with another realm," Bob explained.

"Not every race," Emmett blurted. He pulled his sleeping wrap tighter around him as the feeling of comparative warmth faded. He couldn't wait for Jewel to get another fireball going to warm up the cavern before they all had to brave the icy air outside.

"Really? What races do you know that do not have myths that are a mix of otherworld beliefs as well as their own?" Bob leaned against the rock wall. Emmett found himself a little envious of his natural protection against the cold.

"There are many in Anabasa and Castus that have long since abandoned such things. Those that are near immortal have learned that there is nothing else out there. Just us and the mortals." Emmett tried to ignore how loudly his stomach complained.

Bob raised an eyebrow at the word 'us' but didn't comment on it. "Abandoned, but not without."

Emmett cursed his slip of the tongue, even though he knew the yeti was intelligent enough to have drawn his own conclusions. "How's the ankle?" he asked, wanting to change the subject.

"Stiff, but I'll be fine." Bob sat back down on the cold cavern floor and Emmett did the same. His stomach protested at its emptiness. At the moment, all he wanted was warmth and food. It didn't take long before Jewel and Kami were stirring. Jewel shivered and pulled the fabric tighter around her. She hurried to start a little fire and they all snuggled in closer to the small point of warmth.

Jewel sighed as she reheated what was left of their meager meal from the night before. "It's getting harder to find the energy to create those." No one had anything to say to that; they could only hope that they would find a reprieve soon. It prompted her to ask the important question. "How much longer until we get there?"

"Answer hasn't changed much—now that the weather has improved, I would like to say only three more days," Bob said. "Of course, that depends on if we lose our way in Jötunndys. Once through, we will cross Gigan Moerus Ridge, after which we will find ourselves at Lasursten Lake, the frozen jewel of these mountains. On the other side of the lake are the great cliffs, where we will hopefully find the entrance to Dwergenhellar."

Kami sighed and poked at her belly. "I feel like I'm going to starve before we get there."

"We're all hungry," Jewel agreed, pouring half a cup of reheated soup into everyone's mug. "But there isn't any use in complaining."

"Here," Bob poured part of his soup into Kami's mug. "Yeti's are designed to do without. I can go longer on less than you can."

Emmett looked at his own small portion of soup and frowned. He had only managed a single sip. It wasn't enough, but it would have to do. He pushed his mug over to Kami and Jewel. "Split it. I'm not that hungry." He ignored the look that Kami was giving him and dug out a small piece of dried fruit from his pack instead. He nibbled on it, hoping that if he ate it slow enough, he could fool his stomach into thinking it was something worthwhile.

Bob wound up the rope. There would be no need to stay tethered together now that they could see where they were going. As Kami pulled down the sheet of fabric that protected their shelter, Emmett was forced to close his eyes to the brightness outside.

"Knew I'd forgotten something." Bob frowned as he looked at his friends. "You guys need to protect your eyes, or you'll go snow blind in that."

"Is there any soot?" Kami asked.

Jewel shook her head, "No, the fire created by magic leaves no trace. We'll have to do this the old-fashioned way."

Kami watched expectantly as Jewel dug into her pack and dragged out a few more random scraps left over from the shelters. "Best we can do, I think. Just leave a small slit to look through and if your eyes start to feel sore, let someone know."

Emmett knew that the light would pose no threat to him, but he still firmly believed that he was better off hiding himself as a human. It was safer for them all if no one suspected what he was, so he wrapped the fabric around his face. He couldn't see much between the folds, but it did make the light a little easier to bear. Bob took the lead again, his larger form breaking a path for everyone else behind him. It was exhausting work as they made their way up the steep hill between the towering cliffs, and Emmett struggled with every step.

It seemed like hours before Bob stopped and pointed at a boulder in which weather-worn words had been carved. He read it aloud in a voice that was barely more than a whisper. "Be warned. Here is the place where giants lie. Turn back." They stood in silence, staring at the centuries old warning for those foolish enough to trek this way.

"There is more, but it's illegible now," Jewel said, as she traced the words with her fingers.

"It's enough," Bob said, shuddering. "I would recommend we travel in silence. It isn't much further to the end of this narrow route. Then you will all understand what awaits."

True to his word, it didn't take long before they could see where the canyon ended ahead of them. Several large boulders blocked their view of what lay beyond. Bob guided them into a narrow opening between two oddly shaped rocks that had fallen against each other. It was still a large enough space for all four of them to be able to see out.

Bob whispered a single word, although it hardly seemed necessary for him to do so. "Jötunndys."

Chapter Sixteen

Above them, the cliffs soared to dizzying heights and stretched out to form a massive canyon. Between them and the other side, snow-covered mounds and bare rock jutted upwards towards the sky. Misshapen versions of broken body parts created a landscape of anarchy. There were no paths through or around the nightmarish expanse.

"Much like trolls, giants also turn to stone upon their death." Bob kept his voice barely above a whisper. "Unlike trolls, who barely qualify as intelligent, the jötun have a rich society with a culture and traditions all their own. One of them is that the dead are gathered into a single place. This graveyard is hallowed to them."

"Why are you whispering?" Kami matched Bob's tone. "I thought you said these jötun things don't come out during the day."

"They don't usually, but that doesn't mean they never do." Bob turned to face all of them. "At the first sign of any movement, take cover. It is not only wandering jötun that we need to worry about. There are many creatures travelling these areas that could be considered dangerous. Some of them may be more of a threat to us than any jötun."

Emmett removed the strip of fabric from his eyes and studied the land before them for movement. For a moment, he thought he saw something high up on one of rocky crags, but he wasn't sure. He stared at the spot until his eyes watered, but the movement didn't repeat. Kami and Jewel followed his lead so that they could see better as well. It was easier to see here with the grey rock breaking through the brilliant white of the snow and ice.

"Any suggestions on getting through this place?" Jewel asked, her attention more on the chaotic jumble of stone ahead of them. Many pieces were larger than the home she had left behind her.

Bob pointed to the far side of the cliff-lined opening where they could faintly see another opening in the basin. "We have to make our way towards that path there. If it were a straight path through, I would say we could make it in a few hours easily."

Emmett frowned as he studied the land. No one needed to point out that there would be no such thing as a straight path through this graveyard. He was so intent on trying to chart a route that he barely even noticed when everyone started down the hill into the impossible maze ahead. Emmett hurried to catch up as quietly as he could.

It was eerie, walking through what he knew was a graveyard, but it wasn't like anything he had ever seen before. He had no idea how many lapidified bodies created the haphazard stone maze, but it was already a daunting journey as Bob lead them down random paths, hugging the edges of the chosen route as best he could.

After a few wrong turns and some back-tracking, Bob came to a stop under an overhanging rock that Emmett swore looked like the face of some horrid monster staring down at them. He looked away from what he was sure used to be a single, bulging eye to the worried yeti in front of him. "I'm having a difficult time navigating my way through here. We need to try something else."

Jewel winced as she spoke to the ground. "I could try to see the route through magic, but I'm so tired that I'm not sure I can."

Bob patted her gently on the shoulder. "That's alright. We could maybe climb up a bit higher to get a better view of things. Perhaps one of us will be able to discern a path that way. Normally I'd have done so already, but I'm not sure I can make it with my ankle as it is. Walking on the uneven ground has been hard enough."

"I've got this. I'm a great climber." Kami grinned, already reaching for a crack in the rock.

Emmett grabbed her by the jacket and hauled her back to the ground.

"There is no way I'm going to let you climb up there," he growled. "It's too dangerous."

"I'll go," Jewel said softly. "I can use my ability as a seer to find a potential route, even if I can't see it as I would traditionally."

"Are you sure?" Emmett asked. She did not look like she was strong enough to climb a rock face half as high as the one they were considering.

"It's the only decision that makes sense." Jewel shrugged. Kami crossed her arms and pouted, but she didn't argue. Bob hefted Jewel up as high as he could so that she could get a good head start on the climb.

"Careful," he called after her. "It may be a bit slippery with the snow and ice."

Jewel glanced down and nodded before turning her attention back to what she was doing. Her lips were a thin red line and Emmett could tell that she wasn't overly keen on the idea of climbing up. Or perhaps she had a better idea than he did of what might wait for them out in the open. He hadn't missed the fact that Bob had chosen paths that had more overhead coverage and that he had pretty much clung to the edges of the trail. Nor had he missed the occasional glances skyward.

Emmett looked up sharply as one of Jewel's feet flung out into the air. He winced and prepared to help catch her, but she managed to keep holding on. She resumed her slow climb upwards to the snow covered top of the outcropping. He continued watching her intently, praying that she could make it all the way up. A few minutes later, his heart dropped as he heard a squeak of fear. Seconds later, she fell backwards from the rock face. He stepped forward, but Bob already had his arms out. He caught her with ease and she wrapped her arms tightly around his neck.

"Hey, it's okay. I got you." Bob murmured softly to her. "It's okay."

"I don't think I can do that again. I'm sorry," Jewel admitted, her face pale. "I feel as though I'm letting you all down. It would be so much easier if I had the energy to see the way ahead."

"It's fine, Jewel," Kami said. "Look, I'm a good climber and I know I can do it. Ice or not, I can make it to the top."

"I'll go," Emmett said, glaring at Kami. "You're reckless and it's already a dangerous task."

"You suck at climbing," Kami growled back. "I've seen you try to climb an easy tree and you barely made it. I can climb anything, and you know it."

"Yeah but—"

"But nothing," Bob interrupted. "Someone needs to get up there and unless you can fly, I choose Kami."

Emmett said nothing about his ability to fly. "I'm worried about her safety."

"You won't have anything left to worry about if we can't get out of this maze," Bob pointed out. Emmett decided it was best not to push. Kami was an amazing climber. If it hadn't been for Bob's nervous glances at the sky, he wouldn't even be concerned.

"Please be careful," he said, as she grabbed hold of the rock to start her climb. She ascended quickly—much faster than Jewel. He kept his voice low so that Kami wouldn't be able to overhear him and turned to Bob. "What has you looking up so much? I think we deserve to know what you're watching for."

"Besides giants?" Bob asked.

Emmett nodded.

"There is a bird that is called a vogehempi. They are attracted to graveyards," Bob whispered. "They are semi-intelligent but not very nice creatures. And they enjoy live food when they can get it."

"And how common are they in these parts?" Emmett asked, glancing around the empty blue sky.

"They are not a fan of the cold weather." Bob frowned. Kami had reached the top and was carefully balancing herself on the ice.

"I feel like a 'but' should be in there somewhere," Emmett added.

"But I've seen them here before, and if you are being hunted down by the Erlkrönig they may be on the lookout for us." Bob glanced down at Emmett. "I'm sorry I didn't tell you earlier."

Emmett didn't answer. He kept looking up at the sky trying to spot anything at all. He had no idea what these birds looked like, but he was sure he would recognize one if he saw it. Kami leaned over the edge to look down at them and grinned. "I think I see a path that might get us part of the way through this mess."

"Great, hurry up and get down here," Emmett barked.

"How about thanks?" Kami asked.

Emmett swore he could hear her eyes rolling. "How about you get down here before something sees you?" he yelled, forgetting to keep his volume low. "Now!"

A heavy hand landed on his shoulder and he looked up into a set of very worried eyes. He immediately covered his mouth, but it was too late. He could hear his voice echoing back at him—along with another, unfamiliar sound. Kami's gaze was fixed on something in the distance as the ground began to tremble around them.

"Jump!" Bob roared, but Kami was frozen.

"JUMP!" they shouted in unison. This time, the words seemed to get her moving. She threw herself off the ridge without looking. Bob caught her as a shadow fell over them. Emmett couldn't see what was casting it, but the rhythmic rumbling told him all he needed to know.

"Which way?" Bob asked, even before Kami had her feet on the ground. "We need to run so we may as well run in the right direction."

Kami pointed at a path to her left, still distracted by whatever she had seen. Bob began running in the indicated direction. She froze again, so Emmett grabbed her arm as he ran past her. She came willingly, and it wasn't long before she was running without him having to prompt her. At the next split, Bob didn't ask which way to go. Instead, he turned decisively to his right—and right into a dead end. He didn't look concerned as he ran up the wall and started throwing stones to clear their path. Emmett glanced behind them. The shadow was gone, and he still couldn't see the creature that had cast it.

"What—" Emmett started to ask, but a glare from Bob silenced him. There was no ignoring the way the earth kept shaking at regular intervals, each tremble slightly stronger than the last. Bob continued to pull rocks out from the rubble. He had already placed a large boulder that looked suspiciously like a toe to the side. As Emmett, Jewel, and Kami cowered, he kept carefully picking away at the pile of collapsed rubble that marked their dead end, creating a small hollow.

Emmett backed up towards the wall as the shadow loomed over them again. Without a word, Bob hauled them all into the small area he had so laboriously excavated. Then, with a quiet grunt of effort, he dragged the large toe-like boulder until it partially blocked them in. Kami and Jewel both held their hands over their faces as dirt and debris tumbled down from the near relentless shuddering of the earth. Between Bob and the boulder, Emmett could see nothing of what was going on outside. The ground was shaking so hard he felt sure that their hiding place would collapse on top of them.

Then it stopped. Kami gasped at the sudden stillness. Emmett reached out to her and she took his hand. They waited in silence, not knowing how close the jötun was or if it was even searching for them. Thunder cracked overhead. As it echoed through the canyon, Bob uttered what sounded suspiciously like a curse under his breath and lowered himself to the ground.

"We're going to be here a while," he whispered. "But I think we'll be okay if we stay relatively quiet."

"No, we can't stay here," Emmett said. "We don't have enough supplies."

"I know that," Bob grumbled, looking more than annoyed at the reminder. "And if I thought we could sneak out, then that is exactly what I would suggest we do, but there is a triune of jötun out there."

"A what?" Kami asked.

"A triune," Bob said, as he pressed his impressive bulk as far to the side as possible so that the others could see past him. "Jötun travel and live in groups of three. No one has really done an in-depth study on the subject though, since they are notoriously murderous to outsiders."

Emmett peaked out of their refuge to see three moving monoliths, one of which was being supported by the other two. Emmett had never seen a jötun before, few ever had. He thought they might look like a big troll, but they reminded him more of half-finished statues. It was then that one of them started to sing. If he could even call the rumbling thunder that emerged singing. It sounded more like a rockslide in a fierce storm. He watched in fascination.

"They'll be here for a few days." Bob sounded as though their last hope for survival had been taken away. "A jötun funeral generally takes that long."

"We'll run out of food..." Jewel whispered.

"Then we leave," Emmett said, turning his gaze away from the monstrosities outside. "One way or another, we get out of here today."

"And I'm the one who doesn't think things through," Kami mumbled. Emmett chose to ignore her as he scrambled to organize a plan. It was hard to think through the cloud of exhaustion and hunger that enveloped his every thought.

"Are they undressing that one?" Jewel asked, fascinated by the ritual that few had ever been witness to. "I have assisted a few jötun in crossing into the Ether, but we never really talk about death rituals."

"Yes," Bob said, "I've been witness to two jötun funerals before. It was the same both times. The two who are healthy undress the third member of their triune as they sing to it."

"It?" Kami asked watching and choosing to ignore Emmett. "Can't you tell if it's a guy or girl?"

Bob chuckled. "Not even sure if they give live birth or lay eggs. Hard to get to know much about a creature that tends to kill those who want to observe it. They may be intelligent, but they are angry."

"They are dying," Jewel said. "Less and less jötun cross into the Ether. It's a trend you see as a race begins to die out. It's been a slow fade from the world, but they are fading nonetheless."

"When did that start happening?" Emmett asked, suddenly interested in the conversation.

Jewel thought about it for a little bit. "Not long after the sælig war."

Emmett nodded his head and reiterated his earlier point with more vehemence. "Whether we try to sneak out while the jötun are distracted or at night when they are less likely to see us, we need to keep going."

"Their eyesight is better at night," Bob pointed out. "They prefer to move in darkness."

"Then we leave now."

"And what?" Kami asked. "Hope that we can outrun a couple of jötun if they see us? Why are you being so irrational?"

"I'm not the one being irrational," Emmett insisted. "You three want to sit and die from starvation. If we stay here, we're dead. And I have not made it this far to die now."

Bob sighed. "You're right, but we're all tired and weakened from lack of food. I'm not sure any of us really have the will to run."

"Then crawl," Emmett said. "Look, the snow is melting. Maybe we can forage once we're out of this area. There must be food somewhere in these mountains."

"Hard to find in these conditions, but we might discover some as we descend on the other side. And perhaps your crawling idea has some merit." Bob grinned as the others stared at him in confused silence. "The snow is melting, there is plenty of dirt and dust around here. If we were to coat ourselves as best we could with this mud, we could blend more easily with the rocks around us. We can go slow and steady. Their eyesight isn't the best during the day, so it might be enough to fool them."

"I suppose it's worth the try," Jewel conceded, although the look on her face said it was not an idea she was entirely happy with.

"Um," Kami started, "doesn't that mean we would be covering ourselves in mud made from dead giants?"

Bob snorted. "More or less, yeah."

She shrugged. "Okay."

Chapter Seventeen

They hugged the rock as they crawled away from their dead-end refuge towards the triune of giants. Pausing every few steps to reassess the situation, it took them twenty minutes to make their way back to the previous fork in the path, a route that had taken them only a couple minutes to run earlier in the day. Emmett looked back at Kami to confirm it was the right direction before making the turn. Once again, they were moving closer towards the three jötun as the route meandered its way to the other side of the canyon. Emmett kept the slow and steady pace until they reached a small clearing where he dared go no further.

"Shit," Jewel whispered, as she crowded up behind Emmett. At this distance, the jötun appeared more massive and terrifying. Their sonorous singing sent stones crashing to the ground from the walls above them.

"Which way now?" Emmett asked Kami, determined to go on even if they had to crawl over giants' feet to get out of this place.

Kami shook her head. "I don't know. I can't remember."

Emmett took a deep breath and tried not to be annoyed with her. They were all tired, hungry, and scared. "Guesses anyone?"

His question was met with silence. With no suggestions forthcoming, he decided to take the first path they reached. The sooner they could be away from the mourning jötun, the better. Even more carefully than before, he led the way along the edge of the clearing. He almost wished that he could stop and watch the strange ceremony that was taking place less than a hundred meters from where they crawled, but he didn't dare pause for longer than necessary. Every few steps, he looked back to make sure that everyone was keeping up.

Before they could turn onto the path, the singing hit a note that made his ears ache and his bones tremble. He closed his eyes in pain and the moment he could hear again, Jewel shouted a single warning.

"Look out!" She was staring up at the jötun, one of which was rapidly coming towards them. It took too many precious seconds for him to realize that it wasn't just coming towards them—it was falling.

"RUN!" Bob hollered as he grabbed Kami and dashed back the way they had come. As the earth shook violently under him, he fell. Dust shrouded his view. Jewel grabbed his arm and they clung to each other until the air cleared. Their eyes searched the other side of the newly created rubble pile for Kami and Bob. Then, the unmistakable, rhythmic shaking began again. The two remaining jötun were coming.

Emmett yelled, hoping they would hear him over the sound of the approaching jötun. "Kami! Bob!"

He heard Kami scream before he could see her. He rushed forward, only to find his way blocked by the remains of the fallen giant. He turned to Jewel, her face staring up in horror at a giant foot descending towards them. They were nothing more than a couple of ants compared to the jötun.

Emmett froze, unsure of what to do, when the descending foot halted and reversed direction. He was thrown to the ground as the footsteps shook the earth more violently than ever before. He watched as the jötun ran in the other direction—away from them. He quickly picked himself back up and helped Jewel to her feet.

"Vogehempi," Jewel whispered, her voice quivering as she stared up. Emmett brought his gaze to the sky above them and he caught his first look at the fearsome bird. Its dark grey wings stretched nearly five feet across as it dropped solidly on to the cliff above them. Inky eyes stared sharply and its naked head swiveled around to take in the scene below.

"It's just one," Emmett pointed out.

"It's never just one," Bob huffed. He crawled his way to the top of the rubble that was the dead jötun. Kami was right behind him and Emmett relaxed a little knowing she was safe. "They travel in flocks and they are servants of the Erlkrönig. It's the only reason that jötun would run like that. Even they fear the birds because of what they stand for."

"And what giants fear, so should we," Emmett finished, as he held out a hand to help Kami down. A hand that she ignored completely as she leapt from the last boulder to the ground. "I'd forgotten what they were called."

"Someone explain why the giants are terrified of those damned ugly birds?" Kami asked, eyeing the one that sat above them. It stared back at her, cocking its head from side to side as if it wasn't sure what it was looking at, screaming and thrusting in her direction as it did so.

"Walk and talk," Bob said, brushing some dried mud from his face before reaching down to massage his sore ankle. "In the unlikely event that no more vogehempi come here, the jötun will return to finish the ceremony."

Kami glanced at the bird and nodded her agreement. "Promise you'll tell?"

"Have I lied to you yet?" Bob asked.

"No. You definitely have never lied," Kami said. "Not even a half lie, come to think about it."

"Of course not, little girl." Bob gave her a clap on the back that sent her stumbling forward a few steps. "Not in the nature of the yeti. We're honest folk."

Emmett looked around at their choice of exits from the clearing. "Before story time, what way are we going?" With the jötun gone, they could choose any path now.

Bob pointed across the clearing from where they stood. "The exit we need is over that way."

Emmett nodded and headed for the nearest path that took them in that general direction. There was little that he could do about the story Bob was going to tell. He could only hope that he didn't go into detail about the war. It was not a topic that Kami needed to hear about yet. Still, a part of him was curious about what people said about the war. So much time had passed; he was sure there was much that people had forgotten.

"Now those jötun may seem like fearsome creatures—and to most of us they are—but a long time ago, a dark power rose in the land of the fae," Bob began, as they picked their way through the maze. The vogehempi hopped from rise to rise, following them. "Not many could tell you about how that happened exactly. Fae are normally good about keeping their own in check, which is a good thing since some of them can be very powerful.

"The fae I'm talking about was stealing his power from other fae. He was dark and terrible and should have been stopped. Now, kiddo, some of this is speculation because the fae keep to themselves, but I have my sources."

Emmett wondered at who or what his sources might be, but he didn't interrupt the story. So far, the yeti had been right about the basics of Asèth's rise to power.

"This fae, he wanted to conquer the worlds—all of them. Before this, the vogehempi did not even exist. They are a creation of the Erlkrönig, a blending of life from Immortui and Mythos. He used them as spies and weapons; always willing to do his bidding and be his eyes. The vogehempi would flock upon their victims, tearing them apart. Any who dared oppose the Erlkrönig were brought down. They numbered in the thousands during the dark days. Always watchful, always ready." Bob shuddered.

"Thankfully, I was not here for that, but there were many tales to be told of them. When the Erlkrönig was defeated, most of the birds disappeared. They no longer had that powerful, unnatural magic keeping them alive. How those few survived, I guess we now know. He was never really defeated... and some of that magic remained."

Bob paused as he eyed the bird that was still silently following them.

"So, he wasn't always this evil, dark shadow thing?" Kami asked.

"No one starts off evil," Bob replied. "The Erlkrönig was once as real and alive as either of us. He grew strong and powerful in the secret world of the fae before he dared attempt to conquer Mythos and the realms beyond."

"So, other than the fact that these vogehempi things are unnatural creations and serve this big, bad dude, why are the giants so scared? You said most of them are gone now," Kami asked. Emmett felt a rush of relief as her attention turned away from the war and to her original question.

"Ah, yes," Bob said, scratching his chin as they pondered another turn in their path. "Well, a large enough flock can rip a jötun to rubble in a matter of minutes. They are fast, strong, agile and vicious. I don't think the jötun have forgotten this. And it is in these lands that most of the vogehempi have stayed."

Kami glanced back up at their follower, reassessing the sharp, curved beak and finger-long talons. As big as the bird was, and as ferocious as it looked, she still had a hard time believing that they could damage something as big as a giant. "Still, I would think that seeing just one would not send a couple of giants running the way those ones did."

"The jötun are a hostile race and they were not keen on their homes being invaded by those that chose to serve the Erlkrönig. They were as hostile to him as anything else that would enter their mountains. So, they attempted to destroy him and were nearly wiped out because of their defiance."

"Oh," Kami said. She let the subject drop as they backtracked down another dead-end route. No one suggested that they try to get a better vantage point this time. Not with the vogehempi following so close.

Emmett wished there was something they could do about it, but he knew that it wasn't worth the risk.

"I think we need a rest," Jewel said, after climbing over yet another pile of rock. "I know I do."

Emmett wanted to argue because they were so close to the end, but even he was exhausted. The vogehempi screamed at them as they sat down, like it was angry at their lack of progress and their need to rest. It flapped its wings but did not fly away. Emmett stared up at it and it stared back with vaguely intelligent eyes. It dismissed him as it screamed again.

"I wish it would shut up," Kami mumbled.

"Might as well wish for food to fall from the sky," Jewel said. "Pity vogehempi are not good eating or I would suggest one of us try to kill and cook it."

"I don't think we should rest here too long," Bob suggested, as he pushed himself back onto his feet with a groan. "It may be calling to its flock and the last thing we want is to be trapped by those things in here."

"It wouldn't matter where we were," Emmett muttered, noting the look that Kami gave him. He sighed. There would be questions later. "I agree. We should keep moving," he added, a little louder.

Jewel wasn't listening. She was staring into the distance, back the way they had come, her face a mask of pure horror. Emmett turned to see what she was looking at, fearing the jötun had returned. It was worse than that. Instead, the sky was speckled with dark shapes that were moving quickly in their direction. As he watched, his ears registered the sound of the large flock of approaching vogehempi.

"Run! Hide!" Bob shouted, barely audible over the horrendous screams. He pulled Kami to her feet and launched himself down the nearest path. Emmett followed him, pushing Kami into a run before she had even managed to catch her balance. Jewel needed no prompting to get moving. As hard as he looked, there seemed to be no spot big enough to hide from the quickly approaching swarm. Emmett felt the air stir behind his neck. He flipped around and stabbed blindly upward with his sword. A putrid smell filled his nostrils as a blood curdling screech pierced through the raucous calls of the other birds.

He struck out with his sword again and again, hitting something with nearly every swing. There was nowhere to run; they were surrounded by vogehempi—and more were coming. Emmett stood his ground and gripped his sword tighter. It had been a long time since he had used a weapon, but his body seemed to remember well.

He tried to block out the screams the birds made as he fought frantically against their onslaught. His foot slipped on the intestines of one and he was nearly set upon by several others as they sensed his weakness. He managed to gain his balance and fight them off. A different type of scream caused him to whip around to see Kami smothered by them—her sword lying on the ground out of reach. He charged in, using his body weight to throw as many birds off her as possible before stabbing and swinging to kill those that he hadn't injured enough in his charge. He could see Bob out of the corner of his eye, managing well enough with tooth and claw to fend them off. Jewel was nowhere to be seen, though.

"Jewel!" he called, as he swung at another bird. Kami was struggling to get back on her feet, and he kicked her sword towards her as he finally caught sight of Jewel. She was wedged into a small crack in the wall—her sword jabbing out to dissuade the vogehempi from following her inside. Only occasionally did one of her jabs strike a bird. She was safe for now, but he had no idea for how much longer.

Emmett turned back to where Kami was and saw her pinned again. He ran back to help and found himself knocked roughly to the ground before he could reach her. He watched his sword slide to a stop in a snowbank, out of reach. Kami screamed and Emmett struggled harder as more birds added their weight to the one that had knocked him off his feet. Thick talons dug into his arm and a sharp beak poked at his face.

There was no help for him. Kami was pinned and he could no longer see Bob. More talons dug at him and he was almost surprised that he was not yet dead. Obviously, their master wanted something more than his death, but that would not save Jewel or Bob. If he did nothing, then the kindness that these two strangers had shown him would be for naught.

"No!" Emmett shouted, as he swung his elbow into one of the vogehempi. He had a task to fulfill and that was exactly what he would do. He had wanted to avoid using his full powers, but things had progressed to a point where there was nothing else that he could do. It wouldn't go unnoticed by those who watched, but if the vogehempi had found them, then the Erlkrönig already knew where they were.

It took only a second of concentration for Emmett to release everything he had been holding back for so long. This was the real him that he had kept hidden for centuries. Energy and light poured forth from him in an unrelenting wave. The vogehempi that had been closest to him were nothing more than dust now. He felt his strength return as he pushed himself upwards, launching into the sky. He did not fly far.

Disoriented, the raucous cries of the remaining vogehempi echoed throughout the canyon. As they came to their senses, millions of malicious eyes turned to where he hovered. He was the threat, their primary target. They flocked towards him. A few stayed back to keep an eye on those they had pinned or cornered.

They did not stand a chance. Not a bird could get near him as he dove towards Kami. The birds still pinning her to the ground crumbled in on themselves. There was no need for his lost sword now; he was the weapon. Semi-intelligent, it didn't take long for the birds to decide that this was not a fight they could win. Only a few were able to escape the unstoppable force that had appeared in their midst.

Emmett dropped to the ground and turned to watch them leave, fighting the urge to chase them down and destroy them all. He turned to see Bob helping Kami to her feet, but all eyes were on him. He stared back, glad that he did not see fear in any of their hearts—only awe. Even Jewel, who had known what he was, seemed to be looking at him with new eyes.

"I see you, Emeniel," Asèth said, his voice ringing clearly in Emmett's mind. "I see you and you will pay for all you have done. I swear it. You cannot win this time."

"You can never win," Emmett replied, sending the thought with all the force he could manage. "I stopped you once. I will stop you again."

No words came in response. It was a silent scream that built into a blinding pain. It tore through his head and his vision blurred as he tried to block it out. With an incredible effort, Emmett pulled his true self back inside. No wings. No light. No power. Just frail, human weakness again. He collapsed to his knees. He could hear his friends trying to say something to him, but he could not make it out.

With the last of his strength, he forced the words that they needed to hear from his mouth. "He is coming."

Chapter Eighteen

Emmett opened his eyes to darkness. He stayed as still as possible, listening to someone softly snoring off to his left. Two other people were taking the soft, slow breaths of sleep. It eased his mind to know that they were no longer in any immediate danger. He took stock of his condition. Every muscle ached and his head pounded, but he was otherwise okay. Those last few moments of consciousness flooded back to him.

He had hoped that Asèth would still be weak; unable to manifest to that extent within this realm, but that was clearly not the truth. He had felt the power behind the attack, and for the first time since they had found themselves in Mythos, he was worried. He had to get Kami away from here. Asèth's power had grown too great and he needed to keep her safe until he could find a way to defeat him again. And this time, he wouldn't hold back. This time, he would kill him. The price he would pay would be worth it. There would be no rest for either of them until Asèth was gone.

He sat up, ignoring the waves of dizziness that attempted to overwhelm him. He didn't have time to be weak. "Wake up, we need to go."

"Hmmm? What?" someone murmured as a fireball brilliantly lit the inside of the cave. "You're awake?"

In the blink of an eye the fireball transferred from Jewel's hand and become a miniature sun above their heads. It was enough noise and light to wake both Kami and Bob.

"What's going on?" Kami mumbled, rubbing her eyes as she sat up. Her entire demeanour changed when she saw Emmett, wide awake and staring at her. "Em!" She scrambled over and threw her arms around him. Emmett grunted, not expecting such an enthusiastic greeting, but happy about it nonetheless. She sat back to give him a good look over. "Are you okay?"

Emmett nodded. "Yeah, just exhausted."

"Good, I'm glad you're feeling okay because I have something to say to you." Kami's expression changed from one of concern to one of annoyance as she punched him hard in the arm. "You're an asshole for scaring us like that."

"Ow."

"Apparently you're an angel. A legit, came-down-from-above angel, or so Jewel tells me. Not that I had any trouble believing that after the display you put on yesterday. So, what the hell, Em?" Kami crossed her arms as she glared at him.

"It isn't something I can talk about. If people knew, we would be in even greater danger," he explained, ignoring the rest of her outburst. Kami glared at him. "What more do you want me to say?"

"Maybe you can try apologizing. I think I deserve that. You keep saying you're my best friend, but then you keep something like this from me. Jewel had to explain to me why you were unconscious because I was worried about you. Do you even understand what that feels like?"

Emmett said nothing. He was sorry, but now that she had asked for an apology, he knew it would sound hollow. In his silence she continued.

"I had time to think on the way here and I'm tired of being kept in the dark, of not knowing what is happening around me. I need more than that. I need the truth."

"We don't have time for that," Emmett said.

"Really?" Kami asked, her eyes narrowing. "That's all you have to say?"

"There isn't much else to say right now." Emmett tried to push himself up but quickly lost his balance. He would have to settle for staying seated. "This isn't the time or place for a conversation like this."

"Then when, Em?" Kami asked.

"Later." He knew it wasn't the answer she wanted, but anything short of a full confession would only infuriate her.

"I followed you. I tried to trust you despite that fact that since we got here you've been hiding something big from me—and I'm sure it's not just the angel thing. It's been like pulling teeth to get a straight answer most of the time. I'm sick and tired of you lying to me. So please, tell me something true. Something real." She was practically begging.

"I'm your friend," Emmett said softly, hoping it would bring her back from the edge of the anger that stemmed from her fear. "Anything else that needs to be said will have to wait. We don't have the time. Using that kind of energy causes something akin to a ripple effect. Those that are sensitive to these things will have noticed. There is a reason I haven't used much of my powers until now."

"That doesn't even make sense to me, that is how far in the dark I am," Kami said, her voice getting louder as she spoke. "You keep expecting me to understand and go along with things. I can't do it anymore."

"I'll explain it later," Emmett snapped. "Right now, we don't have time. He's coming."

"So what?" Kami crossed her arms in defiance. "Let him come."

"No," Jewel said, shaking her head before Emmett could answer. "I don't think you understand how dangerous the Erlkrönig can be."

Bob looked at him sharply. "He doesn't know what you are, does he?"

Emmett stared into those large, dark eyes, not wanting to answer the question. He had wondered when this would come up. He looked to Jewel to see the same intense look on her face. They wanted, and they deserved to know, the answer. He couldn't look them in the eyes as he said the words. "He knows."

"We went as far as we could, but, even with what little magic I have, I should have known. We shouldn't have stopped..." Jewel didn't bother finishing her sentence as she put her pack together. "We need to hurry."

Emmett was relieved to see the resolve in her eyes. She wasn't going to run from the situation in which he had entangled her; she was still willing to help. He looked at Bob, who was gathering his pack as well.

Bob smiled. "You heard the little lady. Time to hustle."

"I'm not going anywhere until someone," Kami said with a pointed look at Emmett, "tells me what is going on."

"We don't have time for this!" Emmett insisted.

"Make time, because I'm not going anywhere until someone explains to me why. Why is this thing chasing us, why is it bad that he knows what you are, and why is everyone so scared of him?" Kami said. "You keep talking around the truth. Telling me just enough to keep me going. Saying that it's a bad time to discuss it, but we almost died back there. So, when is the right time to tell me? After one of us is dead?"

Emmett rubbed his temples, the ache in his head magnifying with every word she said. He wanted to keep her moving, but he knew that wasn't about to happen. She wasn't going anywhere until she got an answer that satisfied her. He wished that, just this once, she would listen to him and not question everything. Of course, if she did, that then she wouldn't be the Kami that he knew and loved.

"Please," he pleaded, "can we talk about this when we're somewhere safer?"

"No."

"Kami," Jewel begged, "we really do need to go. It's not safe here for any of us. Surely, you don't wish to endanger us all?"

"No, I don't. So, go," Kami snapped. "I don't care. I will sit here until I have an answer."

"Don't be so unreasonable," Emmett barked.

"I'm being unreasonable? Me?" Kami shouted. "You're the one who keeps expecting me to follow you blindly like a little puppy. You're the one who has spent their entire time skating around the truth. And here you are, once again, just expecting me to act like a good little puppet and do as you say. Do you really think you've been reasonable and fair to me during all of this?"

"Well, I..." Emmett stammered, trying to come up with a good response.

"Well, nothing!" Kami shouted. "I deserve the truth. Why the hell am I this special thing you're protecting? What is it about me that is so special? Am I even human?"

Emmett ignored the surprised look from Bob and the slightly less surprised look from Jewel at Kami's revealing questions. "This isn't the time to talk about it. Kami, please, we need to go."

"I don't care. All I want is to not have to walk out of this cave as blind as I was when I walked in here," Kami insisted. "I've put up with far too much at this point. My entire life, everything I've ever known, has been torn apart. I can't even be sure that I'm who I am anymore. I'm tired and hungry and, most of all, I'm so overwhelmed by it all that I just—I just don't know anything anymore."

Emmett stared in astonishment at the tears that flowed freely down Kami's cheeks. He'd known her for her entire life, and he could barely even remember that last time he had seen her cry like this. It was the only thing that could have changed his mind. They needed to get going, but he couldn't ignore her tears. He couldn't push aside her pain any longer—not when he was the one causing it.

"You're still you," Emmett said. He reached for her, but something told him to hold back, so he let his hand drop into his lap. "You've always been you, but there is more to you than you know. We don't have time to go over hundreds of years of details and history for you to completely understand, but, no, you're not entirely human. You are éstesælig, the last éstesælig."

"You don't mean that she's..." Jewel's voice dropped off.

Bob looked between them, shocked. "Well, damn."

Kami ignored their comments; her focus was entirely on Emmett. She wiped at her tears. "I don't know what that means, but what about my parents? Are they my parents?"

He winced. It was one of the many questions that he had hoped would never come up. "The moment we no longer existed in Mundialis, we were forgotten. If we go back, it would be as if we had never left."

She reached for where her locket used to hang around her neck, the one that she had used to buy their passage out of the Baksüz Bog.

"It wasn't from your grandmother," he admitted. "It was a charm used to hide any energy that you may have emitted. It's why even a non-magical being like Bob can sense that you aren't really human."

"What am I? And don't say that word again. I need to know in a way I can understand."

"You're a fae." Emmett watched Kami closely, not sure what she was going to do with this new information. She took a deep breath and closed her eyes. Without a word, she shoved herself to her feet, spun around, and walked out of the cave. Emmett pushed himself to his feet and rushed after her, afraid that she might do something stupid and impulsive.

He was glad he did. She tried to stop before the edge of the cliff they were on, but the ice and snow betrayed her balance. He grabbed her arm and hauled her back on to the ledge.

As soon as her feet were under her again, she pushed him away. "No, no you don't get to do that anymore. I'm done. I don't need you trying to keep me safe anymore because this isn't real. This is a dream. I fell out of a tree and hit my head, and this is all a stupid dream."

"If only it were so simple." Emmett was trying his best to get her to calm down, but he wasn't sure how. "This is real. You are the last éstesælig and, one day, you will be the Elsgodin. You aren't now, but the potential is there, and it is my job to keep you safe until that day."

"Your job?" Kami asked. "And who hired you to do this job?"

Emmett paused at the question. "I did."

Kami shook her head and began to pace on the narrow ledge. "I'm seventeen years old. Seventeen! How could I possibly be this Elle's Gooding thing?"

"Elsgodin," Emmett corrected.

"I don't fucking care!" Kami screamed at him. "What I care about is getting back to my own life. I don't want to be a part of any of this. Why can't you just let me have my life back?"

"That's what I want for you too," Emmett insisted. "That's what I've been trying to do this entire time. I didn't want to tell you any of this because you're not ready for it, but there is nothing I can do about your involvement. You are what you are, just as I am what I am. We can't change who we are, all we can do is make the best of the situation we find ourselves in."

"I don't care. I don't want this," Kami insisted again. Emmett could see the fear and uncertainty in her eyes as she tried to understand what he had told her. "I just wanted to go to college."

"None of us wanted this, Kami. No one wants their life decided for them, but I need you to understand something important right now. We're in very real danger if we don't get moving. He will find you and kill you to get at the power of the Elsgodin." He didn't see any point in mentioning the fate that he or their friends might meet at the hands of Asèth.

"I thought he just wanted to take me back because you stole me?" Kami asked.

Emmett was silent. He hadn't meant to tell her just how dangerous this journey was, but she had forced his hand. It was time to lay it all out on the line. "No. If he was a reasonable creature that would be a possibility, but you cannot reason with him. I won't lie to you anymore. Our lives are at risk if we stay here. It's why I'm trying so hard to get you home."

"Home?" Kami snorted with a shake of her head. "I don't even know what home is anymore."

"Back in Mundialis," Emmett said, and corrected himself as Kami glared at him. "On Earth."

"Do you know what the worst part of all of this is?" Kami turned on him and shoved a finger into his chest. "You. My entire life you've been lying to me. You may pass it off by telling yourself that you were doing it for my own protection, but that doesn't change the fact that you lied. Would you ever have told me the truth?"

"No," Emmett admitted. He didn't want to argue with her anymore. Already the eastern sky was lightening, and they needed to get going. He knew Asèth would be searching and planning his attack. If they hurried, they might make it back to Mundialis before he could get to them. He needed this conversation to be over, but no matter what he said, it just seemed to make things worse.

"That's what I thought. I went along with everything in hopes that I'd understand later. Because you were telling the truth when you said I was your priority, but it's not me you care about, is it?" Kami asked, her voice calmer now. "What you care about is that Elsa God thing that's hidden in me."

"It's not hidden in you, it's a part of who you are. Even when that part of you was weak, when you were more human than fae, I cared about who you were. Every lifetime made me love and cherish the human you are as much as the Elsgodin you will become." Emmett wanted badly to slap some sense into her, but he refrained from doing so. "You are my friend, Kami.

Not for the potential of what you could be, but for who you are right now."

"I'm sorry, *lifetimes*?" Kami asked.

"Vogehempi!" Emmett called out in surprise. He reached for Kami's arm to drag her back in the cave, but she ducked his grasp. Bob and Jewel had rushed out of the cave at the sound of Emmett's cry. It was a single bird sitting high above them on a crag, just staring at them.

"Shit," Jewel mumbled. "Do you think they'll attack again?"

"I don't know," Bob said. "It didn't work out well for them last time. They are intelligent enough that I don't think they will try to flock us again."

"We need to get moving. How long was I out for?" Emmett asked.

"Not that long. Two more days to make it to Dwergenhellar at the rate we've been covering ground," Bob said. "I would recommend we do not make camp tonight."

"Agreed, I don't like the looks of this. We need to get out of this realm." Emmett backed towards the cave, his eyes not leaving the single vogehempi. It watched their progress just as intensely. He was surprised to see Kami following his lead as she headed into the cave with the rest of them. They spent as little time as possible to pack up camp.

Once again, Bob led the way as they scrambled up the mountainside until they were standing upon Gigan Moerus Ridge. Panting to catch his breath in the thin air, exhaustion gave way to awe at the stunning vista below them. From here they could see out over Jötunndys and the valley beyond.

"I never thought I'd be climbing a mountain in this life. Glad I got the chance," Kami said, fixated on the view. Her eyes drank it all in, as if she might never have the chance to do so again.

"Yeah, it's incredible," Emmett agreed. He ignored the death glare he got for daring to even respond to her comment. Sooner or later, she would come around.

It was the muffled scream of the vogehempi that reminded them to hurry. It had followed them up the mountain. Emmett tried to throw a rock at it, but it landed a few feet short. It glanced at the rock and then back at Emmett before screaming again.

"Let's keep moving," Bob nudged—as if they needed it. He continued to break a safe pass for them along the snow-covered ridge, keeping a good pace. Despite their exhaustion and hunger, no one allowed themselves to slow down. In every direction they could see beauty from the ridge, but they did not stop again to stare at it.

Darkness came on so slowly that none of them noticed until it was too dark to see clearly. Bob stopped. They had not quite reached the other side of Gigan Moerus Ridge yet, but they were close. He pointed out the obvious. "We could use light."

Jewel shook her head. "I can't. There's no way I could sustain that kind of effort right now. I'm exhausted."

"It's a full moon," Emmett said, shrugging. "It's as much light as we're going to get. We can't stop now."

Bob said something under his breath that Emmett couldn't hear, and he didn't see any point in asking as the yeti turned to continue. Every now and again, Emmett found himself watching the trail behind him, wishing he could hide their passage somehow. Not that it mattered with the vogehempi shadowing their every step.

"What are you staring at?" Jewel asked, as they reached the other side of the ridge and the ground before them widened.

"I don't know." Emmett admitted. "I just feel like something, or someone, is following us. Something that is not the vogehempi. Something worse."

"The Erlkrönig?"

Emmett frowned. "I don't know." He turned his attention forward to the two minor peaks they were about to pass in between. Maybe it was the pale moonlight or an overactive imagination, but to him they looked more like living things than peaks of the mountain. He watched as a small avalanche slid down the side of one—away from them, thankfully—and wondered if the mountain itself had moved. He shook his head and tried to focus his attention straight ahead. He was tired, he told himself, and his mind was just playing tricks on him.

Chapter Nineteen

Daylight found them descending below the treeline. Emmett noticed that their pace had slackened, but he didn't mind. All he could do to keep his feet moving was to put a conscious effort into every step. Lost in thought, he walked into Jewel before realizing that they had come to a stop. He looked up to see what was going on and saw two more vogehempi ahead of them. Emmett looked closer at the grove of stunted and twisted growths they were perched on. It did not look like an inviting place to be.

Emmett sidled up closer to Bob. "What do you think?"

"Not much." Bob pointed at the grotesque excuse of a forest. "However, I'm not surprised to see them here. Vogehempi congregate in places associated with death. And, in a way, this is such a place."

"In a way?"

"This is where Fornagavern Altes took place," Bob said. "Or so the histories say."

"That's a myth," Emmett snorted. "Ancient ones. It's silly."

"And yet the vogehempi choose this place as one of theirs," Bob pointed out. "And to the people on Mundialis, I'm nothing more than a myth as well. Remember that."

"Yes, and so am I, but I've lived a long time," Emmett said. "A very long time. I've never found anything that indicates the ancient ones existed. Just stories based on nothing more than superstitions."

"And the sælig?" Bob asked. "Are they not a myth to humans? How can you stand here and deny that there cannot be more than the realms we know with logic that can be so easily disproven?"

"Because if there was a god of any kind, don't you think my people would know of them?" Emmett asked, his tone far harsher than he intended. "I've been around longer than many, and there is no realm of ancient ones."

Bob shrugged and pointed off to his right. "There's a path that skirts around the end of this valley. I suggest we take fifteen minutes to rest and eat and then continue on."

No one bothered to question that suggestion. They all collapsed to the ground. Emmett closed his eyes. He needed rest more than anything right now. He was so far past hunger that even the thought of eating made him nauseated. He laid his head on his pack and closed his eyes. He could faintly hear the thunder of a thousand feet running but dismissed it as his imagination. He switched positions and people cried out in tongues he did not understand. He tried to push himself up but couldn't move. He saw people, new and strange to his eyes, brandishing weapons he had never seen.

He could feel the earth tremble below him as a bright light flashed across the grounds. He closed his eyes against the blinding brightness and when he opened them again there stood only trees. Twisted and angry looking, they had replaced the people on the field who had been fighting only moments before. Another flash of light and the ground trembled. Once again, people fought each other, knocking down their foes with such anger and prejudice that Emmett almost felt sorrow for them.

A figure, unlike the others, walked calmly through the fray, tossing aside any creature that dared swing at him with an invisible hand. He stared across the field at a woman, much like the man, who walked untouched through the fighting figures. They met in the middle as the war waged on and talked as though there was nothing happening around them.

Once again, the fighting creatures turned to trees. He could see the looks of anguish and pain as their feet became rooted to the ground and their many arms flailed helplessly until they froze in place. Soon, all that remained of the great battle were those trees. The same trees Emmett had seen the vogehempi sitting on, but there were no vogehempi now.

The two who remained stood tall above the trees and turned to look at him. They stepped up above the tallest branches and walked toward him through the air. He noticed a few of the branches twitching as they passed. They stepped down to the ground not far from where he lay, unable to do anything besides watch the scene unfold before him. They chatted to each other as if he wasn't even there.

"It does not belong here," the female one spoke.

"It is weak and broken, Gudinne," the male being responded. "It is likely not even sure it is here."

"Perhaps," she said, "or perhaps it is in much need of council that could not be found where it is. Do not assume that what you know is what you know, Theós."

"You speak truth. Advice, that is what we're best at."

"Yes, advice for the traveller. Or perhaps a warning is better."

"Oh, it heeds no warnings, of that I'm sure. It does not believe in anything but the balance."

"There is truth in that, for the balance must be kept." Gudinne crouched down and Emmett could feel the warmth of her touch. "Yes, you have a path that you must travel and many choices to make, but we cannot tarry here."

"We must go, but we will give it the guidance that it needs." Theós knelt as well, also placing his hand on Emmett.

"Your path ahead to us is clear, and to see the truth you must not fear," Gudinne recited, her words drawing him in and forming pictures that he did not understand.

"A choice remains to stand or fall, choose wrongly and you'll lose it all," Theós continued.

"Trust in the things that you hold dear, for in their light things will be clear," Gudinne said, her words coming faster and faster.

"And when you see no hope remains, and all that's left for the world is chains," Theós' words had sped up as well; they both seemed to become thinner and less substantial.

"That is the time to make your stand, to say the words that have been banned," Gudinne said, disappearing.

"Do not fear to ask the dead, to take you where no others tread," Theós said, disappearing as well. His words faded like a bad dream. Emmett felt the ground shake again. He struggled to push himself up to his feet, eager to leave. This time, his body responded to his commands and he managed to roll over on to his side as he scrambled up.

"Whoa, easy," Jewel said. Emmett looked around to see trees that were nothing more than trees. She was standing back from him a bit, looking concerned. "Are you okay?"

He shook his head and took another look around. "Yeah, it was just a strange dream, that's all."

They wasted no time in heading off. Emmett was grateful that Bob had chosen to go around the forest. He glanced at it every now and then from the corner of his eye. Once, he swore that he saw them moving, but he kept that to himself.

As the ground grew steeper on the other side of the grove, their pace slowed. It was hard to find the energy to climb another mountain. Only the unrelenting stare of the three vogehempi kept them moving forward. Emmett wasn't even sure how long they had been going for, but it had been too long for all of them to be without rest or food.

"At the top," Bob spoke between gasps for air, "we will find Lasursten Lake and the entrance to Dwergenhellar on the other side of it."

Emmett took great joy in those words. Soon, they would have a chance to treat themselves to dwarven hospitality. It was something to look forward to. Emmett hoped that they would find temporary refuge there. He tried not to wonder how long it would last. At this point, all he wanted was to sleep like the dead. He did not even have the energy to appreciate the brilliant, shining teal of Lasursten Lake when he saw it. He plodded along behind the others and prayed that they could rest soon.

Bob took them straight across the frozen lake to the giant cliff that marked the far side of the valley. He stood in front of the giant stone wall and hesitated, looking down the wall and then back at the lake. He did this a few times before sitting down on a large boulder. "I'm not sure I can remember where the entrance is."

"What do you mean you don't know where the entrance is?" Kami slumped to the ground. "We've come all this way and now what? We wait until Sneezy comes by and shows us the way?"

"I'm not entirely sure I get that reference," Bob said. Emmett could clearly hear the frustration in his voice. If the even-tempered yeti was starting to reach the end of his rope, then they were all in trouble.

"Maybe I could use my powers to find the way?" Jewel offered, although she looked in no condition to be able to do so much as lift a feather.

"Or we could follow the wall until we find a door," Emmett suggested, hoping that they didn't listen to him.

"It's as good a plan as any." Bob stood up, swaying slightly with exhaustion. Emmett could only imagine how hard this journey had been on him. It had been Bob who had led the way, even with a sprained ankle. He was the one who had plowed the path through the snow for them. It was no wonder he was ready to collapse.

"Or we could rest?" Emmett suggested, knowing full well that it was not a wise choice.

"We continue," Jewel insisted, even as she leaned against the rock for support.

Kami sighed and stumbled forward. "Well, if we're going to keep going then we might as well go now."

Bob picked his way along the rock-strewn path that existed between the lake and the cliff. Every few moments he would stop and press his ear against the rock. Every time he frowned and continued to march further on. Emmett followed blindly, not paying much attention to anything until he heard the cry of a vogehempi in the distance. He looked up to see them circling high overhead. Five of them this time. A shiver travelled down his spine.

"Oh," Bob exclaimed loudly. "I remember now. Yes, I do remember. This way."

His excitement seemed to spur the group on a little faster. He slowed as they approached the midpoint of the cliff along the lake's edge. Here, the rock dipped inward a bit. Bob ran his hands over the rock. "I know it's here somewhere."

Emmett waited and watched as Bob pressed at various outcroppings. It was hard to believe that the yeti might have made a mistake. Emmett wanted to say something, but he stayed his tongue. For now, he was sitting, and that was something he was happy to be doing. He glanced up to see that another vogehempi had joined the others.

"Where are you?" Bob muttered, more to himself than anyone else. With a fierce cry he slammed both fists into the wall. Dust showered down on his feet, but no door appeared. He slammed again and more dust fell.

"I don't think it'll do much good to beat a way through the rock." Jewel took Bob's hands in her own. "And hurting yourself is not a good thing either."

"I was so sure I had found the right place," Bob said, as Jewel took two strips of fabric from their rapidly dwindling supplies to wrap his bleeding fists.

"It must be near here somewhere." Bob glanced up and down the wall. "I'm sure of it."

"Then we will find it," Jewel said. "I know we will."

"How does the door open?" Emmett asked, curious now.

"If you know where it is, you have simply to ask for it to open, but if you don't know, then it is a matter of whether they'll let you in," Bob said, grinning sheepishly. "Trying to beat it in does no one any good. I guess I lost my cool there."

"Ya think?" Kami turned to face the cliff. "Hey you. Little people. Could you maybe let us in? We're tired, we're hungry, and we're only passing through."

Emmett watched the wall with amusement.

"Think you can do a better job, angel boy?" Kami sneered. It was a definite challenge and he considered if it would be worth it. It was the thought of food and a good bed that tipped his hand towards carelessness. He placed his hand against the stone and focused what little energy he had on a single thought, speaking in a language he had not used in far too long. "Ol iolci elasa adagita ooaoana!"

He stepped back and looked up at the wall. Nothing. His gaze turned back to the sky to see even more vogehempi circling overhead. He had no energy left to spare and little hope as he sat on the cold ground. It had been worth a try. He expected Kami to say something disparaging when the cliff rumbled and dust flew at them. Emmett covered his face until the rumbling stopped. When he looked up again, two giant wooden doors stood before him where there had been rock before. He clambered to his feet to join the others.

"Shit," Kami whispered as she looked up. "Those are huge."

"Yeah, small in stature but big in construction." Bob grinned and patted Emmett on the back hard enough to send him stumbling forward. "Dwarves are amazing creatures." He knocked on the door with all his strength. It swung open in answer. No one stood there to greet them. Emmett looked to Bob and Jewel for guidance. He had never met a real dwarf before, and he had no idea what to expect.

"Let's greet our hosts," Bob said, striding confidently into the darkness.

Chapter Twenty

Last to cross the threshold, Emmett was barely inside when the door slammed closed, leaving them in complete darkness. They all knew Jewel was too weak to produce any light, so they stood still, waiting. He wasn't sure how much time passed, but eventually a single pinpoint of light approached them.

"Stay behind me," Bob whispered.

"I thought you said the dwarves were friendly?" Emmett asked, as he took a step forward instead. If someone was coming to greet them, he figured it would be best if something less imposing than a yeti was standing in front.

"And most of the time they are, but not always."

As the light grew closer, Emmett could make out a single figure holding what looked like a traditional torch. The light flickered in a natural way and threw strange shadows on the nearby walls. It made him smile a little. With all the magic at the disposal of this world, these underground beings still used traditional flame.

Bob leaned down to whisper in Emmett's ear now that they could see each other. "I've dealt with the dwarves before and it has always been good. One or two may even remember my visits. Shall I speak for us?"

Emmett shook his head. "No, I will."

"Then wait for him to address us first. Do you have the gift?" Bob asked, his eyes on Jewel. She dug into her various pockets before she found a small pouch, which she held out for Emmett to take. He placed it carefully in his own pocket and then turned back to face the approaching greeter. He had never seen a dwarf before, and he took the time to study it as it advanced.

He had expected something far hairier and shorter than the being that he saw. Of course, his only point of reference was ancient folklore that had been re-interpreted and filtered over centuries. One thing held true; the dwarf was of a stockier build than the average human, but he could have easily fit in among the modern world of Mundialis.

"Greetings friends and strangers," the dwarf said, his voice booming and echoing throughout the cavern. "Why hast thou come to Dwergenhellar on this day?"

"We're travellers seeking rest and hospitality," Emmett responded. "We have heard many wonderful things about the great halls and generosity of the dwarves. We bring a small token, a gift, as a thank you in advance for your kindness."

"Wonderful things indeed," the dwarf chuckled, taking the small gift with barely a glance. He dropped his booming voice, his eyes twinkling in the light of the torch. "I'm called Koson. I'm told that one of your number spoke a forgotten language to ask for entry. We were not expecting guests from on high."

"Uh," Emmett hesitated, not sure how he should address the comment. "We are not from on high. My name is Emmett, and this is Bob, Jewel, and Kami."

Koson snorted and came a few steps closer to get a better look at the others. Emmett noticed the small, intricate sword that hung from his belt. For all he knew it was ceremonial. And, he reminded himself, he was armed as well. "Let us not quibble about origins. What matters most is that the doors have opened. Your intentions must be good. Welcome to Dwergenhellar!"

At his words, the cave lit up to show them a splendid hall and many more dwarves staring down at them from above. Gold, silver, and jewels decorated the pillars and archways. Emmett turned a small circle as he looked up. It was far more magnificent than he could ever have imagined.

"I think you shall not find our hospitality wanting," Koson continued. "You all look wearied from your travels. Perhaps you would like to rest, and then you can tell us why you are so far away from the villages that your kind typically choose to dwell in."

"Sleep does sound good," Bob said. "It has been a hard trip, but we're always delighted to meet new friends."

"As are we," Koson assured them, with a little leap in his step. "This way."

None of them spent time looking at the magnificent chamber Koson brought them to. The moment he left they all found a bed to call their own. Emmett would have been happy to sleep on bare rock. When he sunk down into the feather tick bed, he nearly sighed with pleasure. Sleep overtook him.

It was to dim light and rhythmic snoring that he opened his eyes. He stretched in the luxury of the soft mattress and tried to fall back asleep. This time it didn't come, and he had to admit that he felt fully rested for the first time in days. It was a great feeling, if only he could ignore the persistent grumbling of his stomach. Since he didn't want to move and disturb anyone else, he took the time to study the intricately carved ceiling. It was formed to look like the branches of a tree arching over them. Each leaf was delicately painted with silver, gold, and copper. It wasn't something he had expected to see in Dwergenhellar; such intricate beauty didn't match what humans or angels thought of dwarves.

As interesting as the ceiling was, it wasn't enough to keep his attention away from his now grumbling belly. Sleep had brought back his appetite with a vengeance. He tried to remember the last thing he had eaten, but the memory didn't come to him. He rolled over to see if anyone else was awake yet and was happy to see that Jewel had also joined the land of the living.

"Morning," he said with a grin.

"Afternoon, I think," Jewel responded. "There are some fresh clothes there for you. It seems dwarven hospitality is all encompassing." She stood up and did a little twirl, her tunic flying outwards to show a comfortable pair of lilac pants, intricately embroidered with silver thread. "They're quite comfortable and I don't know what the fabric is, but it feels absolutely decadent."

He rolled over to see a pile of green and gold clothes neatly folded beside him. The fabric was buttery smooth. He pulled off his own filthy shirt and traded it for the undershirt and tunic with gratitude, then glanced up at Jewel with a sheepish grin. "Do you mind?"

"Mind what?" she asked, as she sat on her bed watching him.

"Not watching me change my pants."

"You've got a hang up about that?" Jewel laughed. "Seriously? How much time have you been spending among humans, angel boy?"

"A lot, but modesty is one of the foundations of the Ángelosi," Emmett said, trying not to be annoyed with her.

"Right, the dudes with the golden wings that emanate an intense light from every pore and can smite you where you stand. A race so powerful that they can cross through realms without a portal and make their voices echo in empty fields. They're *modest*?"

"Ever seen an angel do any of that?" Emmett asked, crossing his arms.

"With the exception of your wings and your little light show?" Jewel thought about it for a bit. "Well, no. You are the first of your kind that I've ever met."

"And I'm telling you we're modest, so please turn around."

Jewel sighed and turned to face the other way. "Fine, whatever."

Emmett quickly changed his pants, amazed at how well they fit. He looked around and noticed no shoes of any kind, but the floor, though made of solid rock, was warm to the touch. He considered putting on the well-worn boots that had done so well for him since they had left Abernath, but decided he was enjoying not having the weight on his feet.

"Food?" Emmett asked.

Jewel took his question as her clue to turn back around. "Nice threads, very flattering," she said, joining him on his side of the room. "They didn't leave any, but we could go for a wander and see what we can find."

Emmett looked at the still sleeping Kami and Bob. He doubted that she would want a wake-up call and he wasn't foolish enough to attempt to rouse a sleeping yeti. "Yeah, let's do that."

Jewel beat him to the door and threw it open. Two dwarves stood guard just outside, their spears crossed over in front of it, barring their exit.

"Oh!" Jewel exclaimed, jumping back a step.

One of the dwarves turned around and looked up at Jewel. "Hello friend."

"Hello," Emmett said. "We were wondering if we could find some food."

"A feast shall be fetched for you," the other dwarf responded. "Koson will be here soon to speak with you all."

"Okay." Emmett wasn't about to make a big deal about the guards as he gently closed the door. It didn't bother him that the dwarves wanted to keep them contained. They were still strangers whose motives were unknown. Still, it made him think too much of the hospitality of the elves. Their accommodations there had been very comfortable, but it had still been a prison. He did not relish the thought of another fruitless attempt at escape, and hoped that the dwarves were only being cautious about their visitors until they had determined their intentions.

"What do you make of that?" Jewel asked. "Think it's the elves all over again?"

"Those were my thoughts exactly," Emmett said, "Although I'm hoping for a far better outcome."

"And a better outcome is sure to happen," Bob said, his voice booming through the cavernous room, causing them both to jump. "Last time I was here it was much the same, but the dwarves are far nicer than any elf I've ever met."

"Then let's hope nothing has changed," Emmett said. He looked over to Kami. She was still asleep—or doing a good job of pretending. He was pretty sure she wasn't acting—exhausted as she was, it would take an army to get her up.

"Ah," Bob inhaled deeply and nodded towards the door. Emmett turned to see a parade of dwarves carrying platter after platter of food into the room. As respectfully as he could manage, he walked towards the long table that the food was being set on. He didn't try to count the number of dishes that covered the table or make a plate with all the items, he simply dug in to the nearest dish.

"Easy, Emmett," Jewel warned from the other side of the table. "If you eat too fast you could get sick. We've been without for a bit." As hard as it was, he forced himself to slow down. She was right; he would be foolish to gorge himself on the rich food.

"Fooood," Kami groaned from her bed. He tried not to grin as she stumbled towards them, still half asleep, but he couldn't contain his laughter as she reached blindly for something to eat and missed. She tried again and successfully grabbed on to a plate of some salted meat.

As the frenzied feeding slowed in pace, Emmett asked Bob the question that had been weighing on him since he had opened the door. "Do the dwarves usually assign their guests a representative?"

"Well, they did the last time I was here. Since everything has been much the same this time, I would say yes," Bob said, between bites of some strange, green gel. "They will want to know why we're here. If they deem it a good reason their hospitality will double, but if they think that we seek to steal from them or do something that is against their best interests, then I hear they can be very vindictive."

"That is one way to put it," Koson said, as he walked through the door that none of them had heard open. "However, you have been good friends so far and that will count well in your favour."

He hopped down in a chair and grabbed a chunk of meat. "So, friends, what brings you here? You are not passing by, because there are easier paths through these mountains. Therefore, you must have chosen to come here."

Bob held up his hand before Emmett could start speaking. "It's a long tale. I know your people are very connected to nature and nature is all about balance. We're on a mission to help maintain the balance of all the realms."

"Now that is interesting," Koson said, helping himself to more of the food. "And how are you planning to do that?"

Bob looked at Emmett who looked at Kami. She was more awake now and was paying close attention to the conversation. For the first time since their fight on the cliff, she met his gaze. He knew that she still had a lot of unanswered questions that she deserved to know the answers to. Still, he hesitated, and the room fell into an awkward silence. Koson waited patiently for an answer.

"That is a hard question to answer without endangering your people or betraying confidences," Bob said, when it was obvious that Emmett wasn't going to explain.

"Suffice it to say that we're trying to take something to a realm where it will be safe from those who wish to destroy it and upset the balance," Emmett added, his eyes not leaving Kami's. "We're heading for the rift into the realm of Ether."

"That is quite a trip to make for the still living," Koson said. His voice betrayed nothing of what he was thinking.

"It is a trip the living should never have to make," Jewel responded. "I know better than most, as I used to work in that realm."

"You were a guardian of the dead?" Koson asked, showing true interest in the conversation now.

"Yes, I served as one for many centuries before I retired to this world for my second chance," she smirked. "It is one of many benefits of serving the Ether."

"Yes, I've heard that is the benefit if you choose not to move on to an afterlife," Koson said. "I've considered serving once this life is done."

"Most are not privileged with the ability to remember their time served in their next life," Jewel said, shrugging as if it was no big deal. "My situation was special."

"Ah, that is a pity," Koson said. "So, why the Ether?"

"It's the best way for us to move between the realms," Jewel explained. "It is the only place that is fully connected and truly neutral, so we'll be safe from those that seek us."

"And where are you hoping to go to from the Ether? Surely you will not be allowed to stay there," Koson asked, scratching at the stubble on his chin.

"It would be safer for you and your kin to not know such details," Emmett said. He wasn't sure he entirely trusted Koson. He knew little about the dwarves other than what Bob had told him. He trusted the yeti, but no one could know the intentions of others.

"Of course," Koson nodded sharply. "I will take this information to the council. They will make the decision on where to go from here. In the meantime, I shall declare you our honoured guests and we shall feast tonight in the great hall. Songs will be sung, and the drinks will flow like the great rivers to the north."

"There is nothing so memorable," Bob said. "I think it was a good fifty years ago that I last attended a party thrown by your kin."

"Ah, then you know the delights that you are in for," Koson said, winking. He hopped out of his chair and strode towards the door. "I shall have boots made to go with your new clothing. Soft and subtle, but as strong as the dwarves themselves our leather is. They will do you well."

"Thanks for your wonderful hospitality," Jewel acknowledged, standing as Koson left. She turned to the others as soon as the door shut behind him. "Well, what are we thinking?"

"My instinct says these guys are a lot more trustworthy than the elves," Bob said. "I mean, they were nice to me the last time I was here. They treat every friendly visitor as an excuse to celebrate."

"I'm inclined to agree with Bob, but I have my reservations." Emmett leaned back from the table, his stomach stretched full for the first time in days. "He seemed far more genuine than any elf we encountered."

"Not to mention, they didn't greet us with weapons drawn," Kami pointed out. "I'd like to take that as a good sign. So, new clothes?"

Jewel laughed. "They should be by your bed. It's nice to be in fresh, clean garments."

"Oh, sweet! Yes!" Kami exclaimed, holding up her dark blue tunic. Embroidered silver stars decorated the supple fabric. "It's like the sky at dusk. I love it." At her insistence, they all turned away so that she could change into her new garb. "Okay, how do I look?"

Emmett turned and held back a gasp of astonishment. At first glance she reminded him so much of the Elsgodin he had once known that it was almost like he was looking at a mirror through time. As everyone else gushed over how flattering the new garments were, Emmett just stared. Physical resemblance was only a small part of it. His own people had told him that she would not be ready for another lifetime yet, but as he stared at her, he wondered if they were wrong.

Kami didn't seem to be upset by his lack of input. She was obviously still angry with him and he was okay with that for now. He had learned a long time ago that a little distance between them was the better alternative. It could be dangerous for them both if he forgot himself. He turned his attention back to the food and tried his best not to let his mind wander down places it didn't need to go. He glanced back once to see if he was just imagining it, but the essence was there. It wasn't just the missing locket. There was something more.

For a little longer, Kami could continue in blissful ignorance. None of them needed to know the whole truth. *It will be okay. It is always okay*, he reminded himself. It was the closest he could come to meditation and all he could do to keep his mind off the what ifs.

Chapter Twenty-One

True to Koson's word, supple leather boots arrived for them all. How the dwarves knew exactly what size each of them wore was a mystery, but Emmett was sure there was some sort of magic involved. Although the guards no longer stood outside the doors, they decided to stay put in their suite.

It was, Emmett guessed, well into the evening when Koson returned to fetch them. He was all smiles as he arrived. "Things went well with the council. They are deliberating, but I'm sure it shall go well. Should they decide to let you pass through to the rift, we will make sure you are prepared for the journey. Now follow me; many are looking forward to meeting you all. It's been a while since we've had visitors."

Koson kept talking about what they could expect until they arrived at beautifully carved wooden doors with writing chiselled into the rock above. He stopped and his grin grew impossibly larger. "And here we are, the great hall. Please feel at home and do not be overwhelmed by your greeting, friends. It is a custom of ours."

"Overwhelmed?" Emmett asked. He received no answer as the doors threw themselves open. An uproarious cheer from what seemed like hundreds of gathered dwarves greeted them. They entered in awe, met by handshakes and back-claps as drinks were pressed into their empty hands.

Long tables groaned under the weight of their food. Stacked barrels filled with various drinks towered between them. Everywhere he looked precious metals and jewels decorated the room. Intricate scrollwork amazed his eyes. Dwarves talked amongst themselves in both dwarfish and the common tongue, but they all took the time to engage their guests as well. After he was done eating, he circulated through the crowd, chatting and getting to know more about them.

At one point, he passed by Kami chatting with Koson and lingered nearby as she asked him about why the myths she had grown up with depicted dwarves as short and ugly when they were only slightly shorter than the average human and, for the most part, quite pleasant to look upon.

"Ah, that is quite a tale to tell. Our ancestors were afraid that if they were too nice, humans would come and steal all their valuables. So, they decided to always look fierce when dealing with your kind," Koson explained, his arms waving as he spoke, his ale splashing in all directions. "Of course, that was just a glamour. Now you know the truth, but don't go telling everyone about it. It certainly doesn't need to be common knowledge."

Koson winked at Kami and she giggled. Emmett couldn't help but smirk, happy to see her and the others enjoying themselves. He wandered off to a corner, tired of socializing, but still wanting to keep an eye on things. As the possibility of crossing the rift grew, his worries about doing so consumed more of his thoughts.

"Can't even enjoy yourself at a party, can you?"

Emmett jumped at the unexpected voice of Kami coming from beside him. From where he stood, he could clearly see her out among the dwarves, trying to learn some sort of dance. He studied the Kami that stood beside him and could see no difference at all. It was an amazing likeness, but it felt wrong to him. There was a darkness to the figure that stood beside him. He knew who it was from that feeling alone.

"What? Are you just going to ignore me?" Not-Kami sneered at him. Emmett did exactly that, not sure if this was a hallucination or something more sinister. That didn't stop not-Kami from continuing. "You know, you are such a failure. All you had to do was keep her safe and hidden and you couldn't even manage to do that."

"You're not really here," Emmett said, as he edged a step backward.

"Oh, but I am." She took a step towards him, blocking his view of the crowd. "Emeniel, you know the truth of this. You can feel me breathing down your neck."

Emmett winced. He turned to face the not-Kami. "You may have found a way back, but I can feel how tenuous a hold you have on this life. This time I won't just banish you."

"Big words, but no power to back them up." She reached out, her hand brushing against the back of his where the dark mark still showed. "I can feel it."

Emmett pulled away from the icy touch. "You have no right to wear her face."

"Does it bother you?"

Emmett didn't answer; he just wanted the conversation to end. It didn't stop not-Kami from continuing.

"I look forward to destroying everything you have worked so hard to preserve. I look forward to taking what you denied me so long ago."

Emmett clenched his fists and tried to keep his voice calm. "You shall always be denied that power. You cannot win. I will stop you."

"You and what army? We both know the truth of your situation." Not-Kami melted into another image, one that was just as fake. A young man with purple eyes and long chestnut hair stood now where not-Kami was before. His narrow features and glittery skin were typical of a fae.

"You have no power, Asèth," Emmett said. "You are weak. It will not take an army to stop you."

"Are you so sure of that?" The apparition faded away, but the words still echoed in Emmett's ears. He searched the crowd for Kami to see her still dancing as if nothing was happening, as if their lives weren't in danger. As far as she knew, they weren't. It was better that way.

A klaxon sounded, startling Emmett from his thoughts. He closed his eyes as a grim smile played upon his lips. He could almost appreciate the timing of this attack. Asèth hadn't been lying when he said that he was breathing down their necks. This was his doing. Emmett's smiled faded as he opened his eyes to Jewel's concerned face running towards him.

"What's happening?" Emmett asked, as soon as she was close enough to hear him.

"There are trolls at the gates," she sputtered. She managed to compose herself as she caught her breath. "I don't think we're supposed to know, but the dwarves are arming themselves and preparing to defend Dwergenhellar from the threat. We should get back to our room now and get our stuff. Permission or not, we need to get out of here for the sake of the dwarves. This attack is not random. I'm sure the Erlkrönig is behind it."

"Yes," Emmett agreed. He glanced past her for Koson. The last thing he wanted after such hospitality was for any more innocent people to die. He had to prepare them for what was about to happen. Asèth was still weak, but he was growing more powerful. He glanced down at the mark on his hand. Asèth had mentioned a connection of some sort. He wondered if this was where he was drawing that strength. "We will, but I have to do something first."

"You know more than you're letting on. Maybe it's time to share," Jewel demanded, grabbing his arm to keep him from going anywhere. Emmett could have shaken her off easily enough, but he had more respect for her than that.

"At the risk of making you mad at me too, I'll tell you." Emmett put a hand on Jewel's back and guided her along. He was thankful when she walked with him willingly. "You know about the Erlkrönig and Elsgodin. You know about the war. You were around for all of that. What you may not know is that I was involved in that war, not as a watcher the way my kind normally is."

"What do you mean involved?" she asked. He could hear the fear and suspicion in her voice. He continued to search for Koson and Kami through the crowd, ignoring the helpful dwarves that tried to urge them towards the guest chambers. Jewel came to a sudden stop, still gripping his arm. "You're not…"

"I am," he said, dragging her forward, "and he knows the limits of what I can and cannot do. He knows my weaknesses."

"And you know his, right?" she asked, barely managing to keep up with him. "Right?"

He stopped and shook his head. "If I could do more than just keep Kami safe and hidden, don't you think I would?"

She was silent as she searched his eyes for the truth, but there were no answers there. "Are you telling me that with all your power, you can't stop him this time?"

"No," he admitted. "For more reasons then I have time to explain, I cannot."

"But..."

He pulled his arm free and continued to hurry down the hallway as he searched for Koson or anyone who looked like they were in charge.

"Wait, what does this mean?" she asked, running to keep up.

"It means that I need to warn them before their blood is on my hands, because he will never quit."

"That doesn't tell me anything and I can't see what is going to happen here. There are too many variables," she said, panting now.

He stopped. "Go help shore up the defenses or get everyone ready to run." He grabbed her by the shoulders and looked her straight in the eye. "Go now. There's no more time for questions."

She hesitated for a moment before heading back the way they had come. He watched her leave, then turned to hurry down the hall.

"Whoa there, friend!"

Emmett skidded to a halt at the sound of Koson's voice and whipped around. "I've been looking for you."

"We're in the middle of an emergency right now, I would advise that you—"

"I know the threat you are facing. It followed us here," Emmett interrupted. "You have no idea what you are up against."

"I would say we have a good idea of how to defend ourselves from trolls. Although I doubt that they followed you here," Koson said, looking amused now. "They are not that intelligent."

"Those are only a distraction from the real threat that we're all facing." Emmett struggled not to shout at Koson in his frustration. He needed to make him understand the true gravity of the situation and he needed to do it quickly. He knew only one way to make someone give him their undivided trust and attention. "This is the work of the Erlkrönig."

"Really?" Koson crossed his arms. It was easy to see that his patience was wearing thin. "He's come back from the dead to attack our enclave?"

Emmett sighed and focused a small portion of his energy, just enough to bring out his wings and make his voice boom in the small hall. Everyone within range turned to see the confrontation. "I do not say this lightly, but you are all in grave danger. The fate of the realms balances on your decision. He was never dead; he has been sleeping in the shadows. Even as you are distracted by the dangers in front of you, he sneaks in through the back doors. Heed my words." Emmett relaxed and allowed his wings to fade away from view. He had hoped to save every bit of his energy for the inevitable confrontation, but sometimes it took putting on a show to make people understand. Silence descended on the hall and all he could hear was the sound of the alarm echoing. All who had seen stood in awe of what was before them.

Koson recovered from the shock quickly and stepped forward. His voice was barely more than a gruff whisper, but it echoed in the silent hall. "I will take you to the council."

Emmett could hear the frantic activity resume as they walked away. It would not take long for the rumour to spread through the community, he was sure of that. It was hard to keep such good gossip under wraps, and it limited the amount of time they had. He only hoped that no details of their plans made their way to Asèth.

Koson led him into a chamber near the hall. Eleven dwarves were leaned over a table, talking rapidly in dwarfish. The council was as busy preparing to defend their home as the rest of the dwarves. He had to respect a people whose leaders did not think themselves above those they ruled. Koson cleared his throat as way of announcing their arrival but said nothing.

An older female looked up at Koson and, with mild surprise, at the guest that stood beside him. "What is so important that you interrupt us whilst we are planning for war? Have you not heard that a troupe of trolls are attempting to knock down the great gates of Dwergenhellar?"

Koson dipped his head in respect. "I beg your pardon Arlesa, but our new friend has something that weighs far more heavily upon us than the trolls."

"What could possibly be that important?" Arlesa asked, as everyone else stopped to stare at them.

Koson glanced up at Emmett and nodded. He took a step further into the room and fumbled through imitating the nod of respect that Koson had given. "I'm known as Emmett. You know why my friends and I are here: to access the portal to Ether that exists deep within your caves. However, I left out the important reason we must do so."

"That has been a topic of some discussion," a decrepit old dwarf responded. "It is a very odd request."

"We're trying to keep something important out of the hands of the Erlkrönig. It is he that has organized the trolls to distract. He will send other servants through the back gates; a direct assault is not his style."

"And what makes *you* an expert on the ways of the Erlkrönig?" one of the other dwarves asked.

Emmett had prepared for this. With no hesitation this time, he revealed his wings. "Because I was there when he first rose to power and I was instrumental in his downfall. I know him far too well for my own liking. So, trust me when I say that this is no random attack."

The eleven dwarves reverted into speaking dwarfish as they argued amongst themselves as to what to do. They did not waste time on staring at him in awe, for which Emmett was grateful. He once again allowed his wings to disappear beyond view and reach. Every time he pulled at his power the easier it became, but it still drained him.

It did not take them long to reach consensus. It was Arlesa who addressed them once again. "We're choosing to believe your story. You and yours shall make for the Forbidden Caves and enter the rift. We will call upon those few of our kind who are gifted in magic to defend us from the Erlkrönig."

"No," Emmett said. "Do not defend yourself against him. He is vindictive and will not hesitate to destroy those who try to stop them. Save yourself from the trolls, but anything else should be ignored. You have not officially aligned yourself with us; you can claim ignorance as to what we were doing here. Say that we were looking for a way to a new realm, but do not say which one. Please, I could not stand the blood of your people on my conscience. "

"So be it." Arlesa nodded tersely. "Koson, show them the way and do not let them stray from the correct path."

"Yes ma'am." Koson hurried from the room with Emmett close behind him. "Most likely your friends will have been urged to the guest rooms," he said. "Collect what you need and then we will leave."

Emmett pushed through the door and was greeted by the drawn swords of his friends.

"It's good to see your face again," Bob said, sighing in relief.

"I've explained the basics of the situation to the dwarf council, they are letting us use the rift. You're all ready to go?" Emmett asked, as he noticed the few supplies they had were already packed up.

Jewel tossed him his sword. "This may not see much use with you, but sometimes just the sight of a weapon can put someone off."

Emmett strapped it on with a grimace. "Thanks."

"Hurry!" Koson shouted.

"You heard him. We're going to the rift now," Emmett said.

"Is he coming?" Kami asked. Emmett softened a little.

"Yes, but we will get you safely to the Ether. It's going to be okay, Kami." Emmett wanted to reach out and touch her, to try to reassure her, but he was pretty sure she would not allow that yet.

"Hurry now and stay close," Koson said, leading them from the room. He took them deep into the caves and as the air grew colder, it did not surprise Emmett that they saw no one else. It was obvious that they were going somewhere that most dwarves did not go. He remembered that Arlesa had referred to the area as the Forbidden Caves. Here, other than their own footsteps and breathing, the only sound was dripping water.

Koson stopped at a plain wooden door. A single unlit torch sat beside it. Although there was no dust to be found, Emmett had the impression that it had not been touched in a long time. He watched as Koson removed the torch from its holder and tapped it once against the ground. "Incinderus."

Koson smirked at the questioning look that Emmett gave him. "Just because we're not talented at the magics does not mean we cannot make use of the simplest of spells." He pushed open the door but did not enter the cavern beyond. "Beyond this door is the area we call the Forbidden Caves. We do not enter lightly, for not only is there a rift to the Ether here, but creatures that were once awoken in this darkness. They are a race known as the grootslangs and, while my people warred with them until we came to an agreement, there are many that remain hostile. I recommend that you keep your weapons drawn and your eyes open."

"Grootslangs?" Bob asked.

"Large, cruel, clever creatures. They are intelligent, and they prefer to dwell deep in the darkness, hiding from the gods that seek to destroy them. They are believed to be a great mistake that the gods made. They were never supposed to escape," Koson explained, as he walked into the cave beyond the door. "Their eyes glow red with hate, unblinking. They have claws half as long as their arms and a long serpent-like tail. Their back feet are cloven, but soft, and they are covered with a natural armour."

"I can't even imagine," Emmett said. "I've never heard of such a creature."

"Neither had anyone else until we found them deep in the depths of the earth," Koson explained. "Although, that was long before my time."

Emmett stared into the darkness. This time, no friendly dwarves would be greeting them on the other side.

"This is as far as I go," Koson said, after they spent a few minutes staring into the dark cave ahead without moving. "I must join my family in defending our home."

"Of course." Jewel stepped forward and took the torch from Koson. "I will lead us the rest of the way."

"I wish you luck and safe journeys," Koson said, nodding. They watched as he turned and hurried back the way they had come.

"Into the abyss we go," Jewel joked. None of them laughed.

Chapter Twenty-Two

No one spoke as they wandered deeper into the Forbidden Caves. All eyes and ears were on alert for the creatures that Koson had described. Emmett peered into every dark crevice trying to see if those unblinking red eyes were watching. He hoped that it was just an old myth, but he had a feeling that it was more. He could only hope that they were not aligned with the side of chaos.

Jewel navigated the twists and turns with confidence. Eventually she came to a stop, her head cocked to one side as if she could hear something. "I can feel the rift. It is close, perhaps in the room ahead."

"Then why did you stop?" Emmett asked.

"I would think you know," Jewel said, as she took a step into the cavern ahead. "Only a reaper can guide anyone through the rift—living or dead. Although, we normally only take the dead."

"Is that why you came with us?" Kami asked, as her eyes danced around the cave trying to keep an eye out for the grootslangs that Koson had told them about. She crowded closer to Bob as they went deeper.

"It's not that simple an answer, but it is one of the reasons." Jewel stopped again in the middle of a large cavern. Here, the light from the torch didn't reach the walls.

"What are you waiting for?" Bob asked, as they continued to stand where they were, completely exposed.

"An active reaper is bound by their neutrality, but I'm retired and can choose sides," Jewel said, pausing for a second to look around. She walked a few steps before stopping again.

"Jewel…" Emmett let her name hang in the air, neither demanding nor asking for an answer.

"I can't actually open the rift myself. I can sense them, I can find them, but I need a nearby death to open it for me. Something with a soul," Jewel admitted. "We're fortunate that the dwarves will be fighting the trolls up there."

"Fortunate indeed," Emmett mumbled.

Jewel wandered over towards a glittering pillar of stone that was as wide as the yeti was tall. "Yes, this is it." She brushed her hand over it and smiled. "Now, we wait."

"We wait," Bob repeated. Had it been any other place, Emmett was sure the yeti would have sat down, but after the warning about the grootslangs, no one was letting their guard down.

He felt Jewel's hand gently squeeze his arm before letting go. "It'll be fine."

Emmett said nothing in response because there was nothing to be said. They would either make it through the rift or they would not. There were no other options. He had no more energy left to spend worrying about it. What would be, would be. He kept his mind active as he watched the darkness for any movement.

"Waiting seems a little counter-productive," Bob said after a while. He lowered himself to the floor of the cave. "I don't think I want to meet any of these grootslangs and the longer we're here, the more likely that is to happen."

Emmett turned to stare at the wall, tired of looking at the darkness. He tried to feel what Jewel sensed was there, but he got nothing. It was just another piece of rock, like any other place they had passed. None of them had much to talk about so they fell into silence. The sound of dripping water echoed through the tunnels. It seemed an interminable amount of time before Emmett thought he heard something else. He perked up and tried to find the source of the sound.

Bob seemed to be trying to hear something as well. It came again, and this time, Emmett swore it was closer. He sidled up to Bob and tried to keep his voice low, but it still managed to echo in the cave. "Did you hear that?"

"Hear what?" Kami asked. Emmett shushed her.
Shuffle, thump.

There was something out there in the darkness. Jewel and Kami stood, their swords at the ready. Emmett stood his ground but didn't draw his sword.

Bob stretched and cracked his knuckles. "If it is one those grootslangs, and Koson was right about their level of intelligence, then I'm pretty sure we're going to get that portal to the Ether open soon."

"Eyes," Kami whispered, her voice shaking. Emmett saw it too—an unblinking red glow in the darkness that could not be mistaken for anything else. He withdrew his sword as more eyes emerged. He doubted that it would dissuade any of these creatures, but he could hope.

"Hope? You cling to that useless concept still?" a smooth, seductive voice whispered into Emmett's ear. "You can't even harm one of these beautiful servants of mine and you believe there is hope."

"Go away, Asèth," Emmett muttered, hoping no one else would hear him over the sound of the approaching grootslangs. "You have no power here."

An icy finger touched his chin and Emmett turned his head to see Asèth standing there, grinning as if he had already won. "You cannot tell me I have no power here when you are so weak, Emeniel."

"Emmett, what are you looking at?" Jewel asked.

"Nothing," Emmett said, and turned his gaze back to the red eyes of the approaching grootslangs.

Asèth stepped closer, placing both hands on Emmett's shoulders, sending shivers down his spine.

He was glad that no one else could see what he could see. He was here for him and no one else.

"You will fall. I've seen it," he whispered. A vision came unbidden to his mind. An image of himself, broken, battered, and dying. Huddled in a corner in the dark. Rivers of blood flowed, and the dead passed by. They were his friends, those who had been so kind as to help him. Emmett stood frozen.

"Do you see what I see?" Asèth asked, moving to stand in front of Emmett, his fingers tracing an icy line. No longer was he seeing the image of a young Asèth; before him stood the terrible magnificence that was the last of the gesælig. He knew that there was no way Asèth could really be here, but that didn't stop him from wanting to strike out at the mirage before him. Even though he knew it was in his head, it held him captive. He could not shake it, even as he watched the first of the grootslangs launch itself towards his friends. It was then he saw the scar that marred that beautiful face and smiled.

"Even as nothing more than a spectre, you carry my gift," Emmett said.

"A gift I plan to return," Asèth sneered. "You will fall, and I will rejoice in it."

"Em!" Kami called. The spectre faded slightly as her voice broke through. "Emmett! Help!"

"You will rejoice in nothing!" Emmett yelled. He charged through the spectre to where Kami was struggling with one of the creatures. It looked far more horrendous than Koson had described. His body slammed into the much larger creature, sending it flying back into the darkness. He pulled her to her feet and saw that Jewel and Bob were having nearly as difficult a time. There weren't many of the creatures, but they were large and ferocious.

"We need that portal open now!" Emmett yelled, as he pushed Kami behind him and away from the grootslang that was already charging at them again.

"It won't open until something intelligent dies!" Jewel shouted. The grootslang she was fighting managed to avoid her swinging sword, striking out with its claws. Jewel ducked and just missed it. Kami screamed from behind him and her arm was tugged out of his grip. He swung around to see a grootslang sniffing Kami intently as he held her immobilized in his prehensile tail.

"Then be ready!" Emmett shouted back at Jewel. He was not about to fail so close to their goal. He drew his sword and let loose all the energy and frustration that he had been holding inside. He put all his focus into a single swing and cleaved the grootslang in two, even as he heard Jewel shouting for him to stop. She knew enough about the Ángelosi to know that it was forbidden for him to kill any creature with a soul, but there was no other option. They were too strong, too fast for anyone else to stand a chance—even Bob was struggling. Light bathed the dark cave as the portal opened. He turned his attention to the retreating beast that held Kami in his grip and launched himself at it as fast as his wings could carry him. He severed the tail with another swing. Kami dropped to the ground.

"Get to the portal!" he yelled. She pushed the dead coils off as he took another swing, beheading the grootslang. It finally stopped moving and he turned his attention to the creatures that remained. Jewel needed help first. Once again, he slayed the grootslang with a single blow. "Get her across, keep her safe!" he commanded.

"Emmett, you shouldn't have…" Jewel cried. He herded her towards Kami and the wall where the portal was beginning to widen. "Why did you do it?"

"I wouldn't have been able to cross," Emmett said, urging her towards the portal. More red eyes advanced, seemingly impervious to the light that came from the door to the Ether.

"We could have found another way," Jewel insisted, even as Emmett pushed a confused Kami into her arms.

"Go." Emmett turned to Bob, still locked in combat, an equal in strength with the grootslang. He looked down at his hand, covered in inky black blood, and remembered the dream. It was clear now. There was no other option; he had to save everything that mattered most to him. He had to save *her*. He swung at the grootslang with no hesitation.

"Hurry! You need to get out of here," Emmett said, helping an exhausted Bob to his feet. He watched as the eyes in the darkness moved closer. There were so many now, more than he could possibly fight himself. It didn't matter. Jewel stood in the portal watching him, even as she kept a tight grip on Kami's arm.

"Please try," Jewel begged, as she stepped further into the portal to let Bob in. Kami yanked her arm from Jewel's grip and ran towards Emmett.

"What is going on?" she asked. Emmett didn't answer, he just wrapped his arms around her and hugged her tightly. For a moment, time stood still.

"I'm sorry," he whispered. He didn't want to let go.

"Get them." This time it wasn't just Emmett that could hear his voice. It rose clearly above the rest of the noise and Jewel's eyes went wide.

Kami looked up. Although she said it quietly, Emmett heard her clearly. "I know that voice."

"Go now!" Emmett yelled, as the grootslangs rushed towards them, howling and chittering.

"No, I'm not leaving you here alone." Kami moved to stand beside him with her sword drawn.

"Not this time." Emmett dropped his sword, picked her up, and threw her into the portal. Bob caught her and held her as she struggled to return. "Close it! Now!"

He turned to face the overwhelming onslaught of grootslangs. He scooped up his sword and charged, striking blindly. He didn't know how long it would take to close the portal, but he planned to make sure Jewel had all the time she needed. He struggled until his feet were taken from under him and he hit the ground. From there, he could see Kami calling to him. Her face was the only thing clearly visible through the shrunken portal. He couldn't make out what she was saying, but her eyes spoke volumes, pleading with him to come even though it was already too late.

A claw tore across his face and he heard her scream. The sound was cut-off as the portal closed and he was left in darkness. He struck out as he had with the vogehempi, trying to drive the creatures off him, but he didn't have enough energy left. He wasn't sure he ever would again if he survived. With Kami safe, he had no reason to keep to fighting. He ceased his useless struggle and drew his power back in, becoming nothing more than a human; weak and helpless as the grootslangs tore at him. His only consolation was not letting them hear him scream.

"Enough. I need him alive," Asèth commanded. The attack came to a halt. Emmett struggled to stay conscious, but he could feel it slipping away from him. Asèth's mocking voice was the last thing he heard as pain and exhaustion combined to send him drifting into a world of nightmares. "You're a short-sighted fool, Emeniel."

Chapter Twenty-Three

Pain coursed through his body. It consumed him as he lay on the cold stone, shivering. Pain told him that he was alive, and he hadn't expected that. It didn't tell him much else, but he hung on to a single thought. *They made it.* He opened his eyes to see where he was and bright light assaulted him. Even that hurt. He was not in the caves anymore.

It took several attempts to push himself into a sitting position. Something tugged at his ankle as he tried to crawl towards the nearby wall. He looked down to see a short, iron chain attached to a cuff on his ankle. It was bolted directly to the floor and kept him captive in the centre of the room. He yanked against it with as much power as he could summon, but it didn't budge. He should have known it would be enchanted. Exhausted from the effort, he laid back down and stared up at the room—the windows were high and narrow, and the door looked far more solid than he liked.

He raised a hand to his face and stared at the blood that covered it—both his and the creatures he had slain. However long he had been here, it was enough for the blood to dry completely. His belly rumbled. He was surprised at his ability to feel hungry with the worry and fear that filled his mind. There were very few reasons why Asèth would want him alive, and none of them provided him with a sense of hope for his situation.

Emmett knew that he would be waiting and watching. He wondered when he would show his face. If it was psychological torture he was going for, Emmett would not give him the satisfaction of watching him sink into despair. He was stronger than that.

"I know you're there, Asèth," he called out. "I've known you far too long to think otherwise. Know that I will not despair. You've failed. She is safe beyond your grasp."

"What makes you think I've failed?" Asèth asked, as he materialized in front of Emmett. He didn't bother to wear the mask of who he once had been. He stood as he had the last time he had walked in this world; handsome, despite the madness in his eyes and the scar that twisted one side of his face into a permanent sneer. He crouched down, wearing a look of immeasurable pride as he faced his prisoner. "There are many paths to success."

"You failed," Emmett insisted.

"You keep saying that." Asèth stood up and began to stride around the circular room, his cloak drifting behind like smoke, the hem wavering in and out of sight as if it was just as insubstantial. "Are you so blindly confident that you can't see that I've secured a far greater treasure? You may be a sentimental fool, but you've never been an idiot."

Emmett watched him but did not answer. He knew of a few reasons he could still be alive, and the one Asèth was mostly likely referring to filled him with a heavy dread that threatened to drown him. He couldn't bring himself to say it, but he had a feeling that Asèth would tell him anyway.

"A single angel's feather is worth more than every soul that walks the realms. So much power to be gained from one and yet, they are nearly impossible to come by. No one can tell an angel apart from whatever race they choose to appear as—unless they reveal themselves." He knelt again, his lips twisting into a grin. "Even when you find one and capture it, they won't hand over a feather willingly. It tends to be a bit of a problem."

"That's true. So, why not cut to the chase and let me go," Emmett said, knowing the false bravado in his voice was fooling no one, "or perhaps remove this chain and I will show you my wings willingly."

Asèth laughed as though it was a great joke. "You must know that I have ways to get what I need from you. Once I have that, there will be nothing that can stop me."

"Even if it takes my dying breath to make it happen, I will see you dead." Emmett meant every word of it. Asèth grabbed at his face, the icy touch sending shivers down his back. He could feel those ghostly fingers pressing against his chin, holding his head firmly in place. A spectre should not have been able to touch him but, somehow, Asèth had grown strong enough to take form.

He stared into Emmett's eyes, searching. "No. You won't. No matter how far you've fallen, you don't have the killer in you. Too much heart, too much honour."

Emmett jerked his head away from Asèth's grasp. "How?"

"Oh, Emeniel, did you really think banishment into the nothing between the realms would stop someone as powerful as myself?" Asèth stood up and stared down at him. "I thought you would have realized by now how I escaped from that nightmarish nothingness that you trapped me in."

Emmett looked down at his hand, at the dark mark he had worn since their arrival. It had not faded in the least. He was sure the mark was part of it, but it didn't explain how Asèth managed to find them in the realm of Mundialis. "You had help?" It was terrifying to think that there was anyone out there that would willingly help someone like him. Asèth was not one who considered any his equal or friend; in his mind there was only those who served him and the dead. "Who?"

"You're not as arrogant as you look," Asèth said, grinning. "They're dead. I needed a willing sacrifice. After that, it was only a matter of finding a source of energy strong enough to draw from. It took me a long time to find you."

Emmett stared, speechless. He had already figured out the last part in Dwergenhellar, but he couldn't wrap his mind around the idea of anyone willing to help Asèth that would have access to that kind of knowledge. He didn't think that he would learn the answer even if he asked.

Stepping back, Asèth snapped his fingers. More chains appeared from nowhere, snaking their way across the floor. They lunged at Emmett, their metallic jaws snapping at his wrists and his free ankle. He tried to fight them off, but he was still too sore and weak from the battle with the grootslangs. He slammed hard against the stone floor as the chains tightened sharply. From beneath him a platform rose, the chains loosening only enough to allow him to rise with it.

Asèth strode to the side of the table and looked down at Emmett as he thrashed. He grinned, triumphant now that his captive was fully restrained. "Tell me now how there is always hope. Speak to me now of the light in the darkness. When I'm through with you, there will be nothing left but a darkness far worse than the one you trapped me in."

"It means nothing," Emmett said, giving up his struggle. "You won't get what you want."

"We'll see about that." Asèth clapped his hands together and the door opened. A fae entered, a normal sælig, but she had been ritually scarred and blinded—a tràor. It was something he hadn't seen in a long time and had hoped to never see again. "Once I get what I need from you, I'll be able to fully cross over. By the time anyone realizes what is happening, it will be far too late. For them, for you, for all the realms."

True fear shot through him as he watched her place a tray beside him. He couldn't identify half of what was there, but their purpose was obvious. He wasn't going to give up yet. Asèth drew an icy finger down Emmett's chest. "This is going to hurt, and I will enjoy it."

Emmett closed his eyes, not wanting to know what was going to happen. Burning pain ripped through his torso. He struggled not to cry out. His back arched upwards as far as the chains would allow him to, while his fingers dug deep into his palms. He could taste blood in his mouth, but he kept it shut. He would not give Asèth the satisfaction of hearing him scream in pain.

His skin sizzled as bright white heat drew lines of lightning across his body. He tried not to gag at the smell of burnt flesh and fabric, but he couldn't help himself as the fumes engulfed him. Eyes watering, chest heaving, he could do nothing more than glare at Asèth as he laughed. He flicked his hand at the tràor who, although blind, could sense the movement and placed the tool she had been using back on the tray.

"And to think, we're only beginning." Asèth brushed his hand over the charred flesh and smiled. "You're strong, but even the strongest will break eventually. This will be neither quick nor easy. I don't want to cheat myself out of the one thing that kept me from losing my mind in the nothing—making you pay for everything you did to me. And I'm going to enjoy it so much."

Tears came unbidden to his eyes and Emmett could not stop them. He tried to pull away as Asèth reached out with a single finger to brush away the tear. Where he touched Emmett's cheek, the cold burned into him.

"So much fun..." he whispered.

Days flew by, blending and blurring together. Emmett's world was reduced to the tiny room, his time only marked by the sessions of torture and unconsciousness. He huddled on the cold stone floor—battered, bruised, and broken. If there was a piece of his body that remained undamaged, he could not feel it.

And through it all he kept his vow of silence.

Once again, Asèth hovered over him, studying the results of his latest handiwork. Emmett tried to catch his breath as the pain subsided. "What do we do to you next? I've grown weary of this game. I want my feather. Resist all you want, but I will push you to the point of self-preservation and those wings will show."

Asèth dragged a finger along the length of Emmett's body, setting off little sparks of pain. "What do I do now? There is hardly a bit of you left that I haven't done something to."

He stopped as he came around to the other side and stared down at Emmett. "Oh, I know. There is one part of you that has escaped my attentions." Asèth leaned over Emmett, his face twisting into a cruel smile. "Look at those eyes that have seen so much time pass. Perhaps they've seen enough."

He snapped his fingers and the tràor appeared with a new device, one Emmett had not seen before. She carefully positioned it until the tip was directly above his right eye. After a few adjustments, a clear drop began to form above him. He could see his face—almost unrecognizable even to him—reflected in its surface.

Then it broke free, crashing downwards. Though he tried to turn his head, he could not. He was frozen. It felt cold when it hit his eye. His vision blurred as sizzling filled the air. Another drop followed and then the pain hit him. It spread outwards, carving lines of agony across his face. He could feel blisters forming as the sizzling intensified. He gritted his teeth against a pain that was unlike anything he had felt before. For the first time in a long time, he began to pray. He didn't know how much more of this he could take in his already weakened state. Still, he held his tongue as another drop joined the first two.

It was the fifth or sixth drop of this unnatural fire that caused Emmett to finally make a sound. He could no longer hold it back and with his one good eye he could see that smug, smiling face.

"You will give me what I want." Asèth allowed a finger to drift over to Emmett's other eye. "I will bring you to death's door a million times over and never let you cross it."

Panting, trying to catch his breath, unable to even move, Emmett watched the machine move to hover over his left eye. Asèth smiled wider. "Enjoy the darkness, Emeniel."

In the reflection of that first drop, he could see the angry red welts that streaked outward from the blackened remains of where his right eye had been. A macabre joy in Asèth's smile was the last thing he saw before the drop broke free. His vision blurred as it hit his eye and began to sizzle. Drop after drop fell and Asèth's laughter echoed in the room. Although he fought it, something broke inside him. In this darkened world he found it difficult to hold on to the hope that had kept him from breaking.

He struggled against the pain, against the surge of power that wanted to protect him. But he had no more strength to hold on with. He was slipping, and he knew that he could not keep his true self contained any longer. It all surged forth from him, lifting him from the table as far as the chains would allow. Equipment crashed to the ground. Over it all, he heard laughter.

Emmett slumped back onto the table as a new kind of darkness welled up inside his soul. His wings lay useless under him, their tips touching the floor below. He could not tell if it was blood or tears that streamed down his face as he felt Asèth pluck a single golden feather.

He was barely even aware of the platform disappearing back into the ground until all but a single chain remained to hold him in place. The echoing of footsteps faded away, leaving him alone in his pain. A door creaked open and there was a pause. "I think I will keep you around just in case. Who knows how long the power this gives me will last. I may find the need for more. I hear your people are quite fearsome fighters—it will take much to bring them to their collective knees. I will have food brought for you."

His heart shattered as the door slammed closed behind Asèth. He had given up everything, defied direct orders, and turned his back on all he had known to do what he thought was right.

And he had failed.

He did not even have the sweet release of death to free him from his disgrace. He would be forced to live as the realms collapsed around him—a blind and broken witness to it all.

Chapter Twenty-Four

Emmett huddled in the darkness, lost in his misery. At regular intervals someone brought him food and water. Now that Asèth had what he wanted, there was no need to make Emmett suffer more. He washed as best he could, but everything hurt so much that it was hard for him to move. All he had left to hang on to was knowing that Kami was safe elsewhere. This wasn't her fight; she wasn't ready for it yet. None of them were ready. He paid no heed to the passing days—they meant nothing to him anymore. It was all the same dark world where nothing changed.

It was a ferocious roar, all too familiar, that pulled him out of his stupor. He denied the possibility that it could be them as the sound of the fighting intensified. All they would succeed in doing was sealing their fate with his.

"Em?" He heard Kami calling his name and despaired. He had hoped the others knew better than to bring her to this place. The door creaked open and footsteps rushed towards him. Someone touched him and he jumped. He hadn't felt such a gentle touch in a long time, but it still hurt him, because it meant his one success was a failure. She wasn't safe.

He turned his face towards her and she gasped. "My God, Em...."

He tried to form words to tell her to go. To leave him. That this was useless. All he could manage was a rusty croak. She embraced him and then pulled back. "You stink."

It was such a Kami comment that Emmett wanted to smile, but he could not will his face to move. She grabbed one of his hands and tugged upwards. He knew what she wanted, but he couldn't. There was no point in moving. He sat there as she tried to pull him to his feet. His chain rattled as someone unlocked and removed it from his ankle.

A different person, Jewel he assumed, grabbed his other hand and tugged as well. "Come on Emmett, we need to get out of here before he finds out."

He shook his head no. It was the closest he could get to telling them everything that he wanted to say. His last hope had come to save him. She was no longer safe, and it had been all that he had left to hold on to. His last hope was gone.

"We couldn't leave you," Jewel pleaded. "We'll explain more later—when we're safe. Right now, we need to get out of here!"

Emmett stayed where he was until he felt himself lifted into the air. Bob's voice echoed in the room. "No time for reasoning with him. Let's go."

He couldn't fight against the strength of Bob, so he didn't. Now that Asèth had the feather, he didn't know where they could possibly be safe. All he could tell was that they were heading south on foot. He knew it was south because he could always tell what direction the compass pointed; even without his eyes, he still had a few senses left to guide him. After awhile, pain and exhaustion got the best of him and he passed out.

He awoke to the wonderful sensation of a soft bed and warm blankets. If it wasn't for the pain and despair that consumed him, it would have been glorious. He heard footsteps approaching, accompanied by the smell of rich foods.

"You need to get your strength back. We'll be safe here for a short while, but we're going to need you back on your feet, Emmett. Things are not good out there," Jewel whispered.

"Feather," he croaked, as she lifted a glass to his lips.

"We know," she said. "That's why this place will not be safe for long. He may have it, but he hasn't figured out how to tap into its full potential yet. It won't be long though, and when he realizes that you're gone, he is going to be looking for all of us."

"Why?" he asked, as the glass was removed from his lips.

"Why what?"

He focused on forcing the words from his mouth. "Why save me?"

"Eat. Rest. Get your strength back." She avoided his question and guided his hand to the tray so he could find the food. "We'll talk later."

He listened to her leave and poked at his food before nibbling at it. It was far more nourishing than what he had been eating. This was the sort of food that was meant to give him strength and help him heal. He pushed it away after a few bites. There was no point in gaining his strength back.

He could hear them talking outside his door, but he couldn't make out the exact words. He could feel their emotions washing over him; they were worried and scared. He had been playing a human for so long he had almost forgotten what it meant to be Ángelosi. Every bit of the world was so much richer when he wasn't limited to only five weak senses. He allowed his mind, as weak as it was, to reach out to sense the people around him. There were four souls outside of his room and nothing intelligent for as far as he could sense beyond that. He could immediately sense Jewel, Bob, and Kami, but the fourth remained a mystery to him.

He relaxed back into himself, exhausted by the effort. Once again, he considered the food, but he couldn't bring himself to eat it. Instead, he allowed himself to drift back into sleep. Sleep was easy, it was very much like being dead—a state he would have preferred as he was nothing more than a liability to his friends.

When he woke again, it was to the sounds of an argument. Kami was yelling at someone, he could hear her clearly, but he could not hear the quiet responses of whoever she was arguing with. All he could tell was that it was the mystery fourth person that had Kami riled up so much. Not that it was hard to make her angry when it was something she cared about.

"Don't stand there and dare to tell me what I can and cannot do. He's my friend, not yours. You know nothing about him."

"..."

"Oh, shove it up your gloryhole because I don't care! You didn't see him when we found him. You have no clue."

"..."

"Maybe not," Kami yelled, "but sitting around here, waiting for him to just snap out of it is useless."

"..."

"I don't care what you think!" Her voice was closer to the door now. "I'm tired of listening to what you have to say because you know nothing."

"..."

"Go suck a lemon."

Emmett smiled at the insult as Kami stormed into his room. The door slammed behind her before she started yelling at him instead. "And you, you bastard, did you think we would go through all the trouble of rescuing your sorry ass to watch you die? Because I don't think so."

Emmett's smile faded and he turned away. He wasn't ready to hear this now. Not from her.

"You are going to eat. You are going to get better, even if I have to shove the food down your throat with my bare hands," she insisted. He felt her drop onto the bed hard enough to make him bounce a little. "You spent who knows how long taking care of me—even when I made that hard for you to do. Now it's my turn to take care of you, so quit acting like an idiot!"

"Kami," he turned to face her even though he could not see her. "It's over."

"That's bullshit and you know it! I don't care how screwed you think we are. You taught me that there is always hope. I've heard you say it a million and one times, so if you give up hope, where does that leave the rest of us?"

Emmett lay there, too stunned to respond, as every emotion she was feeling washed over him. Her anger, her worry, her sadness—most importantly her love. Her love filled his mind and something inside of him reached out for that warmth.

"Well Em? Are you just going to lay there like a useless log or are you going to stand up and fight with us? Fight with me?" She took his hand in hers and held it against her cheek. He could feel the tears that were falling down her cheeks. "Even if everything is hopeless, we should still try. You've always told me the worst thing a person can do is to stand by while everything important to them is destroyed. Don't become what you've always encouraged me not to be. Don't lay here in despair. Stand up and fight with us, with me. Please, Em."

Her earnest plea reached him in a way that nothing else had. It came unbidden, like a giant wave overtaking him, and he began to cry. She held on to him and whispered words he did not hear as his pain and sadness washed over him. He could feel it pouring out with each tear that rolled down his cheek. He drifted off with her holding him like she was trying to keep him from falling to pieces.

When he awoke, Kami was gone and his appetite had returned. He reached for the table to find that food was sitting there waiting for him. He inhaled it, then drank several glasses of water. It was Jewel that came in when he called out for someone. He could feel her happiness that the food was gone.

"Evening." She sat down on the bed beside him and pressed a hand to his forehead. "You seem to be doing a bit better."

"Yes," Emmett said, his voice still rough. He wondered how long it would be until he sounded like himself, or if he ever would again.

"I can bring you some more food if you like, or if you're feeling up to it, a bath?" Jewel asked.

"Yes. Bath." He could only imagine how badly he looked and smelled, and he could still feel the pull of dried blood on his skin.

"Do you want me or Bob to help you out?" Jewel asked.

"Doesn't matter," he answered. "You're fine."

He shuffled to the bathroom with her support. She sat him down in a chair and set the tub to fill with warm water. Carefully, she removed the rags of what was left of the beautiful clothing the dwarves had given him. He could only imagine the condition they were in and was glad that he could not see them himself. She guided him into the tub and he winced as water invaded the more sensitive wounds. He tried not to show the pain he felt as she worked to get him clean. Emmett heard the door open and Bob's voice filled the room.

"I got you some new clothes to wear," he said, as if it was just another day. Emmett could feel a turmoil of emotions boiling up within the yeti, none of which made sense to him. Before he could say thank you, the door shut.

"Is Bob okay?" he asked.

"He's nervous," Jewel said.

"Nervous?"

"Yes, Trillean has been trying to fill our heads with nonsense about what happens to broken angels," Jewel told him. "Bob wants to believe better of you, but he hasn't known you for as long as I have, and none of us have known you for as long as Kami has."

"Trillean?" Emmett asked, remembering the name and feeling a strong sense of annoyance at it. His mind was still too foggy for him to remember the specifics. Jewel didn't say anything to that as she washed his hair.

"Dangerous things, broken angels," Emmett said, drifting back centuries to remember what his kind learned early on. It was something seared into their minds; even now it was easy to recall the words. "When there is no hope left and only darkness remains, an angel will break. When that happens, they must be destroyed at all costs—there is no cure for a broken angel."

"I'm guessing it isn't true?" she asked. "You came back to us."

"It shouldn't have been possible." He covered his face with his hands. "I should be dead."

"Then perhaps there is still hope in you." He could hear the smile in her voice. "And if there is hope in you, then there is hope in us."

If there was hope for their situation, it was nearly invisible. He pushed the thought aside and asked a far more important question. "Trillean?"

"Ángelosi," she explained, with obvious disgust in her voice. "Long story, but from what I understand, your ruling class is right mad about something. She was waiting for us when we emerged from the Ether. I'm no fan of this one."

"Trillean..." he said, as the memory came back to him. "Yes, I remember them now."

"Were you friends?"

"No."

"She tried everything to dissuade us from going back for you." Jewel snickered and punched him on the shoulder. "If all angels were like you, they'd have a far better reputation. You're a good guy."

"Technically," he corrected her, "Trillean is neither female nor male. Ángelosi have no designated sexes."

He heard her pause and he blushed as he realized what she was thinking. "I chose to live as male. It was better for protecting Kami in her various lifetimes."

"Uh huh."

"Shut up." He tried to ignore the burning in his cheeks as she helped him back out of the tub and dressed him. It was a good feeling to be in clean clothes again and he could feel his strength returning, though it would still be a long road until he made a full recovery. He allowed her to help him back to bed and tuck him in. As he drifted off to sleep, he had only one thought on his mind: fulfilling his mission.

Chapter Twenty-Five

He was improving in leaps and bounds. As his strength returned his healing quickened, but his sight did not come back to him. He stretched his abilities in the same way he did his wings, remembering what it was to be Ángelosi. There was no need to hide now. He could tell that his power was not what it once was, but he still had power. He had known that killing those grootslangs would damage his connection to his own realm. Though tainted, he still had his wings. Those who fell were not allowed to keep their wings. When Ángelosi found them, few managed to escape. No one ever talked about what happened to those ones.

Perhaps there was a chance he would be allowed to return if he survived what lay ahead. It was a thought that brought many mixed feelings. There was a part of him that didn't want to leave; he had been in the mortal realms for so long that it felt like home to him now. And of course, even if he could return to Castus, he wasn't sure he'd be welcome there.

Knock, knock. He turned towards the sound and smiled at Kami. "I would say you're looking well today, but the one thing that hasn't returned is my sight."

"Everything else has healed." She gently touched his shoulder so that he would know where she was. "Just not your eyes, yet."

"It's fine. I may not be as powerful as I once was, but I still have a few tricks up my sleeve."

"Good, because it's time to convene the council and figure out the best way to fight an impossible war." Kami led him out of his room and over to a chair. "Sit."

It was a small band of warriors that sat at the table with him. Five pitiful beings against one of the most powerful threats that any had faced was not much of an army; it was a suicide squad. He tried not to dwell on the thought. He had to hold on to hope now more than ever.

"Emeniel." Trillian's terse greeting came from across the table. They had been the only person not to visit him while he had been recuperating.

"Trillean. I would say that it is a pleasure to see you again, but you wanted to let me die and I can't see." Emmett smiled. "Of course, I may have thought the same if our positions were reversed."

"You've been in the mortal realms for a long time. Too long," Trillean said. "And, from what I've heard, you've broken nearly every rule there is. The list of crimes goes back centuries."

"I know what our people consider a crime and I still did what was right." Emmett could feel his anger rising and pushed it down, forcing himself to relax.

"You still broke the rules."

"There are exceptions to every rule." Emmett tried not to let them get under his skin. He could easily see why Jewel and Kami were not a fan of this angel. Emmett got the impression that nothing had changed in the intervening centuries. Trillean had never been the type to look up from their books to participate in field work. He wondered who had given them this assignment.

"We're not here to discuss what was. We're here to talk about what to do about the situation in which we find ourselves entangled." Jewel spoke loudly to drown out Trillean's reply. "Right now, the Erlkrönig has been focusing his attentions within this realm. It won't be long before he finds a way to break through to the others. We know he has his hands on an angel feather, but he hasn't managed to unlock its full potential."

"Which is good for us," Kami said. "It means he isn't all powerful. He was defeated once, and that means it can be done again."

"He was barely defeated," Emmett said, and then wished he had held his tongue. He didn't want to crush everyone's hope so quickly. "It took all the power of a newly anointed Elsgodin and a fully-powered Ángelosi. He may not yet be as strong as he was, but he is growing stronger. And, when he fully unlocks the power of the feather, he will be untouchable."

"Then we need to move quickly," Jewel said.

"And we have the power of not one, but two of the Ángelosi now," Bob added.

"Well, one Ángelosi and the broken remains of a Fallen," Trillean stated, with a smug superiority. Emmett wanted to reach across the table to smack them, a feeling that increased as they continued speaking. "However, I'm not sure I will be of much help to any of you. I'm just here to observe—as per protocol and orders. I'm not to interfere unless no other choice presents itself."

Emmett could feel Trillean's eyes boring into him. He gritted his teeth and struggled to squash his immediate response. There was a good chance that he would regret his outburst if he gave in to it. He took a deep breath before speaking. "Even with the feather, they still won't involve themselves?"

"There is no determined risk to the balance," Trillean stated.

"Alright, so we have an angel and an observer," Jewel said, moving on. "Still, the Erlkrönig will be difficult to beat. What we need to do is figure out how to get him into a position where he is more vulnerable."

"He is self-assured and vain," Emmett said, thinking back on all he knew about Asèth. "I say we play to his vanity and his belief that he will win."

"You know him well, don't you?" Kami asked.

Emmett winced. It wasn't a topic he wanted to talk about in front of Trillean, but he wasn't going to ignore her. "Almost as long as the last of the Elsgodin, but she is not here to speak."

"She, meaning me?"

Emmett nodded.

"Speaking of which," Trillean interrupted, either not noticing or not caring about the awkward silence that had descended, "we should return the Elsgodin to safety, beyond the reach of the Erlkrönig. She should not be risked in this confrontation, as that could tip the scales of balance."

"How about no?" Kami sneered.

Emmett smirked. It was an argument he was used to from her. She had proven that she was more than capable of taking care of herself as she was. She didn't need the powers of the Elsgodin to stand her ground; she had her stubbornness for that.

"Perhaps you do not understand the gravity of the situation, human," Trillean said. "Even if Emeniel's involvement in the situation was against the wishes of the council, they did the right thing in the act of protecting you. That much will be admitted to. Thus, my orders are to make sure you are kept safe until you are ready to be the Elsgodin—even if I have to resort to using force."

"Try it and I'll pluck you like a chicken," Kami said. Bob put a gentle hand on her shoulder to prevent her from launching across the table.

"We're all people of free will and we make our own decisions," Jewel reminded Trillean. "Now, why don't we focus on a plan to stop the Erlkrönig instead of fighting with each other."

"I would say focusing on the most important matter at hand would be a prudent idea," Bob agreed.

Trillean snorted but didn't say anything in response.

"If we want to beat..." Emmett paused not wanting to use a title that Asèth didn't deserve. Even now, when that was how the world knew him, he hated using it. "If we want to beat him then we need to be prepared. We need to fight on our terms and not his. We need to make use of any advantage we can get—no matter how slim. I assume, Trillean, that you have warded this place from attention?"

"Yes," Trillean said. "I follow my orders and for now, they are to observe and protect the Elsgodin unless it is no longer advisable to do so. With the way things are going, I'm tending towards it no longer being advisable to do so. How you put up with that obstinate creature for so long, I have no idea."

Kami spoke between gritted teeth. "Then go. We have something far better than you. We have Em, who is willing to stand for something. When was the last time you stood for anything?"

"That's not the way it works," Trillean said. "There are rules to be followed. They exist for a reason and shouldn't be broken."

Kami stood up and leaned over the table. "Life in these realms isn't all neat and clean cut. It's messy, it's confusing, and nothing ever goes the way you want it to. Do you think I planned to find out I was some sort of fairy goddess thing with a mortal enemy who wanted to kill me? Cause I can tell you that wasn't what I wanted."

"Meaningless," Trillean said. "Wants, plans, needs—they're all meaningless without rules and order."

"You know nothing!" Kami shouted. "If you were half the angel that Em is, you would be ashamed of yourself."

"Half the angel he is?" Trillean laughed. "He is a disgrace to our people. Your current mind only knows of him for not even eighteen years, but I've read the records. I've talked to those who observed the events. He's lucky that they've even allowed him to keep his wings. He is Fallen."

"That is enough!" Emmett shouted.

"Are you just afraid that I'll tell them all what a disgrace you are? How you betrayed your own people?" Trillean asked.

"I'm afraid of nothing," Emmett spat. "I did what no one else was willing to do."

"You were ordered to stand down, but you refused to listen. You ignored the rules and revealed yourself," Trillean hissed. "Worst of all, you got involved. That is not allowed except under the direst of circumstances. How you were not severed there and then, I do not know."

"I'm not going to sit here and argue the actions of the past or the choices of the council with you, Trillean. You made yourself as clear back then as you are now." Emmett leaned back. "Right now, I would rather do as Jewel suggested and focus on a plan to defeat the Erlkrönig before he grows too powerful. If that happens, you and the council will have no choice but to become involved."

"That will not happen," Trillean declared.

"Are you so sure of that?" Emmett asked, anger surging upwards as old resentments were brought to the surface. He wasn't even sure he could stop the power from rising, or if he even wanted to try. "He has a plan for Castus and Ángelosi. Once again, they choose the path of ignorance instead of action!"

"We will not repeat your mistakes!" Trillean shouted. Emmett could feel their power. Trillean was still fully connected to Castus; to even show their wings would be like lighting a beacon, even with the ward. As it was, Emmett didn't have enough energy to hide his own wings, but his power was weak and the ward could mask it.

"Caring is not a mistake!" Emmett yelled. "It is better than being a smug and superior asshole. The Ángelosi are no better than anyone else. They can stand in their realm for millennia, observing and taking their notes, thinking that they are above it all. What they are is afraid. They are afraid to discover that there is more to life than just watching it pass by. Not everything has to fit into neat little boxes.

"Do you even know what is at stake anymore? The Erlkrönig has an angel's feather. Fallen or not, it still holds great power. He will not stop at tilting the scales to darkness and chaos. He will bring all the realms crashing down around him. He would have the Ángelosi kneeling before him in defeat. We're the keepers of the balance, not the ones who sit back and record the fall of the universe."

Emmett took a deep breath and bowed his head. He was sure Trillean was trying to form some perfectly snarky remark, but he needed that moment. It had been a long time since he had even spoken to another Ángelosi and here he was yelling at one. He smiled and looked back up towards the energy that he knew was Trillean.

"I'm more than willing to make those same mistakes again. I will make even bigger mistakes if that is what it takes. What I will not do is stand here and pretend that what is happening does not affect us all." Emmett knew the emotion in his voice would have no impact on Trillean, but he continued. "If the choice is stand for something and fall so completely that the council has no choice but take my wings, then so be it. I will not join those who do nothing in the face of danger. Maybe you think I made the wrong choice last time, and I did, but not the one that you're thinking of. I will not let him win."

"You will fail!" Trillean's voice echoed through the room as they disappeared in a flash of light. Emmett sat back down, exhausted. He knew that Trillean and the council would be watching everything unfold. He could only hope that he would prove his point by not just standing with those he cared about, but by defeating Asèth too.

"Well, I'm not sure whether losing Trillean is a bad thing or a good thing, although I'm leaning towards it being a good thing. Now, how about we come up with a plan?" Jewel commented, once the echoing had stopped.

"What does it mean if they take your wings?" Kami asked.

"Don't worry about it," Emmett said. "It's not important now."

"No," Kami insisted. "I've had enough of the secrets. We're all in this together. Please tell us."

"Trillean was right about one thing. I'm disgraced by the standards of my kind. Maybe you haven't noticed, but I'm weak. And these things," Emmett stretched his wings for emphasis, "are no longer the same rich gold they once were. The true power of an Ángelosi is not in our feathers, but in our connection to our realm. When an angel starts to fall, our connection and power lessen. When the connection is severed, our wings shrivel and die. We are left as the mortal disguise we took in this realm."

"That is a hard thing to give up," Jewel said.

Emmett smiled and shrugged. "It's been centuries in the making. We have more important things to worry about. There is someone out there who needs to be stopped, and we're the only ones willing to try."

Chapter Twenty-Six

"Do you think this is going to work?" Kami asked, as she hovered over the cauldron that Bob was stirring. Bob pushed her back from the pot before she could inhale too many of the fumes.

"Kami, please stay back. I don't want to have to scrape you up off the floor." Bob sighed. "And I don't know for sure if it will work. I've never met a sælig of any kind before. It works on most magical creatures. Since you are a magical creature, it would do you well to stay away from it."

Kami sighed and stormed off. Emmett grinned as he sharpened his sword. He understood her impatience, but it would do them no good to rush in unprepared. They were outnumbered against a powerful foe and there was little likelihood of their survival. They needed every small advantage they could get right now. Still, sitting here and waiting was hard for them all now that a plan of action had been decided on.

"Kami," Emmett called out, as he dragged a finger across the blade of his sword. It took her a few minutes but she came back into the room, avoiding Bob and his cauldron.

"What?" she snapped.

"Jewel and Bob are not the only ones who have things that they need to prepare for." Emmett stood up and held out one of the swords he had just sharpened. "You need to learn to use this properly."

"And I suppose you are going to teach me?"

Emmett smiled at the doubt in her voice. "I may not be able to see in the most conventional sense, but I can still do better in a sword fight than you." He grinned. "Now, put that one away, I just sharpened it. There are a few dull ones we can play with."

"I don't see the point. We'll have the potions to weaken him and Jewel is looking for ways to surprise him. I doubt I'll get anywhere near him." Emmett could sense the frustration and relief that fought for emotional dominance. "Swords against something as powerful as the Erlkrönig seems a bit like trying to cut down a tree with a butter knife. I'd rather have a machine gun."

"Those don't exist here. You would be surprised at the number of beings that a sword can do damage to—magical and not. Even if you do not fight him yourself, there will be many that serve him willingly, as well as unwillingly, within this fight. Even if all we do is protect the others long enough to do what needs to be done, then we have played a noble part in saving all the realms. Follow me."

He had memorized what he could of the little cabin they were hiding out in, and his eyes had healed to the point where he could discern light and shadow. It was enough to keep him from bumping into most things. He led the way into the yard and tossed Kami a stick.

"You want me to learn to fight with a stick?"

He grabbed a stick of his own and held it as he would any sword. "There is no guard to protect your hand, so don't swing hard. I want you to learn the basics. There isn't much time for me to teach you much more than that."

"Copy me," Emmett said. Kami sighed and held her stick up awkwardly. "Your stance is critical. You need to be sturdy on your feet, but ready to dodge your opponent as well. Don't expect any fight to last near as long as in the movies. They are quick, they are nasty and, for you, the most important thing to learn is to avoid anyone or anything that is striking at you with sword or claw."

"Like this?" Kami asked as she tried to copy what he was doing.

Emmett shook his head. "No. Here, let me help you." He stood behind her and moved her body with his so that she could feel the movement and positions he was trying to show her. "Do you see how it should feel? Smooth, easy, and continuous. Remember that time you wanted to learn Tai Chi? It's a lot like that."

"You mean that whole five seconds I tried it before getting bored?"

"Yeah, try not to get too bored this time. Our lives could depend on it." Emmett smiled at the memory.

"Right." She leaned against him and allowed him to move her limbs at will.

He could feel her resistance fade as the movements became more familiar to her. After a few more minutes he stopped and stepped away. "I think you should try it on your own." He watched her shadow dance through the sunlight. Her movements were still rough and unfocused, but he hadn't expected much at this point. He held up his own stick and showed her the movements again. "Go slower until you're comfortable. Like this."

Emmett showed her again. Kami did her best to replicate his motions, moving more deliberately this time. She threw her stick on the ground in frustration. "I'm doing it all wrong. I know I am."

"It's like a dance. A secret choreography if you will. This isn't how you fight, but it is a good way to learn the moves that you will need in a fight. Don't try to imitate the motion." Once again, he showed her the movements, dancing across the yard with the stick in his hand. "You need to be comfortable with wielding the sword as if it were a natural extension of your body. That is what we're trying to do here."

"This is stupid. I'll never even use any of this."

He picked it up and handed it back to her. "Just do it. Close your eyes and make the music for it in your mind if that helps. Move to that. A fight itself will never last long, but the moments leading up to that fight are when you will need this the most. That is when the fight is decided."

She took her stick and gave it another try. This time when she stopped, he could tell she was smiling. "Okay, maybe this isn't so stupid."

"It's not," he assured her. "Now strike me."

"What?"

"Try to hit me." He held his own stick up once again. She shrugged and charged at him with no finesse or skill at all. It wasn't hard for him to deflect her blow and strike her with his own stick. "Don't charge me, Kami. Remember the movements. Dance to me, make each move deliberate."

She approached him again, this time taking some time to move around him before going in for the strike. Once again, he had no trouble diverting her blow and striking her in response. "A sword fight isn't a long drawn out thing. It will move fast, and you need to be able hit your opponent quicker than they can strike you. Even without my sword, your strikes are clumsy and awkward. Try again."

She swung her stick, trying to hit him. He dodged her clumsy strike and hit her lightly in the rear with his own stick.

"You're being defeated by a blind man," he taunted. "You can do better than that."

She snorted and tried once more. He parried her strike with ease, but this time she managed to avoid most of the returning strike from his stick.

"Better, but not great. Think about what you are going to do. Think about what I might do. Watch my feet and see where they point. Judge my stance to assess what moves may be harder for me to do. Go for a strike where my defense is on the backhand. I'll have a harder time coming around to strike you immediately."

She tried again and managed to avoid his strike completely. He grinned. "See? I knew you'd be a natural with a little bit of practice. Before you know it, you won't even need me around to help you."

"As if I've ever needed any help protecting myself."

"Tell that to the last couple of centuries," he said, defending against another attack. "Because I sure could have used a vacation somewhere in there."

Kami stopped in her tracks. "Have you really been watching me for that long? I mean, I learned a lot about the war when I was in the Ether, but it's still so hard to wrap my brain around it all. It seems so far removed from everything I used to know."

"Well, it should have been longer than it was."

"How much longer?" she asked, lowering her stick.

"Maybe another lifetime or two." He waved his stick in her direction, trying to get her back to the lesson at hand, but she ignored his attempts. "Not that it matters at this point. We can't alter what has happened."

"It might not matter to you," she said, "but maybe you've forgotten that it's all still new to me."

"I know." He lowered his stick. "I'm sorry. Eventually it will all come back to you; every lifetime as a human and everything that came before that. And someday you will be the Elsgodin. Until then, I will still protect you. Whether you need it or not."

"Thanks, I think. Maybe you can tell me about this Elsgodin sometime. Seems people are a little vague on the details of fae culture beyond the war. Most people don't even really know how it ended, only that it did."

"Maybe I will." He grinned and raised his stick. "For starters, she was way better with a sword than you are."

Kami grinned as she raised her own stick. "We'll see about that. En garde!"

"I know when and where now." Jewel stumbled into the common room, obviously exhausted. "So many possibilities, but one thing was more likely than the rest. There is still so much darkness and uncertainty in the future. I cannot be sure of success because the path to it is narrow and fragile." She collapsed into a chair and Kami rushed to grab her a glass of water.

Emmett reached out and took her hand. "You should probably rest first; we can talk about it later."

"There is no time." Jewel accepted the glass of water from Kami and gulped it down. Bob joined them as well and they sat around the little table, waiting for her to begin. "He will be here tomorrow morning. He is searching for us as we speak. We can surprise him by being prepared for his arrival."

Kami looked nervous. "Do we actually have any hope of winning?" Is he bringing an army with him?"

Jewel stared at her empty glass, not willing to look any of them in the face. "He doesn't need to bring an army because he can summon one at will. He is getting closer to full strength every day and soon, he will not only tear holes in time and space, but through the realms as well. This is the only chance that I can see for us to stop him. If we fail, the realms will fall."

"That would be less than ideal, but the question remains, do we have a chance? Any chance at all?" Bob asked, not sounding the least bit worried about the fight ahead.

"There is always a chance when there is hope." Jewel looked towards Emmett. He could feel her fear, but knew better than to let the others know. "We need to prepare ourselves for tomorrow. Then I would recommend rest for us all."

"I'll set up some traps," Bob said. "I have a few ideas where I can hide a thing or two that might surprise him. If we can immobilise him quickly enough, we might have a real chance."

"Yes, do that. I'm going to get some rest first myself. I will do my preparations when I wake. There will be time in the morning." Jewel turned to Kami and gave her a slight nod. Emmett felt an emotion he didn't understand passing between them before she stood to leave. He did not let go of her hand as he helped her up from her chair.

"Is there something I should know?" he asked.

"There is not much I can tell you. He will come to us; he has seen through the ward. Save what energy you have left. This will not be easy. Any advantage we can gain brings us that much closer to success." She smiled, her face pale. "I can make it to my room on my own, thank you."

Emmett let go of her hand and allowed her to leave. He wanted to ask her more about what she had seen, but it was obvious she needed her rest. He collapsed back into his seat. He could feel the worries and fears that filled the thoughts of his friends washing over him, and he tried to push them away. He had his own worrisome thoughts to deal with.

"So, what do we do now?" Kami asked, after a moment of silence.

"I guess we help Bob set up the traps and then get some rest ourselves. We'll need to be ready for him when he arrives." He put on a smile to show her that he wasn't worried. He knew she would see through the lie, but he said it anyway. "And when he arrives, we will make him regret ever coming back."

She frowned. "You hope."

"As you have said before—there is always hope."

"Always," Bob agreed. "Now, let's set these traps and get some rest."

Chapter Twenty-Seven

Emmett didn't open his eyes when Kami entered his room, but he awoke the moment she stepped over the threshold. He could sense her fear and apprehension long before she even said a thing.

"Emmett?" she whispered quietly. "Are you awake?"

He briefly considered feigning sleep, knowing she might ask him about things that he wasn't ready to talk about, but with the possibility that they might not live past tomorrow hanging over their heads, he saw no point in avoiding the conversation. His own pain would be a small sacrifice to make. "Yeah, I'm awake."

"I can't sleep."

"Why not?" He scooted over on the small bed so that she'd have a place to sit down. "Are you worried about tomorrow?"

"Aren't you?" she asked, taking the offered spot.

"Of course, I am," he admitted, "but in the end, worrying will do me little good. We will succeed or we will lose—worrying won't change that. Some of us may live, some us may die—worry won't change that either. We've done all we can at this point. We might as well give ourselves the best advantage of all—a good night's rest."

"You make it sound easy, Em. I wish I could stop thinking and worrying about tomorrow long enough to fall asleep, but I can't."

"I've fought this fight before," he said, "and so did you, even if you can't remember."

"Em, I'm scared." She leaned back against him, letting her head fall onto his shoulder.

He wrapped an arm around her. "It's going to be okay." He smiled, knowing she would see it even in the pale light of the waning moon.

"I wish I could believe that. So much has changed since we left Blakely Grove. How long ago was it?" Kami sighed. "Because to me, it feels like another lifetime."

"Yeah, it does feel like forever ago, doesn't it?" He shook his head. "I can't even imagine how hard it's been for you to adjust to all of this."

"I'm not sure I have," she admitted. "I got to learn a few things about the history of the war. About who I'm supposed to be. About a lot of things, but I can't help but wonder..." She let the sentence fade away.

"Wonder what?"

"What really happened last time. No one seems to know more than rumour and myth about how the Erlkrönig was defeated."

He had only spoken of it once before, when he had been forced to defend his actions to the Ángelosi. It had not gone well. He had never considered that one day he would have to tell her. He had settled for the knowledge that when she became the Elsgodin again, she would remember. And then there was a chance neither of them would survive. Perhaps she deserved to know the truth.

"Em?"

He turned his head towards her, wishing he could see more than just a blurry, shadowy outline. He wanted to see the current, and possibly the last, incarnation of the Elsgodin in her human form. He wanted to know more than just her feelings—as revealing as those were. He wanted to look into her bright blue eyes and see the Elsgodin within her as she learned the truth.

He sighed and turned his face to stare blankly at the ceiling instead. Her hand brushed against his cheek. He allowed her to tilt his head toward her again. He could feel her looking at him, studying his face. He wondered what she saw when she was looking at him, because her emotions gave nothing away. "I want to tell you, but it hurts to talk about it. To even think about it."

"Why?"

"Because for me it was yesterday," he confessed. "Every night it happens all over again and that is the way it has been for longer then I care to think about. It is not something I enjoy reliving. It is not something I will enjoy telling. No one wants to be reminded of the time they nearly lost it all."

"Was it that bad?" Kami asked.

"It could have been better." He needed a minute to compose himself. To find a way to tell the story without letting it hurt so much. She didn't need to know those parts of it. She might suspect, but she didn't need to know.

"Tell me the story, please," she pleaded. "One last story. Tell me how we defeated him."

"Okay, but it's not a short story. Would you like me to begin with once upon a time, in a land not unlike this one?"

"Oh, that is a good start." She laid down and snuggled in against him. Emmett smiled and wrapped his arm tighter around her. He took it for what it was, one friend needing comfort from the other. If he could though, he would have held on to her like this forever.

"There was once a fairy with eyes as blue as a clear summer sky who was born into a great household. Her parents called her Kievvah. She grew up, as most mortal beings do, and became a renowned beauty across the lands. She was sweet and wonderful and enjoyed life very much. On her one hundredth birthday, she was given the gift of a prophecy—as is traditional among her people."

"Was it a good prophecy?" she asked.

"It depends on your point of view. She wasn't a big fan of being told how to live her life, but it told of her being the greatest of the Elsgodin and said that she would bring the sælig kingdom out of a terrible darkness one day. Prophecy or not, all fae can choose to walk their own paths and she chose to leave. She wanted to experience life outside their lands. From what I hear, it was not a very popular decision among her people. So she left, but not without a warrior to help protect her—a powerful gesælig named Asèth.

"She travelled far and wide. She had seen within her realm nearly all there was to see, and had learned a great many things when she met her first angel. He had also left his home to spend time among the mortals, as was common for his kind. He had been caught by a necromancer who had designs to steal his wings for their powers."

"Oh, I bet that's a good story too," Kami said. He could feel her throaty chuckle and it made him smile.

"It's a tale of incredible foolishness. The angel learned quite a bit from that little encounter, but it's is a story for another time. Now Kievvah, being the kind soul that she was, intervened on the angel's behalf and he was grateful for her help." He was almost beginning to enjoy himself now. "He was so grateful that against his better judgement, he took her to see some of the other realms. They travelled together for a long time and became very close friends.

"However, Asèth was unhappy about Kievvah sending him home. He wasn't worried about her protection. He had fallen in love with her, but she didn't reciprocate his feelings. He was jealous of the angel, thinking perhaps she was attracted to his power. So, Asèth set out to gain all the power he could. When Kievvah returned to the lands that belonged to the sælig, she discovered that a lot had changed. All the sælig who had become éstesælig or gesælig were dead and most everyone else had been enslaved. Asèth had laid claim to the throne, and he hungered for more power than what he had already stolen from those he killed. By his own hand, he had become the last of the gesælig.

"Furious, Kievvah confronted Asèth about what he had done and demanded that he step aside. Asèth, of course, was not impressed with her demands and refused. He told her he loved her and, that as the last of the éstesælig, it was her job to stand by his side. His words rung hollow. He had fallen in love with power and there was no room left for the love he once had for Kievvah. When she refused, he grew desperate and said he would do anything for her to be the Elsgodin by his side—even change his ways.

"She was horrified at the idea, but agreed to his demands for the sake of the sælig. The angel read deception in Asèth's heart and warned her against agreeing to anything. However, no one could ever tell Kievvah what to do, not even a friend as good as the angel. She knew that balance in the realms was far more important than anything she wanted for herself. She cried the night before her ascension and it broke her friend's heart to see her so, but he had been trained, as all Ángelosi were, that it was not his place to interfere. He was worried and he wanted to stay, but he had been called by his people to return home. He left with great reluctance; he couldn't ignore the demands of those above him.

"On the day of her ascension, she awoke from a vision. She saw the worlds burn and she confronted Asèth about it. As clever as he was, he couldn't convince her that the dreams weren't true. She refused to take part in an ascension ceremony. He was furious. Without an Elsgodin there could be no Erlkrönig. And what Asèth wanted more than anything was power. To be the Erlkrönig was to be the true king of the sælig.

"Asèth tried to bind her into the decision anyway, forcing her to ascend into the Elsgodin. If she would not stand beside him, then he would take her power. He would let nothing stop him from becoming the Erlkrönig. Her friend, the angel, heard her plea for help. He cared for her too much to not turn back. He rushed back to the land of the sælig as fast as he could, even though his own people tried to stop him from doing so."

He paused and she stayed silent, waiting for him to continue the story. He knew she was awake and hanging on every word. So far, it had been easier treating it as a story that was someone else's and not something he had lived through. It was the next part that made his heart ache even now. It was a memory that haunted him in his dreams and caused him to wake up with tears in his eyes. Not enough time could pass to heal that wound.

"When the angel arrived, he found Asèth, who had ascended in to the Erlkrönig, standing over Kievvah and attempting to steal from her the power of the Elsgodin. Without even thinking, the angel pulled out his sword and charged in to protect his friend, but already the Erlkrönig had grown more powerful than the angel had expected. He barely managed to save Kievvah from certain death by distracting the Erlkrönig with a powerful blow to the face—a blow that only served to the scar the Erlkrönig.

"The angel attempted to take her away to the safest place that he knew, Castus, but there she was granted no sanctuary. He was chastised for even attempting to interfere. There was little for him to do but return to the realm of Mythos and try to find a way to defeat the Erlkrönig."

He paused again, collecting his thoughts and calming his own emotional reaction to the story. He wanted to skip over the rest, but that would have been too easy. If they were to die tomorrow, and he knew that there was a good chance that one of them would, then she deserved to know. Not through the memory when she ascended again, but from him. Even if it was only the most basic details.

"And then what happened?" she asked. Instinctively, he knew that the question she wanted to ask was, did they defeat the Erlkrönig, but they both knew the answer to that question.

"There were none who were willing to stand against the Erlkrönig. He had grown too powerful for most mortals to even think that they had a chance against him. So, the angel and Kievvah came up with their own plan to use a mix of sælig and Ángelosi magic to trap the Erlkrönig and strip him of his power. If they could do that, then he could be stopped.

"They ambushed him, but he was stronger than the magic that they used. He managed to break free of the spell before the stripping ritual was completed and he hit back blindly. His curse to kill struck Kievvah directly. The angel had a choice to make. He could save his friend, or he could finish the ritual to strip the Erlkrönig of his powers. For the angel, it was not a choice.

"He could not curse or kill; those things were forbidden for him. He did the only thing that he could think to do in that moment of desperation. He pushed the essence of the Erlkrönig out of the Mythos realm, past the Ether and into the nothing. It was something that had never been done before. He could only pray that it would work. The Erlkrönig attempted to counter the magic, but the raw emotion behind the angel's spell could not be fought and he was banished.

"With his friend dying, he had few options left to help her. She was past the point of any healing spell. He chose, instead, to lift her essence and place it inside a human woman to form a new incarnation. It was a way for her to gain back the strength that she had lost in the Erlkrönig's attempt to kill her. The angel knew that this method would take a very long time, but he could think of nothing else to do. He set himself the task of keeping watch, of protecting her and keeping her safe until her essence had recovered to the point that she could once again become who she was meant to be."

It was as watered-down a version as he could manage. There were so many details that he had left out and he wondered if she could read into the things he hadn't told her. All he knew was how she felt and, right now, even she didn't know. She was still processing a story that was more than just a story. It was her life—and his.

"Thank you," she finally whispered, as she snuggled tighter against him. "If we did it once, then I know we can do it again."

He gave her a little squeeze. He could still feel the fear that had brought her to his room, but there was also a resolve that had not been there before as she relaxed against him. He listened as her breathing slowed and she fell asleep. He only wished that it would come as easily to him. Instead, he stayed awake a bit longer, thinking of all the things he hadn't told her. All the details that made it more than just a story. He hoped that she would live long enough to find out for herself.

Tomorrow was not likely to go well, he knew that. He had planned for that. If it went as badly as he feared, it might mean his plan would be the only thing left for them. He'd had a long time to think about what he would do if Asèth ever returned and, until recently, he had been torn.

As reluctant as he was to believe that his recent dream at that old twisted forest had been real, the idea that had sprung from that encounter could not be ignored. He knew that it was risky, but if all other hope was lost it would be worth the risk. It was one of the last secrets he would keep.

He held Kami a little tighter and ignored the tears that came. He was glad that she wasn't awake to see him cry. After all these years, he thought that he had managed to retain his impartiality, but it was obvious now that he had been lying to himself. Some things never change.

Chapter Twenty-Eight

"Wake up sleepy head," Kami whispered, as she elbowed him in the chest. Dawn had not yet arrived, but already he could see that the sky was beginning to lighten in the east.

"I'm up. I'm up." He yawned. "Stop poking me with those bony elbows."

Kami rolled out of bed and he could hear her joints pop as she stretched. "My elbows are not that bony."

Emmett pushed himself out of bed as well and tried to shake the feeling back into the arm that Kami had been laying on. "If you say so."

"I do," Kami said. Her tone grew more serious. "And thank you. For last night. I'm glad you've been my friend for all these years. I know I'm not always the easiest person to deal with. And it sounds like that may have always been true, so, thank you."

"I'm glad I had a chance to tell you," Emmett said. He stretched out and released his wings. He flicked her with a wing tip. "Now get out so I can get dressed and get ready."

Kami scooted out of the room and Emmett sat back down on the bed. He was not looking forward to the battle. Asèth was coming to them and there was little they could do about that. Emmett closed his eyes and reached out as far as he could, but he sensed nothing. His range of sensitivity was slowly shrinking. It was not a good sign.

He dressed quickly and joined the others at the kitchen table. He took his seat and couldn't help but wonder if this was the last time the four of them might share a meal together. He yearned for a chance at a real last meal, like the kind they had eaten back at the Inn at Abernath, but their meager rations would have to do.

It was mostly silent, each of them lost in their own thoughts about the fight ahead. They knew that their chances of survival were slim, but they all had hope. It was the only thing they had. All their preparations and planning could come to naught or they could succeed beyond their wildest dreams. Only time would tell, and no amount of talk could change any of it.

"Among the reapers," Jewel broke the silence, "there is a saying. Death comes silently for all who breathe the air of the mortal realms, but it is not a thing to be feared. It is a journey to be celebrated, for life does not end at death. Even if we do not survive the fight ahead, we may still see one another in the afterlife."

"I'm not sure that's as comforting as you think it is," Kami said.

"Is there a better quote from your realm?" Jewel asked. "One that will reassure us all?"

"I have had many lifetimes to learn and read," Emmett interjected. "And in all that time, I found nothing that will bring us comfort now. I can tell you one thing, though, we will not fail because we cannot fail."

Bob smiled. "And why do you say that?"

"Because it is not a matter of choice. Winning is a necessity. Mistakes were made once, and those mistakes will not be repeated. Not this time," he insisted.

"You make it sound personal," Bob said.

"It is. For me, it is more than personal. I will not let him win." Emmett looked at Bob as an unexpected thought crossed his mind. "But why are you here, Bob? You hardly even know us, but you've been risking life and limb for us since the start."

Bob grinned. "Well now, there is a very astute question. Was wondering when someone would ask that."

"I never even thought about it," Jewel said. "I just…" She started laughing. "Oh my, how could I forget such a simple thing?"

Bob chuckled with her. "For those not versed in yeti culture, she is laughing because she forgot a simple fact—we have a code among our people. It stems back to our days of living in some of the most inhospitable climates. We help those in need. It is as simple as that."

"I think you have done more than your fair share in helping us already," Emmett said, shaking his head in disbelief.

"I have a lived a long time. I have travelled through the realms. I have had every adventure I could find, but I have never once had the chance to save it all," Bob said. He stood to his full height, his head brushing against the ceiling. "I would much rather stay and fight than run and hide. It is the only right thing to do."

"And pray we win," Jewel said.

"Or die trying," Kami added.

Bob grinned. "Sounds like a normal day around here."

"We should go outside and wait. It won't be long now." Jewel frowned. "I wish I could tell you how this will end, but there are too many likely paths. Still, we have a chance."

Emmett nodded. "And that is all we need—a chance." It was as close as they would get to encouraging themselves as they filed out the front door of the little cottage and took up their stance outside in the clearing. They had time before his arrival, but they stood there anyway. A grim, unmoving wall—this,

Emmett knew quite well, was their last stand. He was glad they were together.

"It's growing darker," Kami whispered.

Jewel adjusted her stance. "It is time. Everyone ready?"

Emmett unsheathed his sword and could hear Kami doing the same. Even with what limited vision he had, he could tell that it had grown eerily dark in the clearing. No bird song came from the surrounding forest. It was an unnatural quiet when he sensed the presence of Asèth within his limited range.

The Erlkrönig stopped when he caught sight of them standing there, ready to face him, and laughed. "You think you are enough to defeat me? A retired reaper, an aging yeti, a pathetic human, and a blind and fallen angel—you are nothing more than dust to me."

"If that were true, you'd ignore us," Bob said, unafraid of the monster that stood before them.

"I'd ignore you," Asèth snapped back at him, "if not for the fact you are attempting to stand between me and something I want. However, I'm not unnecessarily cruel. Give me what I want, and I will spare your lives. Bow down to me, then I will let you go."

"Never." Jewel stepped forward. "We stand strong and united. We will not bow down to someone who is unfit for any company but those of Anabasa."

"Is that supposed to insult me?" He laughed again. "Amongst even the most terrible of creations I will be king. For all realms will bow down to me when I'm done."

Bob took a step forward to stand with Jewel. "But we never will."

"Perhaps some incentive to do so?" As he said those words, the traps that they had set so carefully were revealed and the potions that were meant to subdue his magic were exposed. "I suppose I could give you credit for trying."

"Makes no difference." Kami took her own step forward. "We will still fight. We will not give up quietly."

Emmett stepped forward as well. He had no idea what he was going to say until he opened his mouth and the words came out. "No, we will not go quietly. Even if we're the only ones who dare to stand, then so be it, we will not run away. We will not back down. We have no fear left to give in to."

"Then you die," Asèth stated. Had Emmett been in any other state of mind, it would have sent shivers down his spine. As it was, it only strengthened his resolve. He could tell the others felt the same.

"You first," Kami said. He could hear the smile in her voice. It was just like her to not care about the consequences of her words, but right now he wanted to applaud her.

Asèth only laughed at her bravado. "Even in a human form, you are much the same. I suppose you cannot change some things no matter how many lifetimes one lives," he said, still sounding as though he hadn't a single worry. "One last chance to change your mind. There is no weakness in surrendering since there can be no victory here for any of you. This is not a fight you can win. I give you one last chance to bow down and spare yourselves the pain and suffering."

Emmett wondered why he was being so patient with them. He knew there had to be a reason. Asèth had limited foresight, but there was more to it than this. Emmett tightened his grip on his sword.

"Emeniel," Asèth addressed him directly, "you know better than the rest of them how little hope remains. Let's not uselessly waste lives here. You know this cannot end well."

"Perhaps you shouldn't address your appeals to the dead. Emeniel is no longer. I'm just Emmett, and I think you're stalling. You are not a creature of mercy. You do not give chances to those who defy you."

"I have no reason to stall. Maybe I'm getting sentimental in my old age. Why should I not take a moment to offer four pathetic beings, who don't know when they are beaten, a chance to save their own worthless lives?"

"There will always be hope where there is life," Emmett said. He still couldn't figure out why Asèth was choosing to offer them mercy instead of trying to destroy them. He could feel the strength of the power that he had gained since their last encounter. There had to be a reason for him stalling like this. Or, maybe he just wanted to keep them alive for his own amusement.

"If you choose to fight, then there is no hope. You will not live to see tomorrow."

"You may be right that some of us won't make it, perhaps even all of us, but that does not mean we will just lay down and give up." Emmett took a step closer.

Asèth gave a long, drawn-out sigh and flicked a hand towards them. A bolt of lightning shot towards them. Jewel blocked it from reaching the group, but Emmett knew that it was just a way to get their attention. He was like a child playing with his toys. This was just the beginning of what was about to be unleashed on them.

"Last chance," he said, "give up."

Emmett was done with words. He charged towards Asèth, sword at the ready, with everyone else just a step behind him.

Chapter Twenty-Nine

Like waves upon rock, they crashed into the Erlkrönig and were tossed back with ease before they could reach him. He stood there, confident and unmoving, as the four of them lay on the ground. He laughed. "Such courage... and such a waste."

Emmett stood up and turned to face him. They had expected this, but the first rush had been the test to prove their theory. Already, he had grown too powerful for such blunt methods to be effective. Emmett needed to distract him for the next part of the plan to work. He hoped that everyone was on the same page. All they had to do was stick to the plan. He walked up to Asèth, sword held loosely in his hand. He wanted to stand face to face with him, even if it was a face that he could not see. "It is not a waste to stand for something you believe in."

"Give it up." Asèth turned a small circle with arms outstretched. "I came here unarmed, with no army to back me up. Do you think I would have been so foolish if you had any chance of defeating me? I'm impervious to such a clumsy weapon as your sword."

Emmett sheathed his sword. "Then I guess I don't need it."

"Coming to your senses then?"

Emmett reached out and shoved Asèth back a step. "Not impervious to everything though, are you?"

Asèth reached out and touched him. Pain coursed through his body, but he stood his ground. He had grown used to this kind of torture. "I humour you because I pity your pathetic attempts."

"Pathetic?" Emmett tried not to grin as he brought his sword to bear and swung. He wasn't surprised when it bounced off Asèth's skin. Emmett swung again with more ferocity. He spared none of his waning power for this attack. He needed to save that for later. Right now, all he needed to do was keep Asèth distracted. His attack had the intended effect as Asèth focused on him and nothing else.

With a twitch of his hand, Asèth could have sent him flying, but Emmett moved fast and hard, not giving him a chance to do more than block his vicious strikes. They both knew that there would be no damage but Asèth fought back, not wanting to appear weak by losing more ground. His breath coming in gasps, his muscles trembling from the effort, Emmett struggled to keep up the intensity of his attack. He dug into his power just a little bit, enough to drive Asèth backwards as he rammed his sword against his crossed arms, pushing harder and harder. Digging his heels into the ground, Asèth countered the attack. Emmett stumbled backwards a few steps as he tried to catch his balance. There was no hesitation as he launched himself forward, resuming his attack the moment he had his balance back. With casual waves of his arm, Asèth deflected the sword.

"What are you fighting for Emeniel?" he asked, as he trapped the sword between his hands. "You have nothing left. Your realm has abandoned you. You're dying. There is nothing for you here. Give in, give up. Join me. I have the power to make you whole again. You want that, don't you? To be powerful once more?"

Emmett yanked his sword back and swung again. Asèth grabbed it, gripping it hard enough to dent the blade. He yanked Emmett closer to him. "You could be a dark angel of vengeance. You could make the Ángelosi kneel before you. They never believed in your vision. You could have it all."

Emmett tried to take his sword back, but Asèth held tight to the blade. "It was not them who abandoned me. I abandoned them."

"For what?" Asèth snarled. "For an unrequited love? To spend your time caring for a weak and pathetic human? Don't be absurd. The Elsgodin will never exist again. She will die with the rest and there is nothing left for you here. Listen to me Emeniel, I have the power to make you whole."

Emmett blinked as Asèth's face became clear to him. He could see everything now, the fragrant purple flowers in the trees that surrounded them, the small cottage, the barn that had tumbled into ruin, overgrown with vines. There was no more trying to interpret the movements of the shadows in the light, no relying on his weakening senses to know where people were. Emmett paused in his efforts to release his sword from Asèth's grasp.

"A gift of good will," he whispered, before releasing his grip on Emmett's sword. "Join me and fight by my side. We could rule it all."

"You need me, don't you?" Emmett realized. "As powerful as you are, you cannot defeat the realm of Castus on your own."

"Not yet, no, but soon." Asèth didn't seem to mind admitting to his weakness. "Sooner if you were to stand with me. Give up this fight and I might even let your friends live."

Emmett stared down at his useless, dented sword and then up at Asèth—a handsome face marred only by that ancient scar—and smiled. "I would rather fall to the fates than live forever as a servant to someone who has no idea what love even is."

There was no chance for Asèth to respond as Bob, Kami, and Jewel hit him with several glass vials. As they shattered, Jewel cast the spell that she had been working on for days. Emmett dove out of the way. As he rolled back to his feet, he could see a frozen mask of fury on Asèth's face. It worked as they had planned. Now, they would have a bit of time to find a way to strip him of his power.

"What's that?" Kami asked, and Emmett followed her gaze to the sky. A small dark spot had appeared in the air above them.

"I don't know, but we need to act faster than we thought. He is fighting me with everything he has access to right now," Jewel shouted. Beads of sweat dotted her forehead, evidence of the extreme effort she was putting into holding Asèth. "This isn't going as I had hoped. We need to do something now."

"I have another couple of vials left," Bob offered, holding them up. "I could…"

A horrendous screech filled the air, drowning out whatever Bob had been trying to say. They all looked back up at the sky in horror as the dark spot grew into a narrow portal. Emmett understood exactly what was happening. This was why Asèth had been stalling them. He wanted to shout out at everyone, to tell them to run, but the words froze in his throat. He had no idea how the Erlkrönig had done it, but he had opened a portal to Anabasa.

Creatures that should only exist in nightmares fought to get through a gap that was still too narrow for them. There was no time left for any of their carefully laid plans. Every second that passed saw the portal widening. It wouldn't be long before those creatures could push their way through.

Emmett mourned for them all in that second. No options remained. No chance for them to make it out of here alive. He looked to Jewel who didn't seem surprised by this development. She gave him a single nod. She knew. He wondered if she had always known, but there was no time to ask as Asèth struggled out of the magical bonds and hell poured into the world.

Chapter Thirty

Jewel focused her efforts on the far more critical job of closing the portal. Emmett knew she was already exhausted, but she was the only one who had the ability to stop the hell beasts from pouring into this world in countless numbers. He stayed close to her to help defend her from the creatures who aimed to stop her.

"This was one of the paths I was afraid of," Jewel said, panting from her efforts to close the portal. "We're losing. We're going to lose."

Emmett took a swing at another of the beasts that charged them. He skewered something that looked like a demented nightmare version of a rat crossed with a centipede. "We can't fail. We need to win."

"I can't close it. I can only keep it from opening wider." Jewel drew her own sword. "They will keep coming. I know you have a plan. Whatever it is, do it now."

"I don't know if it'll work," he admitted, as he struck at another beast that parried his blow with a giant claw. Jewel ducked and struck the beast in the belly, spilling its intestines to the ground. "It's a risky plan."

"It's the only plan." Jewel threw a fire ball at a beast before bringing her sword to bear on yet another. "We're all going to die here. Make those deaths mean something."

Emmett struck upwards as a beast came crashing down from the sky towards them. He wanted to argue with her, but there was little he could argue about. Everything that they had counted on had done them no good. He had wanted to avoid the plan that had been brewing in the back of his mind. He asked the only thing that mattered. "All of us?"

"One way or another, yes. Not one of us who walked into this clearing will walk out of it." Jewel ducked out of the way of some slime covered tentacles. "I will keep the Erlkrönig occupied. Just do what you have to do!"

Emmett watched her run toward where Asèth stood looking down on the chaos that he had wrought. Bob was teeth deep in the neck of something that Emmett was glad he could not see in more detail. He searched for Kami. He couldn't see where she was, but he could sense her presence.

He ran, knowing that what he had to do would be harder for her than him, but he couldn't leave her defenseless. It was a long shot, but it was all they had right now. If they were lucky, it would work, and they might have a chance. Some of them anyway. As Jewel said, death was inevitable now. He heard her scream before he could sense her pain. He reached the beast that had attacked her, burying his sword deep in the creature's head without a second thought. He searched for her as the beast fell and saw her on the ground, a pool of blood spreading from her body, eyes wide open in shock.

Another creature attacked and a spiked tail crashed into his leg and sent him sprawling. He rolled over onto his back to see a mass of teeth and eyes descending on him. He jabbed upwards as it slammed into him, covering him in whatever passed for blood. He tossed it aside and crawled towards Kami. Her eyes fluttered and he hoped her wounds were not as bad as they looked. He stopped short of reaching her, exhausted by the effort, and looked down at his leg. It was a mess, blood pouring from it, but as far as he could tell it wasn't broken. He would still be able to do what he needed to do.

"Kami!" he shouted, trying to get her attention. "Kami, please."

She turned her head to look at him, her face pale as she bled out before him. She tried to say something, but he shushed her. He pulled himself closer and grabbed her hand. He didn't have the power to save her as he had last time. He only had one option left.

He had considered the ramifications of giving her a feather long before this point. Her survival was more important to him than any of the laws of his own people—they had already abandoned him anyway.

"I need you to do something for me," he said, hoping she would not fully understand what he was about to ask of her. "I need you to take some of my feathers. Can you do this for me?"

Her eyes went wide and she shook her head. Emmett glanced around to see that, for now, they were being ignored. As close as he was, he could see that the creature had struck her straight through. It was a wound that would kill her, slowly and painfully.

"Take them." He stretched a wing over her body so she could reach them easier. "You need to take some and use them. You're going to die if you don't."

"No—" she tried to argue, but he wasn't about to have a long drawn out conversation with a dying girl in the middle of a battle.

"Take them now!" he shouted. He had no time for her protests. "You'll know what to do with them. It's instinct."

He winced as she grabbed a handful. He wasted no time. As soon as they were in her hands, he struggled to his feet and lurched towards the Erlkrönig, his sword drawn. It would be useless against Asèth, but the beasts that he had summoned from Anabasa were susceptible to a blade. He fought on instinct alone, trusting his senses to guide him as pain clouded his vision. He needed to reserve what little power he had for what he was about to do, but he still needed to make it to Asèth alive. He heard Jewel cry out; her panic came to him more clearly than anything else. He looked up then to see her ahead, too far away for him to be able to help.

Asèth held her in the air with a single hand wrapped around her throat. Emmett paused for half a second before trying to force himself ahead faster. He knew he wouldn't make it, but he needed to try. He swung at any unfamiliar shape that approached him and barely managed to stop himself from taking a swing at Bob.

He could see one thing clearly, and that was the energy Asèth was taking from Jewel. He was stealing her essence, as he had from countless others. Emmett heard a cry rise from his lips as he used what was left of his battered wings to propel himself forward even faster. He couldn't spare the power, but he couldn't watch his friend die like that. Even though his focus was on draining Jewel of every last bit of her lifeforce, Asèth had no problem deflecting his attack. Emmett flew back through the air and landed hard against the ground. He could feel a wing snap beneath him as he landed awkwardly. He tried to regain his feet, but he didn't even have the energy to lift himself. All he could do was lay there as Asèth finished with Jewel and threw her to the side like a ragdoll.

There was nothing he could do to help as he watched him turn his attention towards Bob, who had not stopped his headlong charge towards him. He grinned in a way that Emmett remembered from so long ago. It was the smile he reserved for those he was about to destroy. He wished like hell that his sight hadn't been returned. He didn't need these moments as his last living memories.

Asèth skewered Bob through the chest with his arm, pulling out the yeti's heart and crushing it with his bare hand. Bob crumpled to the ground as he laughed. It was the laugh that told Emmett that this fight was over. They had lost.

Helpless and nearly hopeless, he watched as Asèth caught sight of Kami. He marched towards where she lay still on the ground. Emmett wanted to scream at her to move, to do anything. It was a far too familiar scene to his eyes, but last time he had been strong. He had been able to save her. Now he was beyond weak. He had no strength left, hardly any power to speak of. He couldn't let that stop him. It was time. One last desperate measure that he wasn't even sure would work. No one had ever tried it before.

He struggled to his feet, ignoring the blood and the pain, and threw himself at Asèth's back. He brought his sword to bear against his neck, knowing that he couldn't cut him. He had something else in mind.

It had the desired effect as Asèth stopped his advance on Kami to turn his attention to Emmett. "Why can't you lay down and give up for once? You can't hurt me. Just die already."

It took most of his remaining strength to stay in position. He reached around and gripped the blade with his other hand, ignoring the pain and the blood that ran down his arm as the edge pressed deep into his own flesh. "I may be dying," Emmett whispered in his ear, too weak to raise his voice, "but I'm not dead. You, on the other hand, are using powers that aren't yours to keep, and I mean to take them away from you."

"You're fallen; you don't have the power." Asèth tried his best to shake Emmett off his back, but he gripped tighter, letting the blood run, ignoring the pain. For this to work, the blood was necessary.

"Zomdv oresa bolape en oresa. Zomdv olapireta bolarpe en olapireta," Emmett chanted. All he needed now was for the dead who could not cross to hear him; to hear the words of an incantation that he should not have known. "A vime de a tolfaglio. Tol q'alunuashi hvbar."

A surge of energy burst forth through him, using him as a conduit. Emmett stumbled backwards. Asèth, still in his grasp, came with him for those few steps. Emmett's knees weakened as a power stronger than any he knew ran through him. His fingers spasmed tighter around the blade; it was the only thing that kept him from collapsing. Asèth held him up for those last few seconds as every ounce of Emmett's waning strength left his body.

Empty, he hung limply against Asèth's back. He wasn't even sure that it had worked. He could no longer sense the others and he lacked the strength to open his eyes. He did not mourn his failure, that was beyond his abilities. All he could hear was the darkness calling to him, dragging him down into its welcoming depths.

A bright fire lit the darkness, pulling Emmett back to reality and sending him soaring backwards through the air. He landed hard on the ground and his eyes flew open to see Asèth's headless body crumple to the ground in front of him. The portal closed with no power to keep it open. It had worked. Emmett smiled even as he knew he was dying. Everything hurt and now, when he wanted most to close his eyes and fall into that darkness, something held him here. It kept him frozen in the moment as salty blood flowed into his eyes and the disembodied head of Asèth stared back at him.

A song he had never heard drifted down to him from somewhere in the distance, ethereal and soothing. He closed his eyes and let go. He had done what he needed to do. Now he could rest.

Epilogue

He awoke to the pleasant sound of rushing water and the rich fragrance of flowers that threatened to overwhelm his senses. Even before he opened his eyes, he was filled with a sense of peace and wellbeing. It was as though everything was going to be okay. He did not know how that could be, but he did not have the will to think past it. Instead, he immersed himself in the feeling.

He smiled when he opened his eyes to see a ceiling soaring to majestic heights above him. Stars shimmered within the décor itself. He had no idea where he was, but he wasn't too sure he cared. He had not expected any sort of afterlife, not for his kind. Or perhaps this was why no Ángelosi had ever passed through the Ether; they went to this wondrous place instead.

It seemed strange to him that he was here. He was Fallen, no longer one of the Ángelosi. No one knew what happened to the Fallen. It had never been talked about, but he did not think that something as pleasant as this place would be the destination for one such as himself. His mind turned to the last few moments of his life. He remembered the surge of energy right before he died, but he didn't know what it had been or where it had come from. Still, he knew one very important thing—the Erlkrönig was dead. He had defeated him.

"Em?" A beautiful, musical voice echoed through the room. He knew it instantly. All the joy from a few seconds ago came crashing down around him. He had thought himself dead—in some sort of afterlife, but if he was then she shouldn't be here.

"Are you awake?" she asked, more insistent this time.

Emmett looked towards the doorway to see the Elsgodin, silhouetted by the sunlight beyond. If this was a dream, he wanted to take in every second of it. "Am I dead? Are you a figment?"

"You're not dead." She laughed as she entered the room. No longer a silhouette, she looked real to him now. She was different, or maybe he was seeing her in a new way. He had felt the touch of the darkness and it had drained him of his life. This was not possible, yet here he was.

"Where am I?" Even his voice sounded strange to his ears. He closed his eyes tight and opened them to see that she was still there—close enough that, if he dared, he could reach out and touch her. He was afraid that if he did, she would disappear. "I don't understand."

"You were dying, Em."

"No, I was dead. I felt the darkness take me. How am I here?"

"You were almost lost to us, but I had a little help from the other side." Kievvah grinned and winked at him. "Sometimes being an obstinate loud-mouth has its benefits, but I can tell you more about that when you've had some time to adjust."

"Adjust?" He stared up into her face and tried to believe her. He wanted to believe her, but still his mind rejected that thought. "You look different."

"Yes, I would." Kievvah laughed. "You know, I remember it all now. So many lifetimes you've stood by my side. How much you gave up because you believed that what you were doing was right and true. After all of that, do you honestly believe that I would let you die?"

"You didn't know that then." Emmett said, confused. "You couldn't have known that then."

She sat down beside him on the bed, her fingers leaving electric trails on his cheeks as she caressed the side of his face. Em inhaled the scent of roses and frangipani that accompanied her. "Even when I was mad at you, I never once stopped caring about you, silly."

Slowly, Emmett reached up to touch her hand and she entwined her fingers with his. "I still don't understand."

Kievvah stood up with a grin, not letting go of his hand. "Not Ángelosi nor human. Those lives are gone. Come see."

He allowed her to pull him up from the comfort of his bed and toward the wall where an ornate mirror stood. She gestured towards it, silently asking him to look at his own reflection. He let go of her hand and stepped in front of it. It was his pale grey eyes that stared back at him, but it was not the same image he remembered from the last time he had looked at his reflection. The man in the mirror was both different and similar to him in many ways. He reached out to touch the vision before him. His hand hit the cold, hard glass and he knew it was no illusion.

"Emeniel is dead. Emmett is no more. I believe that means you deserve a new name to go with your new self—a sælig name. Emias? Do you like that?" she asked. Emmett was still too fascinated by the realization that he had once again been given another chance to live his life. This time as a fae. It shouldn't have been possible.

"Then I can still call you Em, but I shall be the only one." Kievvah stood beside him, grinning, not bothered by the lack of a response from him.

"I still don't understand."

"You should know better than most that the Elsgodin cannot rule without the Erlkrönig by her side. There must be balance in our world. That means that our people cannot be led only by an éstesælig. Asèth was the last of the gesælig. He made sure there could be no others to take the throne from him. When he returned, it was the first thing he did—destroy any éstesælig and gesælig that had come to be in his absence." Kievvah turned him away from the mirror so that she could look into his eyes. "There are so few sælig left, no gesælig wander the realms, and I'm the only éstesælig. There needs to be balance, Em."

He tried to wrap his head around what she was saying. It still seemed more like a fevered dream than reality. He looked back at the mirror and touched his shimmering skin. Far more dream than reality. "I just do not understand how you did it."

"I told you, I had a little help from the other side." Kievvah shrugged. "It has to do with an old myth that goes back to when the fae still crossed over to Mundialis on a regular basis."

"What myth?" he asked, forcing himself to look away from the mirror.

"In Mundialis they used to believe that the fae replaced human children with their own—they called them changelings." She laughed. "You know how so much gets corrupted over time in other worlds. We do have changelings, but not like that. There is the ability to allow those nearing death the chance to live again."

"I wasn't just near death," he said, as he turned to look in the mirror again.

She turned him to face her. "I will not force this on you. You still have the ability to choose this life or walk away from it. I wasn't able to give you a choice at the time, so now, the choice is yours."

"Whether I live or die?" he chuckled at the thought. "I don't think I would choose to leave another chance at life."

"No," Kievvah said grabbing both his hands and searching his eyes for the truth to her question, "will you stand by my side as King? I can think of none better to be a gesælig and ascend as the Erlkrönig than a Fallen who has put his life on the line for me countless times. What do you say?"

He made an act of considering her offer. "I don't know. That's a lot to ask of someone."

Kievvah rolled her eyes. "We're not talking about the end of the world. Not this time, anyway."

He chuckled and squeezed her hands. "I couldn't think of anything I'd rather be doing."

ABOUT THE AUTHOR

Crystal L. Kirkham currently resides in a small hamlet west of Red Deer, Alberta. She is an avid outdoors person, unrepentant coffee addict, part-time foodie, servant to a wonderful feline, and companion to two delightfully hilarious canines - Treble the Standard Poodle and Nahni the Australian Shepherd. She will neither confirm nor deny the rumours regarding the heart in a jar on her desk or the bottle of readers' tears right next to it.

Find out more about Crystal at:

www.crystallkirkham.com

ALSO AVAILABLE FROM KYANITE PUBLISHING

IT STARTS WITH A KISS

J.L. PERIDOT

Celeste is a talented engineer who doesn't realize her job's going nowhere fast. She's a little naïve. She'll cut code and solder cables forever as long as Owen's around. Owen, on the other hand, knows exactly how badly things suck—he just doesn't care. Sure, his skills aren't what they used to be, but they're still better than what Halcyon Aries deserves.

Then it happens. The company's toxic management team finally cross the line. As both techies race to upgrade the station and to free the team from their oppressive contracts, they come to learn that life—and love—can only ever be what you make it.

Strap in for a steamy office romance in space, because sometimes It Starts With a Kiss!

ALSO AVAILABLE FROM KYANITE PUBLISHING

Blues singer Nicole Giordano is terrified of a past she can't remember; moving from town to town and always looking over her shoulder. Her only comfort is the beautiful and sexy Logan Moretti who haunts her dreams; claiming to be her Guardian and guiding her every move.

But when Logan suddenly appears on her doorstep it triggers an explosion of suppressed memories. Her mother's hatred, her father, Dimitri's abuse, the existence of Other species, and her ultimate destiny; a prophecy foretold hundreds of years ago.

With the help of their friends, Nicole and Logan fight to stay hidden until the prophesied time when she will come face to face with her greatest fear; all the while struggling to control their raging desire. A desire if unleashed too soon could destroy them all.

COMING SOON
FROM KYANITE PUBLISHING

Cursed with a past she can barely remember, Astrid fills her role as an assassin with ease. When Michael draws her into a rebellion, secrets begin to come out, and the worst one might belong to the life she forgot. As she starts to remember and Michael tells her the true reason he's been able to survive for so long, Astrid finds out she won't just have to save the city, she will also have to decide what it truly means to be human.

COMING SOON
FROM KYANITE PUBLISHING

SAM HENDRICKS

THE
ASSIMILATION
AGENT
BOOK ONE

Rae Sorano leads an ordinary life until the CIA tells her she's been selected for a special government-run program. While she learns the truth about her world, a war brews two miles underneath the New Mexico desert. Desperate to save the planet and herself, Rae must act as a double-agent, investigating her own government and the aliens she's been trained to help.